He's single, he's wealthy,
and he ca

"I believe that Mr. Arbuthnot
Miss Quince when she took her seat at the breakfast table the following morning. "His fever has broken, and he has taken some nourishment. *He is asleep again*"—raising her voice as her colleagues rose with the obvious intent of visiting the invalid— "so we must allow him to rest, undisturbed, until the doctor arrives. I have taken the liberty of sending the kitchen boy to Dr. Haxhamptonshire's and requested he look in on Mr. Arbuthnot this morning. I have also determined, through conversation with the house staff, that a lame horse has been found wandering about in the village streets. No doubt it belongs to Mr. Arbuthnot. I am told," she said, "that it is an exceptionally fine mare, a thoroughbred."

"Ah!" exclaimed Miss Winthrop. "I knew it! O, omniscient Providence!" she said, clasping her hands together and looking toward the heavens. "You have seen fit to reward our efforts here in this out-of-the-way place! A man of considerable means—and, er, no doubt, cultivation and high moral stature—has been guided to our doorstep. What a wonderful thing for the school!"

OTHER BOOKS YOU MAY ENJOY

A School for Brides

Books by

PATRICE KINDL

ᕀ

Owl in Love

The Woman in the Wall

Goose Chase

Lost in the Labyrinth

Keeping the Castle

A School for Brides

A School for Brides

A STORY OF
MAIDENS, MYSTERY,
AND MATRIMONY

PATRICE KINDL

speak

SPEAK
An imprint of Penguin Random House LLC
375 Hudson Street
New York, New York 10014

First published in the United States of America by Viking,
an imprint of Penguin Group (USA) LLC, 2015
Published by Speak, an imprint of Penguin Random House LLC, 2016

THE LIBRARY OF CONGRESS HAS CATALOGED THE VIKING EDITION AS FOLLOWS:
Kindl, Patrice.
A school for brides : a story of maidens, mystery, and matrimony / Patrice Kindl.
page cm
Sequel to: Keeping the castle.
Summary: In the early 1800s, in a remote corner of England with almost no eligible
young men, the eight students at the Winthrop Hopkins Female Academy uncover a
mystery while learning all the skills necessary to become a good wife.
ISBN: 978-0-670-78608-4 (hardcover)
[1. Boarding schools—Fiction. 2. Schools—Fiction. 3. Marriage—Fiction.
4. Courtship—Fiction. 5. Mystery and detective stories.
6. England—Social life and customs—19th century—Fiction.
7. Great Britain—History—1789–1820—Fiction.]
I. Title.
PZ7.K5665Sc 2015 [Fic]—dc23 2014028087

Speak ISBN 9780147513953

Printed in the United States of America

1 3 5 7 9 10 8 6 4 2

TO MY MOTHER,
Catherine Q. Kindl, with love

"I should not like marrying a disagreeable man any more than yourself; but I do not think there *are* many very disagreeable men; I think I could like any good-humored man with a comfortable income."

—*The Watsons*, Jane Austen

CHARACTER LIST

❧ TEACHERS AND STUDENTS AT THE ❧ WINTHROP HOPKINS FEMALE ACADEMY

Miss Eudora Quince, teacher and headmistress

Miss Clara Hopkins, teacher and headmistress

Miss Prudence Winthrop, teacher and headmistress

Miss Ariadne Evans, age 19

Miss Emily Asquith, age 18

Miss Rosalind Franklin, age 18

The Honorable Miss Jane Crump, age 17

Miss Millicent Pffolliott, age 17

Miss Cecily Mainwaring, age 16

Miss Alice Briggs, age 15

Miss Violet Victor, age 12

❧ SERVANTS AT THE SCHOOL ❧

Robert, the footman

Mrs. Grebe, the housekeeper

Annie, a chambermaid

Jim, a groom

Cuthbert, the head gardener

Cook, the cook

❧ VISITORS TO LESSER HOO ❧

Mr. George Arbuthnot, an injured gentleman

Mr. Arthur Hadley, his friend

The Honorable Mr. Henry Crabbe, his friend

The Honorable Reverend Mr. Rupert Crabbe, younger brother to Mr. Crabbe

Mr. Gideon Rasmussen, a stranger at the inn

Miss le Strange, a lady governess

Maggie, her maid

❧ THOSE LIVING IN AND AROUND ❧ LESSER HOO

The Frederickses of Crooked Castle

Lord and Lady Boring of Gudgeon Park

The Honorable Mrs. Westing, Lord Boring's mother, of the dower house, Gudgeon Park

Sir Quentin and Lady Throstletwist of Yellering Hall

Mr. Godalming, a local landowner and the district magistrate

Mr. Bold, the vicar

Dr. Haxhamptonshire, a physician

Mrs. Hodges, the postmistress

Mr. Lomax, a shepherd

Wolfie, a sheepdog

❧ SERVANTS AT CROOKED CASTLE ❧

Greengages, the butler

Agnes, a nurserymaid

Gladys, a maidservant

Tom, a kitchen boy

A School for Brides

1

"MARK MY WORDS. If something drastic is not done, *none* of us shall ever marry. We are doomed to die old maids, banished to the seat farthest from the fire, served with the toughest cuts of meat and the weakest cups of tea, objects of pity and scorn to all we meet. *That* shall be our fate, so long as we remain in Lesser Hoo," said Miss Asquith.

Extravagant as Miss Asquith's mode of expression was, her fellow scholars at the Winthrop Hopkins Female Academy could not help but feel that she had a point. They nodded in solemn agreement, and Miss Victor, who was only twelve, began to cry.

The other young ladies frowned and attempted to turn and regard Miss Victor with disapproval at her outburst. This was rendered difficult by the fact that all eight were bound to backboards, wooden devices that forced their necks and spines into an erect posture. The backboards required them to rotate their entire upper bodies when they wished merely to turn their heads.

"Oh, I do beg your pardon, Miss Evans," said Miss Asquith. "I am afraid I struck you with my crosspiece."

"Not at all," responded Miss Evans, and then pivoted, mindful of *her* crosspiece, to regard Miss Victor with some severity. "Control yourself, Miss Victor, and do not wail so when your elders are conversing."

"Yes, Miss Evans," said Miss Victor. The backboard prevented her from using her handkerchief, and her tears therefore continued to flow unchecked, albeit in silence.

The young ladies, ranging in age from twelve to nineteen, had planned to while away their daily hour of posture training with a chapter from *The Castle of Otranto*. However, by a minor mishap, Miss Asquith, who had been reading it out loud, had lost her grip on the novel and it had slipped out of her reach. Although the book remained on her lap, her attempt to recapture it was frustrated by the fact that the backboard pinned her elbows to her waist.

Cautiously, Miss Asquith had leaned forward and read all the way down to the bottom of the right-hand page, arriving at the passage at which the virtuous Isabella attempts to repulse her amorous father-in-law:

> *"Heaven itself declares against your impious intentions!"*
> *"Heaven nor hell shall impede my designs," said Manfred, advancing to seize the princess.*

Here Miss Asquith halted. She was obliged to leave off at this tantalizing moment, being unable to turn the page. After some moments spent speculating on the events likely to occur after such a fearsome line, they began thus to discuss their future:

"Perhaps one of us should consider marrying Mr. Cruikshank," mused Miss Asquith. "He reminds me of a dear little leopard frog dressed in green and black. He leaps about so, you know, when he is teaching us to dance. And I *believe* he is a single man."

Her fellow scholars erupted into nervous laughter. "Really, Miss Asquith," said Miss Evans. "I know you speak in jest, but I certainly hope that no one here would so forget what we owe our families as to consider bestowing our hand on a music master."

"Quite right, Miss Evans," replied Miss Asquith. "I had much, much rather bestow my hand on Robert the footman."

Here, several of the ladies erupted into *very* unladylike shrieks. Unable to cover their mouths with their hands, they struggled to suppress their merriment. Even Miss Evans allowed a brief smile to cross her face. Robert the footman was a *very* handsome young man.

"Ladies! May I ask what is occasioning such a noise?" Miss Winthrop, one of the founders of the Winthrop Hopkins Academy, had appeared in the doorway of the library, drawn by the sound.

"Good afternoon, Miss Winthrop," the young women chorused. "Nothing, Miss Winthrop."

"No doubt Miss Asquith was entertaining you, *as usual*," said Miss Winthrop austerely. Miss Asquith's father owned a distillery; he was therefore obliged to pay a rather larger sum than anyone else to ensure that his daughter be educated with ladies the likes of the Honorable Miss Jane Crump, daughter of a viscount, and the other girls, whose families may not have been particularly distinguished, but who were at least not intimately associated with gin.

"Dear Miss Winthrop, *do* say that you have come to tell us that our time on the backboards is up," replied Miss Asquith, smiling in an attempt to draw Miss Winthrop's attention away from the book teetering on her knees.

"No, indeed, Miss Asquith," said Miss Winthrop. "On the contrary, you have another half an hour left. Do not sigh, I beg you; I am aware of schools at which young ladies are required to wear a backboard *and* a metal collar both day and night. I wonder if we are too lax with you; good posture is *so* important." Miss Winthrop was quite proud of the backboards, which she had had specially made. As they were much more complicated and uncomfortable to wear than the commoner sort, she considered them vastly improved.

Miss Asquith gave an involuntary shudder at the thought of being permanently tied to a backboard with a metal collar, and as a result *The Castle of Otranto* slid onto the floor, coming to rest at Miss Winthrop's feet. That lady bent and picked it up, looking at the title on the spine.

"Reading novels, I see! And such a novel! I do not think this is at all appropriate for young girls. I will fetch my copy of Doctor Barrow's *Sermons*. I think you will find it far more *spiritually* improving than this sort of sensational literature. We must ever keep in mind the impermanence of life and the imminence of the hereafter."

"Yes, Miss Winthrop," the girls chorused again, and watched sadly as *The Castle of Otranto* was borne away.

The Winthrop Hopkins Female Academy had come into being at least partly because Miss Prudence Winthrop, a lady of a certain age in possession of an income that never seemed to stretch quite far enough to suit her needs, had decided that living with her newly married stepsister was less congenial than she had anticipated. Coincidentally, her stepsister and brother-in-law had come to a similar conclusion.

At the breakfast table one morning several weeks after the wedding, the aggrieved bridegroom had taken a stand: "Either she leaves this household or I do," he said, fixing his bride with a stern eye. His complaint was that his new sister-in-law had pilfered his entire stock of handkerchiefs in order to embroider them with some of the more judgmental verses from the Bible.

"It is all very well for you to find it so amusing," said he to his wife, who was attempting to maintain her composure at the sight of the newly adorned linens, "but she has grown quite intolerable. She requires an occupation to absorb some of that crusading zeal. Why cannot she nurse lepers or something of the sort? Surely she could go and harass the deserving poor, instead of lecturing *me*."

"You know quite well that Miss Winthrop of Crooked Castle could never stoop to consorting with the poor, whether deserving or otherwise," his wife objected. "However, perhaps something will turn up. . . ."

Happily, word soon arrived that the house of one Miss Eudora Quince, resident of York, had burnt to the ground. Miss Quince, who operated a small academy for young ladies, was cousin to Miss Clara Hopkins, the dear friend of Miss Winthrop. Miss Quince needed a large house with ample grounds for her school, and Miss Hopkins possessed such a house, as well as a desire for an additional source of revenue in order to maintain it. Miss Winthrop descended upon the pair with a great deal of advice and opinions and the offer of a modest investment of money. Within a short time, she had wrested command from Miss Hopkins, whose house it was, and Miss Quince, whose school it had been, and had changed her own residence from the Castle to the school, with the result that at last the newlywed couple was left in peace.

Poor Miss Quince! The name of the new school did not even mention her, for all she was the only one with any experience of instruction or credentials to offer. However, in Miss Winthrop's opinion, having had the carelessness to allow her house to burn down, she could expect nothing better.

The purpose of the school was the "finishing" of young ladies in preparation for marriage. That is, in addition to the rudiments of a practical education, it offered instruction in the womanly arts necessary to catch a husband. Undisciplined posture was corrected by backboards, undisciplined behavior by etiquette classes. Students danced, gave dramatic readings, wore their fingers to stubs on the pianoforte, drew and painted, netted purses, and decorated lamp shades from dawn till dusk.

Despite the horror with which all decent English people regarded the French—the armies of that madman Napoleon were currently rampaging about the world unchecked—the young ladies also labored to learn how to speak the language of the enemy with a Parisian accent, braid their hair in the French manner, supervise a French chef, and choose French wallpapers and French wines for their dining rooms. The entire Gallic nation might be composed of bloodthirsty, frog-eating barbarians, but one could not deny that they possessed a certain *je ne sais quoi*.

The students at the school were in some ways a misfortunate lot. Each young lady had lost either one or both parents, and her remaining relatives had not troubled themselves much beyond paying the modest fees demanded by the school in return for assuming her care. Within a few weeks, the students discovered that all had experienced loss, and most had known a solitary childhood, tended by servants and little loved by anybody.

Clearly, marriage was their duty, thereby relieving their guardians of the necessity of bothering about them even to the extent of sending a bank draft for school expenses and dress money four times a year. Unfortunately, so little interest had been taken in their fate that no one seemed to notice they had been sent to acquire a husband in a remote corner of England with almost no eligible young men. The small village of Lesser Hoo had no obvious excuse for existence other than the fact that it always *had* existed. The inhabitants were yeoman farmers, with a few shopkeepers clustered around the green; hardly anyone for a gentleman's daughter to marry lived for miles around.

The reality of their situation had not, however, escaped the young ladies themselves. Miss Victor, at age twelve, and Miss Briggs, at age fifteen, were still too young, and studious Miss Franklin had declared herself to be resolved against matrimony. The other five—being of marriageable age and well-disposed toward the wedded state—were beginning to look about themselves and feel a little anxious.

"Miss Mainwaring ought to have married a maharajah whilst she had the chance," Miss Asquith said. Miss Mainwaring, the niece of Mr. Fredericks at Crooked Castle, had been sent to Yorkshire from India several months earlier, after the death of her parents from cholera. "Imagine! He could have given you ropes of pearls and a ruby diadem for a wedding present."

"The only maharajah I ever saw was quite elderly and already had five wives," Miss Mainwaring objected. A pretty girl of sixteen, her eyes and her manner were still shadowed with grief and her own close brush with death.

The Honorable Miss Crump, whose overpowering shyness demanded that she wear both indoors and out an enormous poke bonnet shaped like a funnel, said in her habitual whisper, *"Five wives?* Surely that can't be legal."

"It is if you are a maharajah," Miss Mainwaring said.

"That is what *we* shall be reduced to," said Miss Asquith, returning to her plaint. "We shall have to marry Mr. Godalming, all eight of us."

Miss Victor burst into tears once again.

"Oh, do hush, Miss Victor!" said Miss Evans. "You need not marry Mr. Godalming if you don't want to. Now look what you've done, Miss Asquith! Poor little Victor is terrified."

The only unmarried gentleman of fortune in the neighborhood, Mr. Godalming was known to be looking for a wife, and the students of the Winthrop Hopkins Academy were resigned to the idea that one of them would someday become Mrs. Godalming; it was but a question of *which one.*

"But you see, if we all married him," persisted Miss Asquith, "we should be able to divide him up among us. Miss Victor, you would only have to spend one-eighth of the day with him."

"I do think you are unkind about Mr. Godalming," said Miss Pffolliott. "He's not so very dreadful, only rather unattractive to look at and inclined to talk about sheep. I don't mean that *I* want to marry him," she added hastily. "But one could do worse."

"Not much," said Miss Evans, who would bring twenty thousand pounds and a respected family name to her marriage, and therefore rated her own worth pretty high.

"I agree with Miss Pffolliott," said Miss Asquith. "One *could* do worse, and I expect I shall. I have quite given my heart to Robert."

2

ROBERT THE FOOTMAN stood in the doorway, beaming with pleasure at having a message to deliver that he knew would be so satisfactory to his hearers. "Miss Quince says that Annie and I are to assist you in taking off your backboards, as she is anxious to have everyone take a walk before the rains move in," he said.

"Hooray!" cried Miss Asquith. "Robert, Annie, you are angels of mercy. Do get this Procrustean device off me, won't you?"

"Really, Miss Asquith!" protested Miss Evans. Miss Evans was quite firm about enforcing the rights of seniority, being the eldest student at the school. "I believe *I* should go before you."

"Actually, Miss Crump takes precedence, doesn't she? As the daughter of a viscount, I mean?" Miss Asquith inquired.

Urgent murmurs could be heard from underneath Miss Crump's massive bonnet, the substance of which appeared to be that she did not *wish* to be first, and that no one should mind her in the least.

Miss Evans frowned. "Miss Asquith, you know perfectly

well . . ." She halted, being unable to claim that a senior student occupied a higher rank than the daughter of a viscount.

Annie looked at Robert, waiting for instructions. As Miss Crump seemed distressed by the attention, he, being a natural gentleman, directed his assistant to set about releasing Miss Evans, who chafed her wrists and elbows gratefully.

"Sorry, Miss," said Robert to Miss Asquith, who was impatiently dancing about him, causing her near neighbors to remove themselves to a safe distance. "I don't know what a Procrusty device is, but it'd be easier for Annie to help you, Miss, if you could hold a bit more still."

Miss Franklin, a young lady with an alarming degree of scholarship, stifled a short bark of scornful laughter.

"Procrustes was a perfectly dreadful ogre," Miss Asquith explained as Annie attempted to remove the device, "who captured travelers and either stretched them to make them taller or chopped their limbs off to make them shorter, so they would fit in his bed."

Struck by this bizarre behavior, Robert frowned and paused in untangling the straps of Miss Evans's discarded backboard. "Is that so, Miss? In his *bed*, you say?"

"Oh, *do* hurry, Annie!" Miss Asquith gyrated wildly in her agitation.

"Yes, Miss," said Annie, struggling to catch hold of the apparatus as it and its wearer whirled by.

"Why do you suppose he would do a thing like that, Miss?" asked Robert, his face wrinkled in puzzlement. "It doesn't make any sense."

"Never mind, Robert," said Miss Evans repressively. "There is no need for you to speculate about Greek mythology."

"I'll tell you later," Miss Asquith murmured and, satisfied, Robert began putting the room to rights and restoring the backboards to their usual cupboard.

Not only Miss Asquith had noticed the charms of Robert the footman. Mrs. Fredericks of nearby Crooked Castle, besides being stepsister to Miss Winthrop, was Miss Mainwaring's aunt by marriage. As she and her husband had been persuaded to invest in the school—which had the happy result of removing Miss Winthrop from their household—she considered that she had a right to an opinion on its domestic arrangements. She had, in addition, consented to send her niece as a day student. True, she felt a twinge of guilt at thus throwing the poor girl to the lions (in the person of Miss Winthrop). However, she considered it quite probable that her niece would learn something from Miss Quince, and also that the experience would at least serve as a distraction from her troubles.

"Engaging that boy Robert was a mistake, tho' he is a harmless enough creature," Mrs. Fredericks said. "Why on *earth* Miss Hopkins and my stepsister require a footman is quite beyond me. And introducing an ornamental young man like that into a girls' school, when there are no other suitable objects for their fancy to light upon!"

Footmen were rather an extravagance; the government had levied a special luxury tax on male servants, as if Robert were a bolt of hand-painted silk or a thoroughbred horse. They were generally chosen for a handsome face and a shapely leg, and Robert possessed both. He had been a page at Yellering Hall, petted and made much of by Lady Throstletwist, and taught to read and write by the butler. As a result, he spoke with a much more refined accent than most of the local residents, and in general presented a genteel appearance. Miss Hopkins and Miss Winthrop felt he lent a fine air of distinction to the establishment, which he did, in the sense that wearing a diamond tiara lends distinction to a donkey. He wore (and took great pride in) a fine suit of livery in yellow silk, a powdered wig, and white silk stockings. He looked very elegant and very out of place handing the young ladies into the roomy old black coach that served them as a conveyance.

In short, he was more the sort of servant who should be employed at a nobleman's seat, not in a school in a remote village in Yorkshire. Between their specially designed backboards and their footman, the ladies considered their school the equal of any in London, or, if not quite that, then at least of any in York.

Luckily, Robert was a naïve young man, ignorant of his own value, having never ventured out of Lesser Hoo since birth. He delighted in his new position, opening and closing doors with a flourish and enthusiastically handing round the fish and fowl at dinner, and he regarded his wages of ten pounds per year as a treasure trove of unimaginable wealth.

As he was the only indoor manservant and the most presentable male for miles around, Robert's presence had a beneficial effect upon the behavior and personal grooming of the students. His cheerful, smiling face seemed to demand a smile in return, so the young ladies of the Winthrop Hopkins Academy returned his respectful bows and salutations with great cordiality and arranged their dress and their hair with much more care than they might have done at an entirely female institution.

"Could he not be a prince in disguise?" Miss Asquith wondered aloud as they donned cloaks and bonnets for their walk. "Hidden here by his royal parents for fear of schemers and poisoners at court? Perhaps he could rule over a tiny little kingdom on the shores of the Mediterranean, where they have palm trees and the winters are warm and sunny, instead of alternately raining or snowing as in Yorkshire."

Most of the other girls applauded this happy invention and supposed it quite likely to be true, if only because he was so handsome and agreeable. His one disqualification as the hero of a romantic story was his contentment with his lot.

"He *was* a foundling," observed Miss Briggs who, unlike the others, was a local girl, born and brought up in Lesser Hoo. "The vicar found him on his front step in a basket, and he gave the baby to the cook and butler at Yellering Hall to bring up."

"There! You see?" said Miss Asquith.

Miss Evans, who was sensible and not at all romantic, discouraged this sort of talk. "What *I* see is that his mother was no better than she ought to have been and his father even worse, for all we know to the contrary. He is lucky to have achieved his position here, given such a disgraceful background. And if you go encouraging anybody here to fall in love with him,

Miss Asquith, you will do him no favors. Why, he could be dismissed if any of you begin mooning over him."

The girls sighed at this unsatisfactory conclusion, but admitted it to be just, so any admiration of Robert had henceforth to be indulged in private, or at least out of hearing of the hard-hearted Miss Evans.

They filed out of the house under the watchful eye of Miss Quince and prepared to enjoy themselves as much as they could on an overcast August day. Neat and tidy in a dove-gray dress and pelisse, Miss Quince led the way, followed by four pairs in an orderly line. Their small company presented a pleasing aspect; none were beautiful, but several were very good-looking, and all were strong and healthy (save perhaps for small, thin Miss Crump, who, shrouded as she was, might have had any sort of appearance).

As usual, Miss Quince sought to combine exercise with instruction, and was quizzing her pupils on the nomenclature of local plant life in French. *"Dites-moi, quel est le nom de ces arbres?"* she inquired, gesturing at some stunted-looking pine trees.

"Ce sont des pins, Mademoiselle!" responded the entire group in unison.

"Et ces buissons?" Here she thrust her walking stick into a thick mass of bramble bushes.

"Buissons de—" the girls began, but were interrupted by an agitated cry.

"Oh, I say, that hurt!" objected the bramble bushes. "Er, I mean, *pardonnez-moi, Mesdames* . . . er, *pourriez-vous me dire* . . . Oh, bother it all! Have I somehow been transported to the Continent? I mean, *French*! It's a bit much, on top of everything else!"

The younger ladies hastily removed themselves from the immediate area of the bramble bushes, while Miss Quince stirred them once again with her stick, more gently this time. A white and scratched face, topped by disheveled black hair, peered out through the leafy gap.

"*Parlez-vous anglais?*" it inquired pitiably.

Miss Quince drew herself up. "Young man, come out of there *at once*! What do you mean by frightening us like that?"

"Oh, so you do speak English, Madame! Or, er, Mademoiselle? I say, can you see my horse anywhere?"

"I do *not* see a horse, sir," said Miss Quince.

The young man uttered some sort of an exclamation that he promptly smothered, as it was undoubtedly profane. "Beg pardon, Madame! Only hope she's not injured. She's a fine piece of horseflesh, tho' a mite high-spirited, and I should hate to lose her."

"*Will* you kindly show yourself, sir?" Miss Quince said. "Please, stand up and get out of that bramble bush." Her earlier fright was making her irritable.

"Well, as a matter of fact, Madame . . . By the by, please allow me to compliment you on your excellent English. One would not know you for a Frenchwoman."

The pupils of the Winthrop Hopkins Academy giggled. The gentleman in the bramble bush acknowledged them by doffing an imaginary hat and inclining his head. "Mademoi-selles," he murmured.

"I am *not* a Frenchwoman," said Miss Quince with deci-sion. "Nor are my pupils. But we *are* ladies, and as such you have no business sprawling in front of us on the ground in this way. Pray get to your feet."

"My leg . . . Well, not to put too fine a point on it, Madame, er . . . Madam," the gentleman said, "I think my leg is pretty well broken in half." And he fainted.

"Oh!"

Miss Briggs, being a local girl, was sent off to fetch a sur-geon, while Miss Asquith volunteered to go get Robert and Jim the groom to transport the wounded gentleman to the house. Soon enough, the men appeared with blankets, which they fashioned into a stretcher. Unfortunately, the young man had become entangled with the prickle bush, and he was roused from his merciful stupor as he was torn from its embrace. Miss Quince gathered her charges together and began to herd them away. They obeyed, but not soon enough to avoid hearing a cry of pain as the men jarred his broken leg whilst lifting him onto the blankets. The expected rain began to fall, which further reconciled them to a rapid return to the house.

Not until the young ladies sat down to their simple repast at eight o'clock in the evening did they learn anything more. The surgeon had come and, after a lengthy interval closeted first with the patient and then with the principals of the school, had left. Miss Quince had refused to discuss the situation, but instead produced a great deal of plain mending for them to work on, and proceeded to read *A Serious Call to a Devout and Holy Life* to a restless and agitated audience.

"Robert!" Miss Asquith whispered as they at last filed into the dining hall, "How is the young gentleman?"

Robert looked at the older ladies, but they were occupied with finding their own seats, so he whispered back, "As well as can be expected, Miss Asquith. 'Twas a compound fracture, tho' not a grave one, and he's suffering from fever."

"Oh! And what is his name?"

Unfortunately, at this very moment Miss Winthrop turned her basilisk stare upon them. Ducking his head, Robert sidled away and began to fiddle with the dishes on the sideboard.

At last, when everyone was seated, Miss Winthrop said coldly, "Kindly recall that your family has sent you to our school to learn to be a lady, *not* a kitchen maid, Miss Asquith. And now, you will wish to know the name and condition of our accidental guest. He is a Mr. Arbuthnot from Maidstone, in Kent. We have no doubt he is of a respectable family—certainly his air and appearance are those of a gentleman—but he was too ill to question closely. Mr. Busby insists that we must not move him for the present, and of course we would not dream of it." Mr. Busby was the surgeon.

From Kent! The young ladies looked at one another. Kent was a world away, farther even than London. What could he be doing, passing through Lesser Hoo in the wilds of Yorkshire?

Miss Hopkins was not as immune to the romance of the

situation as her friend. "*I* believe he was traveling to Scotland for the grouse hunting season," she announced, unable to retain a dignified silence. "He said something about Lord Pauncefoot. Of Hurley Hall, you know." She looked around the table with a significant smile and was rewarded by the awed murmur her revelation produced. Even these young girls living so removed from the fashionable world knew of Lord Pauncefoot.

3

LORD PAUNCEFOOT, THAT stupendously wealthy and hospitable Scottish peer, was well-known for his shooting parties celebrating the Glorious Twelfth of August, the first day of grouse season. As the current date was August second, it seemed reasonable to believe that Mr. Arbuthnot had received one of the much-coveted invitations to Hurley Hall, Lord Pauncefoot's hunting lodge on the northern moors. Since Lesser Hoo was not precisely on the road from Kent to Scotland—it was not precisely on the road to *anywhere*—it might be deduced that the young man's journey had involved a side excursion along the way. And as for the fact that he traveled on horseback instead of in greater comfort in a coach and four on such a long ride, why, a man of spirit, with sufficient leisure to stop frequently to rest his horse, might easily do it, and send his guns and sporting kit ahead of him by mail coach.

The Pauncefoot connection meant that Mr. Arbuthnot was not merely a gentleman, but one of the elect. The Prince Regent and his brother, the Duke of York, regularly visited Hurley

Hall, along with a veritable galaxy of the brightest lights of high society.

The ladies, both young and old, regarded one another with a sense of new worlds opening before them. A guest of Lord Pauncefoot, here in Lesser Hoo!

"Mr. Arbuthnot . . . *Mister* Arbuthnot, from Maidstone, in Kent," mused Miss Hopkins. "What a pity he comes from so far away—it will be difficult to ascertain details of his family without seeming to be . . . *inquisitive*. Now, if it had been *Lord* So-and-So, or even *Sir* So-and-So, we should know where we were, but *Mister*—it's difficult to judge."

"The great thing," observed Miss Asquith, "is to prevent him from dying before we can make inquiries."

While the Misses Hopkins and Winthrop disliked being given advice by Miss Asquith, they had to admit that this was sound. They began to bestir themselves, wondering what potions and tisanes they had in their storeroom that might be efficacious in such an extremity.

"For myself, I always insist upon being bled when I am ill from *any* cause. I find it soothing—*cleansing*, you know. Perhaps we ought to call the physician and ask him to bring his lancets and his jar of leeches?" said Miss Hopkins.

"I have heard that in cases of fever it is an excellent practice to douse the patient with *very cold water*," offered Miss Winthrop. "Then one must lay great pieces of ice on his body and all round his head."

"All good ideas, no doubt," said Miss Quince, "but Mr. Busby, who I am sure is a fine surgeon, said nothing about such measures. And you know, in the event that the young man should die from his fever, perhaps his family will be inclined to blame us for being a little *too* zealous. My suggestions are rather more moderate. I would recommend some calves' foot jelly and beef tea, with perhaps a little wine, rather than resorting to such *heroic* efforts."

The other two ladies were offended at having their common-sense methods dismissed in this way. Indeed, each had been about to propose some rather more daring and unconventional treatments, imagining themselves at some future date being hailed by his family as an angel of mercy who had snatched their son and heir away from the jaws of death.

"I believe that Mr. Busby has given him laudanum," pointed out Miss Quince. "It is best to let him sleep. Only think if we were to drown the young man while he was unconscious."

The Misses Winthrop and Hopkins grumbled a bit, but soon subsided.

Miss Quince said that she would sit beside the young man's bedside overnight, to cool his brow with wet cloths and administer calves' foot jelly and beef tea in the event he was able to take it. The offer was immediately accepted, as neither of the other two were prepared to go so far as to lose a night's sleep over the matter.

✦ ✦ ✦

"I believe that Mr. Arbuthnot is substantially improved," said Miss Quince when she took her seat at the breakfast table the following morning. "His fever has broken, and he has taken some nourishment. *He is asleep again"*—raising her voice as her colleagues rose with the obvious intent of visiting the invalid—"so we must allow him to rest, undisturbed, until the doctor arrives. I have taken the liberty of sending the kitchen boy to Dr. Haxhamptonshire's"—(Miss Quince correctly pronounced this as *Dr. Hamster's*)—"and requested he look in on Mr. Arbuthnot this morning. I have also determined, through conversation with the house staff, that a lame horse has been found wandering about in the village streets. No doubt it belongs to Mr. Arbuthnot. I am told," she said, "that it is an exceptionally fine mare, a thoroughbred."

"Ah!" exclaimed Miss Winthrop. "I knew it! O, omniscient Providence!" she said, clasping her hands together and looking toward the heavens. "You have seen fit to reward our efforts here in this out-of-the-way place! A man of considerable means—and, er, no doubt, cultivation and high moral stature—has been guided to our doorstep. What a wonderful thing for the school!"

"If somewhat unfortunate for the young man himself," was Miss Asquith's sotto voce response to this piece of oratory.

"I believe," continued Miss Winthrop on a less elevated note, "that I have heard it said that a *small* amount of arsenic—you know we have plenty in the stable, for the rats—has an excellent tonic and stimulating effect. Do you think—?"

"I think," said Miss Quince, "that we should wait for Dr. Haxhamptonshire. After all, what if we miscalculated the dosage? Recall what even small amounts of arsenic do to rats!"

After this conversation, poor Miss Quince felt unable to go

to her bed for the rest she so sorely needed, resigning herself to a return to the sickroom to defend her patient, at least until after the doctor arrived and gave more authoritative instructions.

The doctor, while admitting the value of the methods proposed, agreed with Miss Quince. "As he is going on so well, I see no need for more stringent methods. Give him a little liquid refreshment from time to time, as Miss Quince has been doing, and we shall see how he shapes." When the other ladies seemed likely to take offense at his dismissal of ice water, bloodletting, and arsenic, he allowed as how, should the patient take a turn for the worse, "we can always try them, either singly or in combination, as it will not matter so much *then*, you know."

And with this the ministering angels had to be content.

* * *

It was not until more than a week had passed that the students were given a second glimpse of the invalid, as he had remained confined to his bed. Since nine-tenths of the labor required to operate the school was performed by Miss Quince and the servants, and they could not be spared for many hours, Miss Winthop and Miss Hopkins, having nothing else in particular to do, were therefore called upon to spend some time tending to Mr. Arbuthnot's needs, with a housemaid under strict instructions to report to Miss Quince if either were to offer him anything not ordered by the doctor.

News from the sickroom was encouraging; besides being rapidly on the mend, Mr. Arbuthnot was reported to be all that was worthy and charming. Robert, who was assisting with the more intimate, and also more physically demanding, aspects of caring for a sick gentleman, confided in Miss Asquith that he bore the miseries of his condition with fortitude, and was of a pleasant and courteous disposition. The three older ladies were pleased to relate how he had repeatedly expressed his gratitude to and admiration for the inhabitants of the Winthrop Hopkins Academy.

All in all it was agreed (if unexpressed aloud by any save the irrepressible Miss Asquith) that the most practical way in which he could express his gratitude would be to fall in love with one of them and offer her a respectable marriage and home.

Mr. Busby the surgeon and Dr. Haxhamptonshire the physician were united in the conviction that Mr. Arbuthnot must not stir abroad for some considerable period of time. A message had been sent to Lord Pauncefoot (the visitor had confirmed that he had indeed been on his way north toward Hurley Hall) not to expect his presence for the grouse-shooting season; now, all that was required was for the young ladies to don their prettiest muslins, practice their best pieces on the pianoforte, and wait to see which he would choose to honor with his attentions.

"He is probably already married," pointed out Miss Evans.

"He doesn't *look* married," objected Miss Victor.

"And how does a married man look, pray?"

Miss Victor consulted the experience of her twelve years. "Married men are always either immensely fat or immensely old," she said at last, "and Mr. Arbuthnot is neither."

"*Ergo*, he is a single man," pronounced Miss Asquith to general satisfaction.

Excitement was at a fever pitch when at long last he was declared strong enough to join them for an hour in the afternoon. Miss Hopkins had found an invalid chair in her lumber room, left over from her late father's final illness, and with his injured leg swathed in bandages and splinted both sides, Mr. Arbuthnot was wheeled out and installed in the front parlor, before a fire that had been lit for his benefit on this sultry August day.

Though he was rather pale and thin, the lines of pain and tension as well as the bramble scratches had been largely erased from his face, and all present were in private agreement that he was a fine-looking man. ("Not more handsome than Robert, of course," whispered Miss Asquith loyally in Miss Mainwaring's ear, "but quite pleasing.")

"Ah, *les demoiselles*," said Mr. Arbuthnot, looking about himself with a smile. "And I had thought it was but a fever dream! However, here you are, as lovely as I recall, but also, thank goodness, as English as I am myself. I cannot tell you how alarmed I was when I heard you conversing in French! I quite thought myself demented."

A look of confusion crossed Miss Asquith's pretty face. "Ah, *pardonnez-moi, Monsieur. Je ne comprends pas*—"

"*Miss Asquith!*" cried several members of the company in unison.

Mr. Arbuthnot had grown even more pale. "*Now* see what you've done," murmured Miss Evans.

"Our Miss Asquith has a rather *wry* sense of humor, I am afraid," said Miss Hopkins, while Miss Winthrop looked daggers at the culprit. "That will be *quite* enough, Miss Asquith."

"Je suis désolée, Monsieur," murmured Miss Asquith, looking down at her hands, which were folded in her lap.

Mr. Arbuthnot regarded her warily. "Er . . . *Ce n'est pas grave, Mademoiselle.*"

"And now, please allow me to introduce you to the students at our school," continued Miss Hopkins. "This young lady to my left is Miss Crump"—here she lowered her voice to a significant whisper—*"only child of Viscount Baggeshotte."*

Mr. Arbuthnot turned to greet Miss Crump with an air of relief, which changed to consternation as he realized that he could see almost nothing of her face. He craned his neck this way and that, rather as if endeavoring to view someone who had had the misfortune to fall into a well. "Charmed, I am sure," he said, attempting a sketchy bow from his seated position. Miss Crump shrank back into her corner as though he had struck her. Staring at the floor, she murmured something indistinguishable and began to twist and pluck at her handkerchief.

Miss Winthrop sighed. It seemed dreadfully unfair that the most notable student in the school should be so timorous. Miss Winthrop was quite certain that, had *she* occupied Miss Crump's position in life, she would have proved an ornament to it, unlike the timid Miss Crump. While normally yielding to no one in her admiration of the workings of Providence, Miss Winthrop was of the opinion that it could use a few pointers on occasion.

Luckily, Miss Evans, next in order of precedence to be introduced, was a young lady of whom Miss Winthrop heartily approved. Handsome, healthy, of good family and fortune, intelligent without being the least bit intellectual, with irreproachable morals and a strong sense of her own place in society and the world, Miss Evans was a compendium of all the virtues that an English gentlewoman of the nineteenth century might safely claim.

The admiring glances directed toward Miss Evans by Mr. Arbuthnot seemed to suggest that he agreed, and once the rest of the introductions had been performed, Miss Hopkins sent one of the other girls sitting nearby off with a message for the cook. This allowed her to beckon Miss Evans to sit next to her, and therefore him. *She* behaved exactly as she ought, smiling and speaking just enough to let their visitor know that she was open to his attentions, all the while maintaining a decent reserve, and *he*, for his part, seemed well pleased.

Miss Briggs was sent to the pianoforte, being the most skilled performer, and instructed to play *very quietly*, so as not to disrupt. The elder three ladies took care to engage Mr. Arbuthnot in conversation, but also to allow the two young people a little time to speak with each other.

"How grieved you must be, to miss the Twelfth of August in Scotland on Lord Pauncefoot's grouse moor!" began Miss Hopkins, with some intent. "I know that you sporting gentlemen look forward to it all year."

Mr. Arbuthnot agreed that this was true. He explained that the reason he was so far out of his proper path toward Hurley

Hall was that he meant to fetch a fowling piece from Sunderland for one of the other guests—a task that now must be abandoned—and had therefore chosen to take the coastal road.

"I am certain that the members of the house party will miss you, as well. And your relatives—how concerned they will be about your accident! Ought I not to have sent messages to your family and friends in Kent, for instance, as well as Lord Pauncefoot?"

"No, indeed, it is quite unnecessary! My parents are dead, and my closest companions were to meet me at Hurley Hall. I am singularly alone in the world save for a few friends—good lads all, but not given to much fretting over a comrade. No hearts would be broken over me, I assure you, if I were to vanish from the earth tonight."

The ladies, young and middle-aged alike, of course cried out against this dreadful idea, while in fact being pleased by its expression. And then, perceiving that he was tiring, Miss Quince called Robert to wheel Mr. Arbuthnot back to his room.

4

MR. ARBUTHNOT'S FRIENDS loved him better than he knew; after only a few days of shooting grouse in the company of the beau monde at Hurley Hall, some of them proposed to quit this agreeable house party in order to cheer him on in his recuperation.

Miss Hopkins had, by some miracle of social connectivity, discovered that Mr. Arbuthnot's friend Mr. Hadley was an old schoolfellow of Miss Winthrop's brother-in-law Lord Boring of Gudgeon Park. Miss Winthrop hurried to the Park to make it quite clear to her sister the Baroness that it was her duty to offer hospitality to Mr. Hadley and to any other of Mr. Arbuthnot's friends who wished to visit.

The Baroness, made more peevish and quarrelsome than usual by the approach of the birth of her first child, complained that it was dreadfully inconvenient and that she loathed having company when the weather was so hot and that sportsmen were, above all people in the world, the most tiresome. Her husband, for instance, was never to be found at home anymore, but was out with his dogs and his gun taking potshots at rabbits from morning until night, so that she barely ever saw him.

Not that she *wanted* to see him, of course; why would she, in her condition? Husbands were utterly selfish creatures, without the slightest comprehension of how much their wives suffered. Her dear sister Prudence had no idea how fortunate she was not to have attracted one.

Her dear sister Prudence eyed her thoughtfully.

"Well, since it would be such a burden to you, Charity, perhaps I ought to ask Althea if she would be willing to play hostess. I am sure—"

"Indeed you will not, Prudence!" exclaimed Lady Boring, sitting up, her complaint forgotten. "You know quite well that Althea is in precisely the same condition that I am. She would not be able to, any more than I!"

Althea Fredericks was their stepsister. As Mrs. Fredericks had married on almost the same date as the Baroness, the two ladies were now equally expecting a blessed event in a few months' time.

"And furthermore," the Baroness added, "Crooked Castle is far too small to accommodate a large group of guests."

"It has eighteen bedrooms," Miss Winthrop observed.

"More than half of them are under construction!" Crooked Castle had suffered a collapse of one wing during a storm and was undergoing major renovations. "And last time we dined there, they gave us aged mutton and stewed crab apples. I cannot *think* why their cook is generally so highly praised. *I* have never had a meal at the Castle that was even passable."

"'Better is a dinner of herbs where love is, than a stalled ox and hatred therewith,'" quoth Miss Winthrop. "And I am sure Althea would love to entertain them as much as you should hate it, my dear. It would be disgraceful to have them staying at the inn—you know how dirty and ill-run the Blue Swan is—and our school is full to bursting. No, no, you must not concern yourself, Charity. I shall ask Althea, as you find it so disagreeable to entertain your husband's friends."

"I never said such a thing, Prudence! You know quite well I did not! I am widely acknowledged as a *delightful* hostess, and I'll warrant there's not a woman in England more devoted to her husband's honor and happiness than I. Er . . . *how* many of them did you say there are?"

In fact, only two young men proposed to leave the amusements of a wealthy and sophisticated household in order to go sick-visiting. The fact that their friend lay ill in such an interesting locale as a school for young ladies was judged by the young ladies themselves to be of no importance; the saintliness of the gentlemen's characters was assumed and much exclaimed-over. The Honorable Mr. Crabbe, who was discovered by a brief inspection of Debrett's *Peerage* to be heir to a barony, and Mr. Hadley arrived by coach a few days after receiving a nearly gracious invitation to visit Gudgeon Park from Lady Boring, with an enthusiastic postscript from Lord Boring, who welcomed any dilution of his evening's *tête-à-tête* with her expectant Ladyship. Having dispatched fifty brace of grouse— or one hundred birds—between them, they arrived with great mounds of the little dead birds in wickerwork baskets strapped here and there over their coach and presented them to their hostess for her cook's use.

"Lord Pauncefoot's chef quite simply refused to accept them," explained young Mr. Crabbe with a winsome smile. "Being French, you know, and sensitive that way. He says he has roasted and baked and fricasseed *les grouses*, and stuffed them and served them in aspic and in a pâté, and now he bursts into floods of tears and begins throwing pots and pans about if you bring any more into his kitchen. I believe that Lord Pauncefoot's guests brought down over five hundred brace last year, so perhaps the cuisine *is* growing a trifle repetitious. But I hope that you, dear Lady Boring, will not look so harshly upon our offering."

Young Mr. Crabbe was *very* good-looking, of aristocratic stock, and possessed a pleasing address. Lady Boring smiled upon him most graciously and assured him that he, his friend, and their birds were entirely welcome.

Indeed, when on the following day the gentlemen wished to walk over to the school to visit their injured friend, with Lord Boring to show them the way, Lady Boring was quite put out, forgetting that they had not been especially invited to amuse her. She complained that she was far too weak and unwell to walk half so far, and that it was quite unkind of them to go off and leave her alone.

Her husband's brow darkened. "My mother would be glad of some company for a change," he observed in a low voice. "Why don't you go over to the dower house and play a hand or two of faro with her? That's no more than a few steps away for you, and you know how she enjoys it."

"Last time I 'played a hand or two of faro' with your mother at the dower house," replied her Ladyship in a furious whisper, "she won half the housekeeping money from me, and we had to live on salt pork and dried beans for a fortnight, as you very well know!"

Mr. Crabbe cast a beatific smile upon this muffled conjugal dispute.

"Oh, my dear Madam, it is so good of you to pretend you do not find us most terribly in the way! But I know what the life of a great lady is: you will be closeted with your cook and your housekeeper and your majordomo all the morning and into the afternoon, and have no time for a pair of inconvenient guests who have been wished upon you at short notice. No, you must *not* fret about us. We will not intrude ourselves until you have a bit more leisure—perhaps later this afternoon?"

Much mollified, Lady Boring admitted that there *were* a number of matters she needed to speak to the cook and housekeeper about, especially with guests in the house. Not that they were not the most excellent servants, she explained, as otherwise she would not employ them, but . . .

"I understand, Madam, and approve," said Mr. Crabbe. "The hand and eye of the discerning mistress; only these can create the perfect domestic felicity that I observe here at Gudgeon Park. Nothing can replace *that*, and we would be ashamed to disturb you whilst you work your magic."

Lord Boring looked positively mutinous at this description of his often tempest-tossed and erratically managed home, and even Mr. Crabbe's companion, who knew of old his friend's skill in managing irascible countesses and difficult debutantes, looked uneasy at this fulsome praise. However, their hostess seemed to swallow everything without the least difficulty; they were not only allowed to leave without further complaint, but Lady Boring stood at the front steps and waved them on their way with a pleasant smile.

Once away from his Baroness, Lord Boring became more cheerful and began to point out, as they walked along, good places for surprising a hare or a quail in season. "I cannot offer you as fine sport as Lord Pauncefoot can, of course, but if you care for some rough shooting I'd be glad to join you, if only the cursed rains will hold off for a few hours," he said, waving his walking stick in a discontented manner at the streamers of fog blowing in from the sea.

At the school, the imminent arrival of not one but two more young men had aroused a good deal of excitement. The students were fidgety, paying no mind to their lessons and changing their attire repeatedly. The invalid had been installed in the front parlor where he might greet his friends, a light repast of fruit, cheese, and bread had been laid out, and the ladies of the house arranged themselves as artistically as possible around him.

Once the lengthy business of introductions was completed and Mr. Arbuthnot's health had been inquired into, conversation became general. The young gentlemen eyed the ladies with interest, and the young ladies eyed them, rather more surreptitiously, in return.

Mr. Arbuthnot abruptly turned to Miss Evans and offered to help her wind up her skein of yarn. Miss Evans had no need whatever to have her yarn wound, but she accurately interpreted this as a way of making clear to Mr. Arbuthnot's friends that *he* possessed a prior interest in her company. She obligingly dropped her tidy skein on the floor, blocking the action with her skirts, and then began to rewind it on the proffered hands of her admirer.

"I must make myself useful," he observed. "These ladies have been far kinder to me than I can ever repay, and, as you can see, one might as well lean for support on a broken reed as on me at present."

"Perhaps we can make good your deficiency, Arbuthnot," said Mr. Crabbe. "No doubt you are not yet capable of escorting them on their walks or running any little errands that might be required, but *we* should be honored to do so."

"Yes," put in Mr. Hadley, "and if the ladies wished an excursion to some local beauty spot—I suppose there must be one around here," he said doubtfully, looking out on the dismal scene observable through the windows, "we should be delighted to convey them."

"Or a little dance?" suggested Mr. Crabbe. "I am sure it would do you good, Arbuthnot, even tho' you could not participate."

The young ladies agreed to each and every suggestion, until

Miss Quince pointed out that this was a school, and that lessons must be taught, long division comprehended, verbs memorized, and flowers arranged. Parties and outings with visitors, no matter how pleasant, must take second place in importance to the education their relations had sent them there to acquire.

"But, Miss Quince!" protested Miss Asquith. She smiled at the young men and continued with an innocence so wide-eyed that it struck misgivings into the hearts of several members of her audience. "*Surely* the fundamental reason our relations sent us to this institution of learning was—"

"To strive to become a source of pride and satisfaction to them, no doubt," interposed Miss Quince hastily.

"To gain household skills that will prove of use when you return home," added Miss Hopkins.

"To be virtuous, industrious and, above all, *silent* when your opinion is uncalled for," finished Miss Winthrop with a glint of steel in her eye.

"Oh, of course!" Miss Asquith blushed. "I merely meant to say that, beyond those admirable goals, our relations wish us to acquire some polish in company and learn to move with ease in the greater world. And I cannot imagine how we could better achieve that than in the companionship of three such accomplished and well-mannered members of good society as these gentlemen. Only think, Miss Winthrop," she added, "you'll not need to pay Mr. Cruikshank to drill us on our dance steps if we are to be provided with proper partners at an actual dance!"

"Hmmp!" said Miss Winthrop.

Later, when Miss Asquith had moved away, Mr. Arbuthnot

confided to his friends in a low tone, "That young lady *seems* all right, most of the time, and I daresay there's no real harm in her. But she's a humorist, I fear; a lady with an alarming wit." And he shook his head.

"Indeed?" said Mr. Crabbe. "You interest me." And withdrawing a monocle on a gold chain from his pocket, he screwed it into his eye, the better to observe Miss Asquith as she pilfered the slice of bread and honey from Miss Franklin's plate behind that young lady's back and began to eat it with an abstracted air.

5

AS THE SCHOLARS of the Winthrop Hopkins Academy made the acquaintance of Mr. Arbuthnot's friends, one of their number was absent on a daily errand.

"Letter for you, Miss. *Again!*"

Miss Millicent Pffolliott blushed as she took the missive from Mrs. Hodges at the post office, feeling certain that the old lady's sharp eyes could see right through the envelope. For Miss Pffolliott had a secret, and feared exposure above all things. The secret required that she volunteer to walk to the post office every day without fail to intercept the mail. The excuse she gave was the need of exercise—"I cannot lace my corset! I am growing stout!" This was nonsense, but since it meant that a servant need not be sent, her instructors were willing to allow her this indulgence.

Sometimes she thought her secret a glorious one, and sometimes she thought it dreadful; the feelings it aroused reminded her of the experience of jumping from the hayloft in the barn at her grandmother's house as a child: one moment of glorious flight followed by a sickening crash and a broken leg.

Like many of the students' at the Winthrop Hopkins Academy, Miss Pffolliott's had been a solitary childhood. Her mother had died in childbirth after a hasty and ill-advised marriage, a marriage that made her grandmother's mouth go tight and grim whenever it was mentioned. Within moments of her mother's death, her father had sent his infant daughter away to be cared for by his wife's family, and then seemed to forget her existence. He was reported to be charming, gay, and expensive in London, Bath, and the great cities of the Continent, but had never shown his face in unfashionable Scunthorpe, where his daughter was being raised. Miss Pffolliott could not even spin the fantasies of a lonely child round his portrait miniature, for she did not possess one. All she had of him was one letter, much read and reread, sent on the occasion of her sixth birthday, which exhorted her to be a good girl and to obey her grandfather (who had in fact succumbed to apoplexy three years earlier).

When her grandmother contracted the last illness of her life, she had enrolled Miss Pffolliott in the newly established Winthrop Hopkins Academy, dying but a few weeks later. Evidently, having foreseen her own demise, she had wished to provide some structure for her grandchild, knowing the girl's father would not. Before sending her away she said, "Now, Millie, your grandfather wrote his will so that your father cannot claim a penny of our money. Mr. Trevelyan"—the lawyer—"will be constrained by the terms of the will, and neither you nor he will be legally able to make over *any* funds to your father. So if the rogue ever contacts you, remember that! You cannot give him money even if you wish to."

However, after her grandmamma's death she did not see nor hear from her father himself. She did hear from his lawyer, who directed her to write to him in the event she needed to contact her father, and that was all. Hers had been a life lacking in correspondence; she could count the letters she had received in seventeen years on the fingers of one hand.

And now, quite unexpectedly, there were a great many letters, and from a secret admirer.

They had begun two months after she had arrived at the school. The first came addressed in an unfamiliar feminine hand, and purported to be from an aunt on her father's side. So little did she know of the man that she might have possessed any number of such aunts without being cognizant of it, so she accepted the letter with simple pleasure and sat down to read it openly and without disguise.

After that brief paragraph, however, the handwriting altered to a man's vigorous script, explaining that the introduction had been written by a friend at his especial request. The true purpose of the letter was to state his unrestrained esteem and approbation.

You do not know me—may I call you my dear Miss
Pffolliott?—yet I know you. At last I cannot refrain
from telling you how much I admire and respect
you. Your lovely face, your delicate, graceful form,
that intelligent eye and placid brow that promise
such riches of mind and heart! I can only beg you to

forgive me for addressing you in this manner, without permission from your guardians.

The last line read: *I shall write again, and can but hope you will forgive my audacity to the extent that you will not burn my message unread.* It was signed *Your Humble Servant.*

As the letter had no return address, she was unable to reply and ask the gentleman to apply to her father before writing again. That she ought not to be receiving such missives without his knowledge she knew very well, but how could she approach such an intimate subject with a man she had never met and whose address she did not even know?

When the next letter arrived, she nearly wept with vexation, realizing that her proper course was, in fact, to burn it unread.

Yet *that* also seemed out of her power. No one ever had said such things to her before; she had never dreamt that such things *could* be said to her. Her grandparents had discouraged any feminine vanities, believing that her mother's rash marriage and early death were entirely due to an appetite for admiration and flattery. They were unwilling to give any praise for her personal attractions beyond a grudging "You would do well enough, if only your hands were cleaner and your hair tidier."

To be called lovely, delicate, graceful! Miss Pffolliott read and reread the words with greedy attention. When her eye fell upon the word *intelligent*, she hesitated and frowned. She was an honest girl, and glimpses in the mirror suggested that she was also a pretty one; but nothing in her observation of life had shown her that she was any cleverer than other girls. However, she reasoned, perhaps the fact that she questioned her own intelligence meant that at least she was more intelligent than those who did not. Beyond this point of deduction her wits would not carry her, and gradually she had begun to take her admirer's evaluation of her worth as the correct one: she was both clever *and* beautiful.

To destroy another letter, which might contain repetitions of those assurances, or perhaps even something new of an admiring nature, was unbearable. In the end she had opened it, and the ones after that, and breathed deep the intoxicating fumes.

"Well? Aren't you going to read your letter, Miss Pffolliott?" Mrs. Hodges's gaze was intent.

Miss Pffolliott blushed again. "I—of course I will, later," she stammered.

Mrs. Hodges produced a grubby-looking lemon drop and pushed a straight-backed chair toward her. "Have a sweetie, Miss, and take a seat," she suggested in an insinuating tone. "Rest thyself after that long hot walk—reckon it'll do you good. And you can have a peek at your letter whilst you sit. Is it from your mam and da, then?"

"No, no, thank you, Mrs. Hodges. I—I'll go now. Good-bye!" She made her escape, heart beating loudly in her chest. Mrs. Hodges obviously suspected something and, starved for entertainment in Lesser Hoo, was anxious to pry it out of her. She walked quickly, waiting until she was out of sight of the keen eyes of the postmistress before secreting her own letter in her pocket, away from the half dozen other missives she carried back to the school.

When she arrived, the visitors had departed and the daily routine resumed. In intervals between her lessons, she felt the edge of the paper in her pocket for reassurance that it was still there. Its mere presence was enough to make her speak crossly to Miss Victor when she asked for help with an arithmetic problem. At last, after tea, she had a few moments of leisure alone in her room. She took it out and broke the seal. Carefully unfolding it, she began to read.

I find that I cannot bear the distance between us any longer. I have struggled with myself; I have tried to reconcile myself to merely corresponding with you, never to touch your hand, or to see your lovely face. But I must beg of you—

"Miss Pffolliott! Do come downstairs. Miss Briggs requires a partner for Italian grammar practice."

With a tiny scream of frustration, Miss Pffolliott tried to shut out the intruding voice. *What?* What must he beg of her? But it was of no use. She had only time to run her eyes over the next half sentence—*tho' well do I know that I am not worthy of such a great*—before she heard running footsteps approaching and she was forced to crush the partially read letter back into her pocket.

She stood and said, "Indeed, Miss Quince, I was just coming."

Never did a list of irregular verbs last so long. Miss Briggs was unbearably stupid about them; she wandered unhappily amongst the conjugations of *andare*, *cadere*, and *avere*, and had to repeat every variation five or six times before she got it right ("I expect Italy is a perfectly horrid country," Miss Briggs muttered rebelliously. "If *I* lived in it I should refuse to speak a word!"). And every time Miss Pffolliott moved, the letter in her pocket crackled in the most provoking manner.

But long before she was able to strain her eyes in the guttering light of the last half inch of candle at bedtime to read the remaining words, she had settled in her own mind what promise her secret lover sought to extract from her.

All that remained was for her to decide: would she, in direct violation of the rules of propriety and decorum, without proper supervision or the knowledge of those responsible for her welfare, consent to meet with him? And, *who was he?*

The last line of her precious missive read: *Look for me when you least expect me!*

✦ ✦ ✦

Miss Crump, alone in the state bedroom down the hall, was already asleep and dreaming. In her sleep she contracted into yet a smaller and smaller area of the bed, until she became no more than a slight disturbance in the coverings on the northwest corner. She had been given the largest and finest room in the house, but she used so little of the space that she could hardly be said to be occupying it at all. Miss Asquith had on more than one occasion looked longingly at the shining, unused surfaces in this elegant chamber, but when she had ventured to hint to the only-too-obliging Miss Crump that they trade accommodations, Miss Evans had spoken to Miss Asquith quite sharply, and the suggestion was withdrawn.

Miss Crump had also received a letter that day, and reading it had caused her to dream. She dreamt of the governess who had had charge of her from the time she was ten years of age. It was not a comforting reverie on childhood past; in fact, rather the reverse.

"Jane, I want you to do something for me." In the dream Miss le Strange was sitting in her high-backed chair in the library, the one that made her look like a queen in a fairy tale. Miss Crump's heart turned over and she whimpered a little in her sleep.

"Yes, Miss le Strange," whispered the dream–Miss Crump.

"I want you to climb to the top of the tower, Jane—"

"Oh no, please, Miss le Strange! Please, not again!"

Miss le Strange leaned back in her chair and regarded the child before her. "Now, Jane, you know we must overcome these foolish fears of yours. And the best way to do that is to *face* them! As I say, I want you to climb to the top of the tower and then, this time, I would like you to get quite up on top of the parapet and *wave your arm*. Wave hard! I shall come out and watch that you do it."

"Oh, Miss le Strange! I cannot bear it!"

"Perhaps you think so, Jane, but you must," said Miss le Strange, smiling. "I know best. Now run along. Wave hard!"

Weeping, little Miss Crump crept up the winding iron stairs of the tower, clinging to the wall to stave off the giddiness that always plagued her in high places. At last she reached the summit of the stairs. Pausing a moment to gather her courage, she took a deep breath and pushed open the wooden door and stepped out onto the roof. It was covered with slippery black slates, and the only protection from a fall was the low parapet that rimmed it.

She closed her eyes, then opened them and inched forward to the parapet. Miss le Strange was far, far down below, her face lifted to watch, red hair and white dress and bonnet standing out against the green lawn and the clipped hedges.

"Very good, Jane!" she called. "Come closer. Closer! That's right. Now, I want you to step up onto the parapet. Go carefully! We don't want you to fall!"

"Oh, Miss le Strange!"

"Do as I tell you, Jane! Do it now."

The sleeping Miss Crump whimpered again. Her limbs twitched a little as, in the dream, she obeyed her governess's command.

"Oh, hurrah, Jane! Very, very good! Wave to me!"

Miss Crump's hand uncurled, lifted an inch, and then lowered. Her entire frame was rigid against the horror of the drop.

"Let me think," mused the tiny Miss le Strange below on the lawn. "What shall I have her do now? Perhaps . . . I think a pirouette. Jane, I want you to do a—"

"Miss? Excuse me, Miss," said a voice. Mrs. Barclay, the housekeeper, had approached, and was standing behind the governess, her face expressionless. "Cook wishes to speak with you about the dinner, Miss."

Miss le Strange frowned. "Now, Mrs. Barclay? As you can see, I am at a rather delicate stage of Miss Crump's training. Cannot you attend to the matter?"

"No, Miss," said Mrs. Barclay, staring at the ground rather than up at the terrified child outlined against the sky. "I think you should come, Miss."

"Oh, very well, if you insist." She called up toward the parapet. "Jane, come down, and *do* try not to be clumsy, I beg of you! Now, what is this nonsense, Mrs. Barclay?"

The dreaming Miss Crump, relieved of the prospect of doing a pirouette on the narrow ledge, woke panting, her brow and palms cold and clammy.

The servants had always done their best for the young mistress, but there was little they *could* do to protect her against the iron whims of Miss le Strange. Viscount Baggeshotte, awed by her lineage, which was of fabulous antiquity and intertwined with the ruling houses of three European nations, had granted her a magnificent salary and free rein over his daughter and the entire estate as well. Having entrusted Jane's care to her, he had fled the harsh winters on the North Sea for his house in Bath. He only visited for a month every summer, during which time he vaguely applauded her efforts to embolden the small, sad mouse who was his daughter.

"Quite right, quite right! Can't have the little beggar afraid of her own shadow! I'm certain you've got the right idea, m'dear. There's good blood in you, Miss le Strange, and good blood will always tell. Glad you've undertaken the care of my girl, poor motherless child!"

"I am pleased to be of assistance, my Lord," Miss le Strange would reply, lifting the corners of her mouth into a small, satisfied smile.

When the Viscount had departed again, Miss le Strange would immerse herself anew in plans for her charge; perhaps she would mount the timorous girl on the evil-tempered, skittish mare in the Baggeshotte stables, a bad purchase that had thrown the last three of its riders. For surely, an English gentlewoman ought to be a fearless and accomplished equestrienne.

Or perhaps she would have Miss Crump enact some of the martyrdoms of the saints. Several might be quite amusing— amusing to Miss le Strange, at any rate, and no doubt morally instructive to Miss Crump.

Really, it was difficult to choose . . .

Had she been asked, Miss le Strange would certainly have asserted that she set these tasks for the betterment of her young charge. She might even have believed this. In fact, she was furious with her current situation in life.

Miss le Strange was of Norman descent; the blood of kings and queens ran in her veins. It was only by sheer bad luck, gender, and birth order that she possessed no title of honor. Her elder sister had married an impoverished Italian *principe* with a run-down palazzo in Venice—that was the closest the family had come to greatness in a hundred years. But their lineage was without fault or stain, stretching back into the dim past.

The peerage of Viscount Baggeshotte was of a much more recent creation; a hundred years ago, her family would have scorned to exchange words with the upstart Crumps. And now she had been hired (*hired! like a common servant!*) to raise this female Crump. Very well. It was her duty to mold this most unpromising material into a young lady of whom the British Empire might be proud. If, in the process, the little Crump girl should suffer any distress, well, that was a sort of compensation for her own humiliation.

However, the years were passing, and with them the opportunity for the brilliant marriage she must make in order to secure the position she deserved. Viscount Baggeshotte's title might be of a sadly modern creation, but it came backed by many acres of fertile farmland, properties in London and Bath, and a solid income. Miss le Strange made up her mind to marry her employer.

Perhaps aware of this decision, and alarmed by the steady gaze focused upon him, Lord Baggeshotte canceled his usual summer visit to his home. Miss le Strange, not to be foiled, countered by dispatching Miss Crump to school and pursuing him to Bath in order, as she said, to settle certain points in the young lady's future.

The letter Miss Crump had received that day, read and reread many times, was to say that Miss le Strange would be journeying back to Yorkshire to resume the care of her charge. No explanations were given; none were expected.

Miss Crump shrank down under the covers and curled into an even tighter knot of misery.

6

IN THE FOLLOWING days, life at the school began to fall into a pattern. The gentlemen might have come calling and stayed from morning through night had Miss Quince not placed a restriction upon the hours of social interaction.

"This is an educational institution, and some learning had best take place, or we shall be guilty of misrepresentation," she said in gentle reproof, shooing the young men out into the open air.

A wall of silent opposition greeted this remark, since, after all, the primary purpose of the school was to help the students into advantageous marriages, and a group of highly eligible young men actually on the spot seemed more to the point than learning geography or painting on ivory. Several of the young ladies rather enjoyed learning for its own sake, but at heart they knew it was an irrelevance to the accepted and avowed purpose of their lives: marriage, motherhood, and the management of a household. Being also subject to the usual human frailties, they welcomed the break in their studies, for they were disinclined to work hard on skills that nobody—not even themselves—ever believed they would put to practical use.

One who agreed with Miss Quince, however, was Miss Rosalind Franklin. Miss Franklin was clever—a great deal cleverer than an eighteen-year-old girl from a respectable family had any need to be, in fact. She expressed opinions on the nature of ether, that mysterious substance in which all of creation was believed to be suspended, and had been known to wax passionate about the composition of light; she had thought deeply upon atoms and elements, and had read Sir Isaac Newton's *Principia* in the original Latin when she was only fourteen.

Neither Miss Hopkins nor Miss Winthrop could understand more than one word in ten that issued from her lips. Both were rather afraid of her, but consoled themselves with the thought that *decent* women did not give a fig about the precise arrangement of the solar system. Indeed, Miss Winthrop on occasion braved Miss Franklin's scornful eye by venturing the opinion that it only stood to reason that the Earth was the unmoving center of the universe.

"Anyone with a particle of sense can plainly see that *we* stand still whilst everything else revolves around *us*," she was wont to say. "And that is precisely as it should be. Now let us hear no more on the subject."

Even Miss Quince, who was rather better informed than her co-headmistresses on the laws of physics and the Earth's place in the universe, sometimes felt a bit daunted at the prospect of attempting to teach Miss Franklin anything, as she appeared to know nearly everything about everything already.

That is to say, she possessed exhaustive information on volcanoes and glaciers, the various types of cloud formations, and the movements of the tides and of the heavenly spheres. However, while she could tell you the proper taxonomy of every plant in the garden, her floral arrangements were a perfect disgrace—a hodgepodge of broken stems, some with and some without blooms, jabbed all anyhow into a jam jar—and while she could describe in detail the workings of the new Jacquard looms, her embroidery was a snarl of broken threads and knots of which a five-year-old child might reasonably have been ashamed.

"Oh, what can it possibly matter!" she would exclaim when her skills at painting a fire screen or picking out a tune on the spinet were found lacking. "Fire screens require no decoration to enable them to perform their function, and music only distracts the mind from rational thought." In vain did anyone protest that these things gave pleasure—and might be an intellectual discipline in themselves. Hers was a mind formed for infinite space and the grandest designs of Nature.

Miss Franklin had pleaded with her mother to send her to school in Oxford or Cambridge, where, although she would not be admitted to the lecture halls of either university, she might be able to attend the meetings of learned societies and take notes upon their discussions. However, Mrs. Franklin had no notion of allowing her daughter to become even more of a bluestocking than she already was, and instead determined to send her as far away from modern scientific thought as she could manage—hence the Winthrop Hopkins Female Academy in Lesser Hoo, Yorkshire.

"Never mind, my dear," said that lady comfortably as her daughter raged. "I am only thinking of your health. You know, the best physicians say that you'll do yourself a mischief overworking your brain like that. Girls ought not to think on difficult subjects; it's well known to make you barren, and I shouldn't wonder but what you'll contract brain fever and go mad. Worse, you will die an old maid." She went on to quote Mr. Thomas Broadhurst, the eminent educator, on the subject: "'Of all the objects that are disagreeable to the other sex, a pedantic female, I believe, is the most confessedly so.'" Miss Franklin's mama was herself singularly ill-read, but over the years she had picked up a few useful references in her long battle with an inconveniently brilliant daughter.

"A pox on the other sex," Miss Franklin muttered. "May the entirety of the other sex—always excepting those who are engaged in important scientific research—fall into the sea and choke itself."

"What's that, dear?"

"I do not intend to marry, Mama," she said more loudly, in what she hoped sounded like a composed and resolute tone of voice.

"Fie, what nonsense! When a woman says that it is because she is not pretty enough, or because she has no dowry. Of what use is a woman who does not marry? She is fit for nothing but to care for other people's children as a governess or a teacher in a school. And look at you! You are no beauty, perhaps, but perfectly presentable, with a tidy fortune. For all you are so clever, Rosalind, you are a fool. Go and tell your maid to pack your clothing. And mind you bring a warm shawl—I'm told that the coast of Yorkshire is deathly cold in the winter months."

The school was all the punishment for female intellect that Mrs. Franklin could have asked for, and more. No one cared for the life of the mind, or for any of the subjects that moved or interested Miss Franklin. The young ladies were a decent enough lot, but mentally negligible, and so she had dismissed them and any friendship they might have offered. And the teachers! Miss Winthrop and Miss Hopkins were, in Miss Franklin's opinion, unqualified to instruct a new-laid egg. Miss Quince she disdained as being no more than their underling, never noticing that lady's intelligent gray eyes watching her.

When first Mr. Arbuthnot and then his friends arrived, Miss Franklin had for the most part held her tongue and sat quiet in her corner, irritably stabbing at her wretched needlework with an embroidery stiletto. Feeling herself out of sympathy with everyone at the school, she did not even try to take an interest in these men, none of whom appeared to care for anything beyond hunting and shooting and flirting with the young ladies. As their visit to Lesser Hoo stretched from days into weeks, however, she was from time to time drawn into conversation with one or the other of them.

Now Mr. Crabbe, observing her assault on her needlework, could not help but wince in sympathy for the unoffending square of muslin.

"Miss Franklin, you quite terrify me," he said. "I feel that you are sitting in judgment upon our frivolity, and I must beg you to leave off tormenting that bit of cloth. May I see it?"

When Miss Franklin handed over the fabric, he examined it dubiously. "Is it . . . Is it meant to be a squid from the briny deeps? Or perhaps the head of the mythological gorgon Medusa? No, no, pardon me, what can I be thinking? Of course it is a flower! And a very pretty one, too."

Miss Franklin regarded him in stony silence.

"Miss Franklin does not care for the decorative arts," whispered Miss Asquith in his ear. "You will not win her favor by pretending to admire her embroidery. Engage her instead on the subject of astronomy or chemistry. Better yet," went on Miss Asquith with an innocent smile, "*explain* something to her. Tell her everything you know about comets; I believe she has long desired greater information on the subject. Such things are quite beyond *my* comprehension, of course, but you, Mr. Crabbe, who are so clever, no doubt will be able to make the matter as clear as day."

In Miss Asquith's opinion, Mr. Crabbe had far too high an opinion of his own wits; he could bear to be humbled a trifle.

Mr. Crabbe blanched. However, he was a man of some intellect, and above all, he was a man who had been asked to display his mastery of a subject by a pretty and vivacious young woman. He rallied. "Comets!" he said. "Miss Franklin, Miss Asquith tells me you suffer from a great longing to know about comets." Here he paused, no doubt hoping to hear her disavow any such interest.

However, after Mr. Crabbe's nonsensical comments upon her embroidery, Miss Franklin had no particular desire to spare him.

"My mind *has* been dwelling on comets a good deal of late, Mr. Crabbe," she admitted.

"Comets are . . . Comets are balls of a mysterious fiery substance that pass through our heavens at unpredictable intervals." He paused, searching for some other scrap of information to augment this admittedly paltry dissertation. "I believe that they occasion a good deal of disquiet when they appear out of nowhere in that unnerving manner. However, *you* must not be frightened by them. I promise that they mean us no harm, and are all too anxious to return to the eternal darkness whence they come as quickly as possible. Does that suffice to answer your questions?" He smiled upon her in a kindly fashion.

"Actually, sir," replied Miss Franklin, "it is the 'least squares' method for calculating the orbits of recurrent comets proposed by the mathematician Legendre that has captured my interest rather than any superstitious fears. Although I must say I find your opinion unwarrantably optimistic—we know so little about comets that I could not, myself, speak with such assurance about their harmless and retiring nature. I should think that if one were to collide with the Earth we would find the result quite disagreeable. However, I do not mean to frighten *you*, so pray disregard my more somber view."

"Ah! Hum," said Mr. Crabbe, and soon discovered a pressing need to decamp to the opposite side of the room and the company of less knowledgeable ladies.

Miss Franklin and Miss Asquith shared a little smile; Miss Franklin's was perhaps a bit frosty, but so rarely had she ever smiled at one of her own sex—or, indeed, at anyone—that it was something of an event.

"I believe my mother is correct, after all," she observed, "in saying that there are few things so disagreeable to a man as a woman who knows more than he does."

Miss Asquith laughed. "I am so sorry—I ought not to have done that, but he is a little too fond of himself for my taste."

Miss Franklin lifted her eyebrows and looked at the flushed and lovely face before her in silence. She had spent little of her life guessing at romances and discovering partialities, but she rather wondered if she was looking at one now. Hesitantly, like a waterbird venturing out onto hostile seas, she said at last, "He will be expected to marry a title, I suppose."

"Oh no, not a title. The family needs money more than prestige. But he will be expected to marry an heiress of a prominent family, certainly. Not," she said as Miss Franklin darted a glance in her direction, "*not* the daughter of a gin distiller—that goes without saying. If I were the daughter of a brewer I might have passed muster, but, while gentlemen do drink beer, it is the poor who drink gin. So," Miss Asquith sat up a little straighter in her chair, "I have nothing whatever to lose by teaching him a more becoming modesty."

"I see," said Miss Franklin, who was beginning for the first time in her life to feel a faint interest in affairs in the sphere of human relationships. "Yes, I see. These distinctions are curious and apparently quite trivial, but the consequences may be heavy for the individuals involved."

Miss Asquith replied, "Yes, a brewer of beer may even earn

a peerage by a little judicious assistance to the political party in power, whereas a distiller of gin—" She broke off as, much to the surprise of both ladies, Mr. Crabbe returned, apparently unquenched and unsnubbed, with an opened letter in his hand.

"Do you know, Miss Franklin, I believe I have taken your conversational measure and I hope soon to be in a position to supply you with a worthy partner."

Miss Franklin raised skeptical eyebrows, but Miss Asquith obliged him by inquiring, "No, really? Who?"

"My brother, the Reverend Mr. Rupert Crabbe, who is rector at Stonyfields, in the West Riding. I have just received a note informing me that he has some business connected with our father that he needs to discuss with me, and my hostess, Lady Boring, has been kind enough to invite him to stay at Gudgeon Park. Being an unmarried clergyman with an ample living and a small parish, he has little to occupy his time and has taken up a study of the natural world. He owns a telescope, I believe, and collects rocks and observes birds and comets and so on. I feel certain you will have much to discuss."

"A telescope! Is it a reflector or a refractor? And what are its dimensions, do you know?" Miss Franklin asked. Mr. Crabbe, however, disclaimed any knowledge about the sort of lens owned by his brother. "Oh, in any case, I do not suppose he will bring it with him," she said wistfully. "One could not wish it to be damaged, but how I should love to see and use it!"

"I shall make a point of telling him that he must on no account show his face without it," said Mr. Crabbe.

Miss Franklin blushed, her breath caught with emotion,

and her speech became most charmingly confused. "Oh, you mustn't—I pray you, Mr. Crabbe—But perhaps he would allow me to examine—Oh, it is good of you!"

Mr. Crabbe smiled benevolently upon her and then cast a triumphant glance in Miss Asquith's direction.

"I believe I win this round?" he murmured.

"You do, sir," Miss Asquith admitted. Then, in a louder voice, she continued, "It *is* very good of you, Mr. Crabbe— poor Miss Franklin is quite thrown away on us. Bringing your brother into our circle will give her someone to talk to. I am astonished at how much that circle has enlarged since poor Mr. Arbuthnot had his accident, and now you propose to enlarge it yet again!"

"Yes, and I believe there is a stranger at the inn in Lesser Hoo, as well," Mr. Crabbe replied. "Of quality, my valet tells me, so perhaps that circle may expand even more."

Half the room away, two pairs of eyes were raised at this remark, and two pairs of ears tuned to his words. Miss Pffolliott pressed the back of her hand to her mouth, blotting out the words that trembled on her lips: *A stranger at the inn!* Miss Crump said nothing, but melted back still farther into the protective environs of her wing chair.

However, there was no further discussion about the stranger, and the two ladies were left to their hopes and fears.

7

MR. GODALMING, WHO farmed some three thousand acres outside of Lesser Hoo and was magistrate for the district, regarded the arrival of these alien gentlemen with disapproval. He was a rather ugly man of few social attainments, but yet was inclined to feel that his three thousand acres and healthy income entitled him to a handsome and accomplished wife. He had looked upon the Winthrop Hopkins Academy as his own private hunting preserve, so to speak, and resented the intrusion of others who might be more accomplished sportsmen, and so carry off all the game.

For a time he stayed away, hoping they would soon leave. When, after nearly a month they had not, he called at the school at a moment he thought it likely he would find them there as well. Once introduced, he made a number of disparaging remarks about the counties of their births, and the inferiority of southerners in general and Oxford men in particular, and was ignored for his pains. Attempts to turn the subject of the conversation toward his one area of real expertise were in vain; no one seemed to care twopence for sheep and their care.

At length he went away, feeling abused. He had not the same leisure as the newcomers; it was mid-September and the grain fields were being harvested. Being a gentleman, he did not wield a sickle or handle the grain himself, but he was a concerned and knowledgeable landowner. He had strong opinions about the proper ways to bring in the crops, and could not be spared during this most critical period in the agricultural year. His wheat, oats, and barley stood second to his wool, mutton, and fleeces in the profits produced by his estate, and he was too good a farmer to allow social affairs to distract him when his attention was required in the fields.

✣ ✣ ✣

The stranger at the inn was soon discovered to be a man of middle age, though giving the impression that he wished to be thought younger than his years.

"Dyes his hair and wears a girdle," murmured Robert in Miss Asquith's ear, having ascertained these details from the maid at the Blue Swan whose job it was to clean his room. The young ladies were in their backboards again, which made it rather awkward as she leaned in to listen. "And he's a great one for the lasses, says Mary," he added. "Can't leave a female alone in a room with him, she says."

"What are you telling Miss Asquith, Robert?" demanded Miss Winthrop. "It is not suitable for you to hold *private* discourse with any of our young ladies. What were you saying?"

"Oh, Miss Winthrop!" said Robert, whose natural friendliness and convivial spirit often led him into these sorts of errors. "I'm so sorry, Miss."

"It was my fault," interposed Miss Asquith, straightening up and pivoting toward her instructor. "I had begged him to hide the last biscuit in the Grecian urn in the hallway for me so that I might eat it later in my room—these backboards cause one to be so clumsy that I could not contrive it myself—and I did not care at all that *poor* Miss Mainwaring would go hungry to bed with no biscuit. He was very properly declining to perform such a wrong act."

Miss Winthrop, who had little difficulty in thinking the worst of Miss Asquith, was ready to accept this version of events until Miss Asquith added, "And then he suggested, most respectfully, of course, that I should no longer walk in the ways of darkness but seek the light, and lift up my eyes from earthly pleasures. It was *most* edifying. Personally, I think the entire incident speaks very well of Robert, but of course if you believe that propriety is of more importance than the salvation of my eternal soul, Miss Winthrop, why then I have nothing further to argue in his defense."

"I believe nothing of the sort!" snapped Miss Winthrop.

"Oh, Miss!" cried Robert. "I never! That is—Pardon me, I shall try to do better, Miss Winthrop. Forgive me." And he withdrew to the corner of the room, standing at rigid attention, his face a blank and his inner turmoil only betrayed by the tiny eruptions of hilarity that escaped him from time to time.

Both Miss Crump and Miss Pffolliott were relieved by

the news of the stranger's sex and age, though neither rested entirely easy. Miss Crump merely supposed that her terrifying governess would arrive in a few days' time; her ordeal was prolonged, rather than ended. Miss Pffolliott, though at first thankful that she need not immediately fear an importunate suitor appearing at the school (for a mysterious admirer *must* be young, if not positively handsome) became, before long, somewhat annoyed.

If the stranger at the inn was not her secret lover, then *why* was he not? Her admirer could not be a local man—none was in a position to address her, other than the unappealing Mr. Godalming, and surely *he* was not writing her secret letters! She could not imagine anyone less likely than Mr. Godalming to be involved in a possible tryst.

Miss Pffolliott knew that the inn possessed very few rooms for the use of travelers. If Miss Crump's governess and accompanying servant (for it had become general knowledge that Miss le Strange was likely to appear at any moment) were to arrive before her admirer, there would be no rooms left for him.

It was most tiresome. She became so annoyed with the man's dilatory behavior that she resolutely shut her mind against him. She found herself able to concentrate on her studies for the first time in weeks, sitting down to a lengthy list of dreaded long division problems with such grim determination that by morning's end she could point with pride to a much-smudged slate with several completed examples, one of which even had the correct answer.

✢ ✢ ✢

One day near the end of September the gentlemen arrived earlier than usual, and in a state of some perturbation. They had been made to feel rather in the way at Gudgeon Park. The Baroness was indisposed—indeed, it appeared likely that she would be a mother before the day was out. The doctor had been duly sent for, but he proved to be unavailable, as he had been called out on a similar mission to Crooked Castle, the home of Mrs. Fredericks.

Lady Boring was therefore obliged to make do with the services of a midwife rather than a fully credentialed physician. This threw her into such a fury, on top of the pangs of imminent motherhood, that the Park, as large as it was, seemed far too small to contain her guests in any degree of comfort.

Since the gentlemen were unable to intrude at Crooked Castle, knowing that similar events were on the move there also, they had gone out to do a little hunting in the rain, and now, disconsolate and wet to the skin, appeared at the school hoping for shelter from both the meteorological and the maternal tempests that seemed to have overtaken the neighborhood. Here, happily, they were welcomed and given hot drinks and seats by the fire.

"I suppose we ought to push off and go back home," Mr. Hadley said uneasily. "We ought to have left before now, really. Boring's got enough on his plate with the Baroness and a new member of the family without having guests in the house."

The assembled company greeted these words with alarm and dismay, while being unable to deny their truth. The young men were enjoying Lesser Hoo, and the young ladies had come to feel that the Winthrop Hopkins Academy without their enlivening influence would be a dreary place indeed. The older ladies, too, had had high hopes that matrimony would deprive them of a few of their pupils, if only the gentlemen could stay a few weeks longer. True, the income of the school would be smaller in the short term, but the disposal of perhaps as many as *three* of the older pupils in advantageous marriages would be an excellent advertisement.

"Oh, but—but, Mr. Hadley," Miss Mainwaring said shyly, "my aunt Fredericks has discussed this with Lady Throstletwist. And Lady Throstletwist has instructed me, in the event you found yourselves not entirely comfortable at Gudgeon Park, to tell you that you must on no account think of leaving the neighborhood, but come to stay with them."

Sir Quentin and Lady Throstletwist were an elderly couple who did not entertain often; it was obvious that the offer had been made because Mrs. Fredericks's niece had expressed a liking for Mr. Hadley's company, and Mrs. Fredericks was determined to keep him in Yorkshire. The obedience of the Throstletwists would not have been a matter for debate; Mrs. Fredericks was a lady with some force of will.

The cheer that these words produced was universal. The young ladies in general were pleased to continue receiving visits that distracted them from their studies. Miss Evans, whose acquaintance with Mr. Arbuthnot was not in any danger of interruption until he regained his full strength, was nevertheless pleased for his sake that he should continue to have his friends nearby. And even Miss Franklin smiled upon Miss Asquith's happiness; she was beginning to discover a real liking for the girl, frivolous creature though she was.

The kindness of the Throstletwists was favorably commented upon, and Miss Winthrop volunteered to visit Yellering Hall and inform them that they would soon be entertaining two young men—nay, three, if Mr. Crabbe's younger brother were to be counted—of whom they had only the slightest acquaintance.

"Oh, you mustn't do that," murmured the young men, while obviously hoping she would, and Miss Winthrop determined to call upon the Throstletwists and remind them of their duty the moment it stopped raining quite so hard.

In celebration of this happy resolution, an impromptu country dance was got up in the school parlor, with Miss Briggs on the pianoforte and the dancers treading on one another's toes and tripping over the furniture in the too-small room. Despite these difficulties, however, they took great delight in the exercise and one another's company, and danced until a wind from the sea blew the rain and clouds away, revealing a bright moon that peered in at them from the windows and drenched the scene with its silvery light.

✤ ✤ ✤

The morrow dawned clear and dry, and good news came from both Gudgeon Park and Crooked Castle: Lady Boring was delivered of a little girl and Mrs. Fredericks of a little boy. While it was too soon to be certain that the dreaded childbed fever would be avoided, the children and mothers alike were pronounced healthy and whole.

Miss Winthrop set out for Yellering Hall with Miss Pffolliott and Miss Mainwaring and a determined glint in her eyes. Miss Pffolliott was to accompany them as far as the post office, while Miss Mainwaring's role was more of a silent witness. Should Lady Throstletwist seem likely to withdraw her promised invitation, Miss Mainwaring could, by her very presence, shame her into honoring it.

However, this proved unnecessary. Lady Throstletwist was resigned to her fate—both Mrs. Fredericks and Lady Boring might be momentarily distracted by family affairs, but they were great ladies in the small society of Lesser Hoo. She could not afford to offend Lady Boring, whose revenge could be terrible, and did not wish to disappoint Mrs. Fredericks, of whom she was fond. She wrote out two gracious little notes, one to the young gentlemen and one to Lady Boring, congratulating the latter on her daughter's safe delivery, and begging the former to look upon her home as theirs for so long as they might wish to remain in the county.

Miss Winthrop, hoping to soothe any fears the lady might have for her housekeeping allowance, assured Lady Throstletwist that the young gentlemen were keen sportsmen and anxious to present their kind hosts with the results for their table.

"Why, I believe that Lady Boring's cook still has not exhausted the birds they brought with them from Scotland," offered Miss Mainwaring. "They are fine shots."

"You're in the right *there*," Sir Quentin, husband to Lady Throstletwist, interposed. "We dined at the Park a week ago. Never ate so much grouse in my life. *Crème de grouse* soup, grouse pie, kippered grouse, grouse cutlets. Even that candied dish they gave us for a sweet—that tasted a good deal like fowl to me, m'dear, no matter *what* you say."

"Yes, yes, dear," said Lady Throstletwist hastily. "You must equip them with your fishing tackle, and perhaps we can introduce a little variety in their offerings."

"Probably foul the lines and lose my flies that I've tied," grumbled the old knight. "*I* know what young men are, nothing but a pack of buffleheads. Most likely get bored and throw my entire kit into the stream—"

"We shall be charmed to entertain Mr. Crabbe and his friends," cut in Lady Throstletwist, fixing her husband with a stern eye. "When one grows older, you know, one has a tendency to become rather *set in one's ways*. It will be good for us to have some young blood around the house for a change."

"Oh, very well," said Sir Quentin morosely, and offered no further objections—at least, not while the ladies' visit lasted.

While Miss Mainwaring was dispatched to Gudgeon Park with the notes and Miss Winthrop walked home, Miss Pffolliott was having adventures. She had collected the mail, partly grateful to find no love letter to embarrass her before Mrs. Hodges, and partly regretful at the same circumstance. She was returning to the school, walking briskly and enjoying the fine late summer day, when a man stepped out from behind a rough stone wall and barred her path.

She shrieked in alarm, dropping her burden of letters and bills on the path before her.

"My dear Miss Pffolliott! I must apologize for alarming you," cried the man, doffing his hat and bowing. "I had no notion that I would startle you so."

"But—who are you, sir?" she demanded, gathering together her scattered wits and correspondence.

"Can you not tell?" he asked in a reproachful tone. "Does your heart not inform you?"

She looked at him in bewilderment. He was a gentleman with the look of a dandy gone a little to seed. His clothes were fashionable and costly, but rather too tight, and he moved stiffly, as if they constricted him. His hair was a dull, dead black that somehow made it look like a wig. His face would have been handsome, if it were a little less fleshy.

"*I* know," cried Miss Pffolliott, pleased to have solved the riddle. "You are the stranger at the inn!"

His face darkened, and Miss Pffolliott clutched the mail to her bosom and backed away.

"No, no, do not go! You are right, of course you are right! I am nothing but a stranger to you. I hoped that you would know—that your womanly heart would enable you to guess my identity the moment you looked at me. But I ask too much. Can you forgive me?" And the enigmatic gentleman dropped to one knee in front of her, spreading his arms in appeal.

"Sir, you are alarming me," Miss Pffolliott said, looking desperately up and down the path, hoping to see a farm laborer or even a villager's child approaching. Alas, she appeared to be alone with the stranger.

"Ah, my ardor is my undoing, I see. I shall leave you. A thousand, thousand pardons for causing the smallest tremor of fear in your mind. Wait!" he cried as she moved to pass him and continue on her path. She halted, regarding him as she might a rabid dog in her path. "Take *this* as a symbol of my esteem for you." He produced a rather disheveled rose from his waistcoat and presented it to her. She accepted it, as there seemed no way to avoid it, and then began steadily edging away.

"I shall see you again, soon! And *then* you will not be frightened," he called after her as she hurried off. She increased her speed, and soon began to feel an uncomfortable cramp in her side. Having rounded a sharp bend in the path, she paused, gasping for breath. Cautiously, she peered around a small stone cottage and found that she could still see him.

"Well *that* certainly went well!" she heard him say. He kicked the wall and began to curse.

8

AS SHE WALKED toward Gudgeon Park, Miss Mainwaring was in a state of mind that nearly approached happiness for the first time in nine months.

Her uncle, Mr. Hugh Fredericks, had written kindly to her after the death of her parents in the cholera epidemic, offering her a home in England with him and his new wife, and she had gratefully accepted. She had left the indigo plantation that was the only home she had ever known, traveling from remote Nadia in Bengal Province to the noise and excitement of London, and then to remote Lesser Hoo in Yorkshire. It had all been rather disconcerting.

But in truth, she had been glad to go. India had become a sad and lonely place, and her parents had always intended to send her to England when she was old enough; the colonial society was limited in Nadia and even in Bengal Province as a whole, and they had thought it best that she attain some of the polish of an English gentlewoman. She could shoot and ride; she could face a prowling tiger or a displaying cobra with a cool eye and a steady hand. Her parents, however, refused to believe that these skills, useful as they were, would be of any utility in attracting and securing a husband.

At the age of eleven she had been utterly scornful of the necessity of making a respectable marriage, preferring to imagine herself climbing the Himalayas or trekking through the desolate Great Rann of Kutch with only a parasol-and-cool-drink-carrying servant for company. However, in the intervening years, she had gradually put away these dreams and had begun to wish for an English gentleman with exquisite manners and a faultless frock coat who would whisk her away from the narrow, stultifying society of back-country Nadia. Her mother and father had been happily married, and now, living with her uncle and aunt, she had the opportunity to observe yet another affectionate and successful marriage. She wondered if a husband and a home of her own would help to fill the empty place that the death of her parents had left in her heart. Since it was the highest ambition a young woman of her station could reasonably aspire to, her own desires began to form themselves to their preordained fate.

But, as the other young ladies in the Winthrop Hopkins Academy had hastened to inform her, Lesser Hoo was every bit as lacking in eligible bachelors as Nadia, Bengal Province—at least, until recently. *Now*, of course, there was Mr. Hadley. Oh, and the other young gentlemen, too, but in Miss Mainwaring's mind the other gentlemen were but a drab background, against which Mr. Hadley blazed like a comet. His manners were impeccable, as was his dress, and he had soon differentiated himself from the others by his intelligent questions about life on an indigo plantation. The English, or at least the English she had so far met, did not seem to know or care about the world beyond the shores of their island; no one else had probed much further into her prior life than to venture the suppositions that India was hot and had elephants.

Mr. Hadley had never been to India, but his father had investments there, and Mr. Hadley was interested in everything she could relate to him. But she believed that he was interested for *her* sake as well, and his attention did not flag when she spoke of personal, private matters—of the endless indolence of the rainy season, for instance, or the play of moonlight filtering through the bamboo forest, or the pleasure she took in her pet pangolin. This could not possibly help him understand the fluctuations of share values in the East India Company, yet he listened and laughed and told stories of his own childhood.

Such inconsequential conversations may be the pebble in the path of the stream that alters its course, the pivot that shunts the lives of young people in one direction or another. Shared laughter and confidences, a sense of recognition between two people who were so recently strangers, and their fate is changed. Miss Cecily Mainwaring was in love, and she believed her love to be reciprocated.

Her eyes were bright and her spirits high as she carried the happy news to Gudgeon Park that Mr. Hadley (and Mr. Crabbe, of course) could remain in Yorkshire indefinitely. The empty place in her heart was close to being filled.

The household was, not surprisingly, in considerable disarray. Lord Boring and the young gentlemen visitors had been driven to a defensive position in the library whence they dared not stir, only venturing forth to attract the attention of a footman to obtain supplies of food and drink. The female portion of the staff had deserted them and was clustered about the nursery and the Baroness's bedroom. Miss Mainwaring was first escorted to have a quick peek at her aunt by marriage and her child, propped up on a multitude of pillows in bed. Miss Mainwaring almost burst out laughing; mother and daughter looked nearly identical, only varying as to size, with indignant, protuberant eyes and thin, wispy curls pasted to their foreheads. After listening to the new mother's complaints about the heartlessness of men, and husbands in particular, for some minutes, she admired the pop-eyed infant and made her escape.

Downstairs in the library, the gentlemen were pathetically grateful to have their tête-à-tête interrupted. They attempted to lure her to a seat by the fire, proffering a cup of lukewarm tea and a half-eaten plate of biscuits. Miss Mainwaring, however, protested that she must not stay. She had delivered her message, and such exclusively masculine company without her hostess or indeed any female present made her uncomfortable; she considered it best to withdraw.

Nevertheless, she could not resist revealing the contents of the note before taking her leave. "Lady Throstletwist begs you please to come and stay with her for as long as you wish!" she said. She risked a swift glance at Mr. Hadley to gauge his reaction.

Mr. Hadley's color rose. He stared, not at her, but at the floor.

"How kind," he said, his voice so low it was almost drowned out by Mr. Crabbe's jubilant cries and Lord Boring's reproaches at being abandoned in his hour of need. "Unfortunately," he said, his voice growing a little louder, yet still looking anywhere but at her, "I shall not be able to take advantage of Lady Throstletwist's delightful invitation. I fear . . . I find that I may be required at home."

The other men fell silent, looking at him in surprise. Then they looked at Miss Mainwaring. Miss Mainwaring turned scarlet and fled.

✦ ✦ ✦

Miss Pffolliott had to give herself a stern talking-to in order to gather up enough courage to walk to the post office again the next day. She told herself that she was prepared for anything and would not be startled again. She left the house with her head high and her stride resolute. However, she had not even reached the drive leading to the main road before the clipped yew bushes parted and a man stepped out in front of her.

Miss Pffolliott shrieked.

"Excuse me, Miss! Oh, beg pardon, Miss Pffolliott, I did not mean to frighten you." It was Robert the footman, looking most uncomfortable and clutching a silver salver, on which lay one folded sheet of paper.

"Oh, Robert!" Miss Pffolliott clasped her hands to her breast and took a deep breath.

"'Tis that a gentleman wanted me to give this to you, private-like." He cast a troubled glance down at the contents of his tray. "Only . . . Only, Miss? I think perhaps you oughtn't to read it. I think what you ought to do is to tell me to give it to Miss Quince." He looked at her with anxious eyes. "Don't *you* think so, Miss? She'd know the proper way to respond to—to whatever it is."

The rapid beating of her heart had slowed during his speech, and she began to collect her wits. Really, it was quite presumptuous of Robert to give her advice on how to conduct her private affairs. It was all very well for Miss Asquith to make a pet of him and chatter away as though to an equal, but he was a *footman*! While she, Miss Pffolliott, was a lady, daughter of an old and respected family.

And if she were to allow Robert to show the note to Miss Quince, that would necessitate all sorts of awkward explanations. Why, Miss Quince would ask, had she not shown the previous letters she had obviously received? No, she would deal with this herself.

"That will do, Robert," she said coldly, and held out her hand for the note. "And I will thank you not to mention this message to anyone else, *especially including* Miss Asquith."

"Oh, Miss!"

"That will do, Robert!"

Defeated, Robert held out his silver salver, and then disappeared once more into the shrubbery.

The note read:

My poor, poor darling! How I must have frightened you! I cannot cease from reproaching myself. I beg

you to believe that it was the last thing I wanted! My
devotion overcame my good sense—it has been so
long that I have dreamt of seeing you. Only tarry for
a moment by the bridge over the stream on your walk
today, long enough to tell me that you forgive me,
won't you, my dear?

                                        Your desolate lover

Miss Pffolliott read this missive and walked on, thinking. So that man *was* the person who had been sending her the letters. Disappointing, really. Somehow she had pictured him as having much better hair. And yet . . . it was so romantic to have a secret lover, one who called her a poor darling and was overcome by his feelings upon the sight of her. It made her feel like the heroine of a novel. Surely it could do no harm to speak to him? She could tell him that he must approach her like a gentleman and ask for a proper introduction.

Yes! That would be best. She began to walk faster.

The bridge, built of local stone, crossed a small stream in open moorland, so Miss Pffolliott flattered herself that she would have plenty of advance notice and would be able to keep her emotions well in check without screaming in that humiliating fashion. She looked around, but could see no masculine figure nearby, or any figure of any kind. Even the ever-present sheep were apparently occupied elsewhere, and the birds had fallen silent and hidden themselves. How long would the "moment" he'd requested last, given that it would require many tedious minutes for him to approach within shouting distance?

She halted on the bridge, looking around discontentedly. The only sound was the faint murmuring of the water below. Surely there never was a place more solitary, more deserted, more absolutely uninhabited by—

"Hullo!"

Miss Pffolliott screamed.

The voice came from *below* her. She peered over the stone parapet to see a head poking out from under the bridge, like the troll in the fairy tale emerging to devour one of the Billy Goats Gruff.

"Egad, I've done it again!" The troll clambered out into the watery sunshine, revealing itself to be the selfsame gentleman who had accosted her on the preceding day.

"Many, many apologies, my dearest! I seem doomed to terrify you. I was—er, I was inspecting this stream, to see what manner of fish it might contain. Might like to put in a bit of time with the old rod and reel, you know! And it was awfully nice and shady." He fanned himself with his hat, demonstrating the need for shade. "However, all that is beside the point." Here he sank onto one knee and clasped his hat in his hands beseechingly. "*Can* you ever forgive me, my love?"

Miss Pffolliott took a deep breath and closed her eyes for a moment to calm herself.

"Sir," she said at last to the kneeling man before her. "I pray you, do get up. You *must* not address me in this manner, you know you must not! I do not even know your name—"

"Gideon Rasmussen, at your service."

"—or your family or anything else about you. It is most

improper of you to seek to meet me without any chaperone present or to write to me without permission. I must beg you to desist. If you wish to know me, please do so by more conventional means. I am sure you can obtain an introduction; the mistresses of the school I attend are most amiable and would be pleased to receive a respectable gentleman who wished to call on one of their pupils."

Here she paused, well pleased with this assessment of the case.

"Hang it all, Miss Pffolliott, I had hoped—"

"No, sir," said Miss Pffolliott firmly, her resolve solidified by the difficulty with which Mr. Rasmussen was struggling to his feet. "Pray do not address me again until you have obtained an introduction. Please allow me to continue on my way unmolested."

As she turned to leave him, she caught one last glimpse of his face. He was scowling; he had evidently expected an easier conquest.

9

MRS. HUGH FREDERICKS gently stroked the fat cheek of her newborn son and sighed with contentment. In possession of an excellent constitution, she was rapidly regaining strength. Defying the concerted efforts of her physician, the midwife, the nursemaid, and her personal maid, she had risen unaided from her bed, fetched her baby from his cradle, and was sitting with him in a chair, looking out over the castle garden.

"What the deuce do you think you are doing out of bed?" demanded her husband, who had put his head into the room to see if mother and child were awake. "And where is that useless nursemaid when she is required?" He came and sat down beside them, ruffling the infant's scant hair.

"I am planning the ball I mean to give as soon as your son allows me a little leisure time," she replied. "Our niece is in love, and a young lady in love *needs* a ball, just as a flower needs the sun and the rain." She continued in a sentimental tone. "*We* met at a ball, if you recollect. A ball is a most tremendously exciting event in the life of a young woman, and I have never been in a position to give one before. I have sent the maids downstairs to consult with Cook about the dinner we shall serve."

"Oh, you have, have you? That will be far too much excitement for *you*, young woman." Her husband frowned. "You know quite well you are meant to remain in your bed for at least a fortnight and think about nothing but your health and the health of our son. I refuse to consider *any* entertainments whatsoever until you have recovered entirely. Say, around about the time young Rodney here reaches his majority, at age twenty-one. That will be *plenty* of time for balls, and we shall no longer be in a state of uncertainty about your well-being."

"You are in the right *there*," she retorted. "There will be no uncertainty, because I shall have expired of old age and ennui. Don't be foolish! It will only be a small dance—I ought not to have called it a ball—just the young ladies from Prudence's school and the Throstletwists and the gentlemen staying with them. Oh, and I suppose we ought to ask the Borings as well, if Her Ladyship is able to leave her couch by then, which I very much doubt. And Mr. Godalming, of course, will come in his character of Only Eligible Local Bachelor. We can hire a few musicians from Scarborough, and there ought to be *some* flowers left in the garden, and—"

"Hush, now, you'll fret yourself into a fever. Cease your scheming at once. *I* shall organize this dance, if dance there must be."

"*You!* Pardon me, my dear, but you couldn't organize a game of hunt-the-slipper for a Sunday school class." Waving away any offers of assistance from Mr. Hugh Fredericks, who, when not fully occupied with being her husband, controlled a vast empire of textile factories, financial institutions, and ship-building yards, she continued, "No, no, I am quite well. Within the week I shall be downstairs and presiding over your dinner table quite as usual, I assure you. But do not tell Cecily about the dance yet. I wish to surprise her."

❖ ❖ ❖

Miss le Strange, governess to Miss Crump, did not think well of the inn at Lesser Hoo. When shown to a room at the Blue Swan by the barefoot child who served as the inn's maid-of-all-work, she began immediately pointing out its deficiencies with the aid of her furled umbrella.

"Dirty," she said, prodding a pitcher on a bedside table so that the water sloshed over the rim. "Dirty," she said, stabbing at the bedcoverings and lifting them half off the mattress. "Dirty, dirty, dirty!" She thumped the point of the umbrella's ferrule against damp spots on the wall. With the toe of one exquisitely shod small foot she curled back a corner of the rug, expos-ing the accumulated dirt, fingernail parings, and bread crumbs that had been swept underneath. A shiny black beetle scurried away to safety under the wardrobe. Miss le Strange raised eyes like ice picks to meet those of the cowering maidservant.

"Do you *really* expect me to sleep in these conditions?" she demanded. *"Really?"*

"Eee, Mistress," quavered the small servant, who was unac-customed to dealing with the Quality, "'tis summat t'matter?" Thinking that it was the beetle alone that was causing dismay, she added reassuringly, "'Tis nobbut a black-clock."

Miss le Strange continued to stare at her. At last she said, "I do not have one *single* idea what you just said. Can you not speak the King's English?"

"Dunno, Mistress," said the girl, who for her part was also struggling to understand Miss le Strange's beautifully articulated vowels. In any case, her attention was on the point of the umbrella, which seemed to be positively trembling in its anxiety to find another object to poke and prod.

"Yorkshire!" muttered Miss le Strange. "It had might as well be Outer Mongolia."

In a fury she dismissed the child and ordered her own maid, who had accompanied her, to strip the bed and replace the soiled sheets with the bedclothes she had brought from the Baggeshotte linen presses.

She had been informed that every bed was taken at the Winthrop Hopkins Academy, so that she could not be received there. In her opinion, the girls should have been forced to sleep two or three a bed in order to free up a chamber, but this expedient did not appear to have occurred to anyone else. However, she did not intend to remain in this disreputable hostelry any longer than necessary; surely *someone* in the neighborhood, of gentle birth and comfortable habitation, could be made to offer hospitality until her business with the school was satisfactorily settled.

The tone of the letter she had received from the headmistresses in response to her announcement that she was coming

to take her pupil away was disquieting. Instead of the immediate compliance she had expected, objections had been enu-
merated and barriers erected. Evidently the schoolmistresses
would not give up their most socially prominent pupil without
a struggle. They actually dared to demand the direct instructions of Miss Crump's papa, the Viscount, now in Bath, and
had refused to accept *her* word, the word of a *le Strange*. When
Miss le Strange protested that the Viscount was ill and unable
to make such a decision, they replied that they would wait until
his health improved.

The most charitable construction Miss le Strange could
put upon this attitude was that, in this barbaric, out-of-the-way
part of the world, the ladies of the Winthrop Hopkins Academy
had never heard of the le Strange family.

"When you have finished, Maggie, I want you to go downstairs and find out who the principal people are in this place,"
she instructed the maid. "And be sure to mention to the other
servants who my great-grandfather was. It is essential that it
become known that I am no ordinary governess, but a person
of consequence. Apparently, we shall have to remain in this
dismal place for some time; at least until we can receive word
from Lord Baggeshotte. Very tiresome, but those ridiculous
schoolmistresses won't give up Miss Crump without it."

"Yes, Miss," said the maid, who knew that her mistress
would be difficult to manage so long as she was forced to
remain in this rather run-down country inn. She made her
way down to the kitchen to order some hot negus for Miss le

Strange and a sip of gin and lemon for herself. While awaiting these items, she rattled off details of her lady's fabled ancestry, and the high esteem, amounting almost to awe, in which Viscount Baggeshotte held her.

"He's that grateful to her for condescending to teach his only daughter, why, you wouldn't believe it," she said, drinking down her gin in the kitchen so that the negus did not go cold. "Practically went down on his knees. Thinks the world of her, he does."

Maggie often found it convenient to forget that she was employed by the Viscount, rather than by Miss le Strange. Although the other Baggeshotte servants disliked the governess and feared for the well-being of little Miss Crump under her care, Maggie found that the lady's cold and imperious temperament matched her own. She flattered herself that *she*, at least, could tell quality when she met it.

Suitably impressed, the staff at the Blue Swan was ready enough to accept Miss le Strange at her own valuation, and in return confided to Maggie a list of those gentry in the area who might be worthy of her acquaintance.

Miss le Strange received this information with satisfaction. She would, of course, have to await an introduction, and the bitter truth was that, instead of being the person of property she was so obviously *meant* to be, she was, in fact, a governess, only one step up from a servant. However, Miss le Strange had never allowed this dispiriting reality to impinge upon her comforts, or upon her sense of her own importance. She faced her future with the steady eye and firm grip of a military commander; she believed that, if called upon, she could produce

the courage and audacity so conspicuously exhibited by her ancestors at the battles of Crécy and Agincourt.

"Once more unto the breach, dear friends, once more; or
close the wall up with our English dead," she said aloud in
thrilling tones, striking the bedpost with a small fist.

Maggie nodded in grave approval of this display of aristocratic defiance. "Yes, Miss," she said, and awaited further orders.

It was annoying to discover that the two great ladies of the
place, Lady Boring of Gudgeon Park and her stepsister, Mrs.
Fredericks of Crooked Castle, were both undergoing confine-
ments after the birth of their first children. Miss le Strange
was made for better things than sick-nursing; invalids were so
demanding and ungrateful, and babies shrieked with such self-
willed abandon that it quite gave her a headache.

Yellering Hall, owned by Sir Quentin and Lady
Throstletwist, was reported to be filled with young men visiting an injured friend, who was in turn recuperating at the
school. It would be quite improper to attempt to insinuate herself at the Hall. Miss le Strange was an unmarried woman and,
as such, must protect her reputation. In her position she could
not be too careful, and young gentlemen were all too apt to
think themselves irresistible. Miss le Strange much preferred
older men, who were grateful for any attention.

Only one possibility remained in this limited set of people.
Lord Boring's mother, Mrs. Westing, had recently moved from
the great house at Gudgeon Park to the dower house, a small
but elegant residence within the Park grounds. All parties involved agreed that the mother-in-law and her new daughter

by marriage would get on better in separate houses, and Mrs. Westing, like Miss le Strange, found the wailing of infants to be extremely trying.

So far as Maggie's information went, Mrs. Westing, who was said to be a lady who enjoyed games of chance to the exclusion of all other entertainments, was not particularly well-bred. She had married into the nobility and had never owned a title herself, being but the mother of the heir to the barony. This did not worry Miss le Strange; on the contrary. She had found that it was infinitely easier to impress those who had only relatively recently ascended in society. Mrs. Westing would do very well for her purposes. In addition, Miss le Strange was not unacquainted with games of chance herself; many a genteel evening of whist had supplied her with dress money in years past. She had no fear of Mrs. Westing's skill.

Blood will tell! she reminded herself, and prepared to bend the unsuspecting inhabitants of this provincial neighborhood to her will.

10

BOTH MISS CRUMP and Miss Pffolliott were in a condition of considerable unease. Miss Crump might not be aware that her governess was even now resident at the Blue Swan, plotting to retake possession of her charge, but given the tenacity and decision of the lady's nature, there was little reason to doubt that she soon would be. The idea made Miss Crump's knees quake and her insides feel queer.

Miss Pffolliott was in a somewhat better state, though suffering from a number of misgivings. Being resolved to behave in a circumspect fashion toward her admirer, she felt that her guilt toward her teachers and guardians was eased. However, the man might reveal to others that he had been writing to her almost since her arrival at the school. At least, she thought, she had not been such a fool as to encourage him in his improper behavior. That would have been fatal indeed! It was bad enough that she had not shown the letters to her instructors, so that they could have dealt with the matter.

And now she could not think of any reason to avoid her

usual solitary walk to the post office, which had become hateful. In vain did she plead with her fellow students to accompany her; no one else wished to be absent at a time when young gentlemen *might* come calling. She considered telling Miss Quince, the most sympathetic of the schoolmistresses, that a strange man had accosted her and that she was too frightened to repeat the journey. But she cringed away from the thought that Miss Quince might send Robert to deal with the matter, and later question him about it.

In addition to this, she had developed a nervous habit of expecting men to burst out of the shrubbery at her at the unlikeliest moments, and it had rendered her skittish. Whenever one of the other young ladies approached her from behind, or placed a hand upon her sleeve, or spoke her name unexpectedly, she had taken to shrieking in an unreserved manner. This had the unfortunate result of giving the other girls yet another reason to decline to accompany her on a long walk across the moor.

She set out alone once again, looking about for any lurking figures as she walked. When a shepherd sitting in the shadow of a stone wall hailed her with a courteous "How do, Miss?" she uttered her now habitual scream.

However, once recovered, her eye fell upon the shepherd's dog, a large, ferocious-looking creature with smoldering yellow eyes. She had encountered Wolfie before, and knew him to be a far more amiable beast than his exterior might suggest. Indeed, he was a much misunderstood animal, having the inner qualities of a lapdog with the outer appearance of one of his namesakes in a particularly nasty mood.

"Mr. Lomax, do you think I could take Wolfie with me to the post office?" Miss Pffolliott begged. "I am rather nervous, as you can see, and the dog would be company for me. I will bring him right back."

Mr. Lomax frowned. Wolfie was a working dog, not a pet, and it seemed a foolish request. What could worry the young lady out on the open moor? Still, she did appear to be rather in a state, and it was unlikely he would require the dog's services for several hours' time; he had been contemplating a long nap in the shade, if the truth were to be known.

"Eee, Miss, take him if you will," he said kindly. "Coom up, lad!" he ordered the dog. "Go on wi' t'lady. Away!"

Wolfie lurched to his feet, giving every impression of being about to leap upon Miss Pffolliott and rend her limb from limb. Instead, he lounged obediently along at her heels down the road, slavering in a disgusting fashion and leering from side to side with such apparent menace that a mother duck and her offspring out for a promenade broke ranks and scattered, uttering feeble cries.

When Mr. Rasmussen appeared—from behind a large clump of gorse bushes this time—her cry of alarm was little more than a gasp; Wolfie gave her courage.

Since her decision to rebuff Mr. Rasmussen required that she avert her gaze and pass by without acknowledgment, she could not savor his expression quite so much as she might have liked. However, it was quite obvious that his jaw dropped upon sighting Wolfie.

"I say! I say, Miss Pffolliott!" the horrified Mr. Rasmussen was at last heard to gasp. *"Do look behind you!"*

Wolfie flicked a hot, sulfurous glance in his direction and produced some noises in his throat that were intended to be genial greetings. He drooled. Mr. Rasmussen moaned and shielded his face from the inevitable carnage about to take place.

"Come along, Wolfie!" said Miss Pffolliott briskly, and the pair strolled onward to the post office, untroubled by Mr. Rasmussen or by anyone else.

✦ ✦ ✦

"Hullo, old chap, good to have you here at last! I see you brought the telescope, as I requested," Mr. Crabbe said, buffeting his younger brother about the shoulders by way of a greeting.

The Reverend Mr. Rupert Crabbe, new-arrived from the West Riding, replied, "Yes, though I can't think why. The weather in this beastly country is nearly always overcast, if not actually raining—I cannot make use of the instrument more than a few times a year. Still, on the coast in September, perhaps we might see *something*. What was it, exactly, that you wanted to look at?"

"Oh, not I!" Mr. Crabbe replied as he led his brother into the main receiving room of Yellering Hall. "There is a young lady here, a Miss Franklin, who has a great interest in astronomy, and nobody to discuss it with her. She is vastly intrigued by your telescope."

"Oh, a *lady*!" Mr. Rupert Crabbe was dismissive. "Depend upon it, Henry, she doesn't care a whit—she is only trying to impress you. Why can't you conduct your amours on your own, without making me drag that telescope all the way here from Stonyfields? I'll wager a quid she does not know a planet from a star in the sky."

Mr. Crabbe smiled. "In that case, I hope you keep a quid handy, as I expect to require it of you soon. Do you know of a man named Legendre?"

"The French mathematician? Clever chap, I believe. What the deuce do *you* know of him?"

"Nothing but what Miss Franklin was good enough to inform me. Something to do with calculating the orbits of comets?"

"Ah!" Mr. Rupert Crabbe was silent a moment. "So, indeed, a definitely learned lady. I cannot think why a woman troubles to be learned. I suppose she is quite hideous?"

"Not at all! Pleasant to look upon and possesses a nice little fortune, or so I am told. She regards me as practically an imbecile, but may feel more respect for *your* intellectual attainments."

"Ah!" said Mr. Rupert Crabbe. "Well, I see you have planned out my time here for me—I am to be a sort of superior entertainment."

"Precisely! We shall have to get up a star party, or something of the sort, on the rooftop of the school. A romantic thought! In addition to you and me, Hadley, and Arbuthnot, it will be attended by any number of lovely young ladies and all the stars that twinkle in the heavens. What could be more delightful?"

"I *knew* it had to do with one of your amours," his brother said in some disgust. "Evidently Miss Franklin is but the pretext for your 'star party.' Some other young lady of the company is your aim. Well, I hope *you* have honorable intentions, and that *she* is plenty flush with funds, for our father is feeling the wind a bit. Between us, he has sent me here to get you to agree to let him sell off some land to cover his debts."

As heir to an entailed estate, Mr. Crabbe needed to give his permission before his father could sell. His voice was cool as he replied, "Oh, he has, has he? Been riding pretty high of late, I believe. When's the last time he spent any time on the property?"

"Not these last five years, not that I know of, tho' he is visiting friends in the area now. There's going to be a great smash-up soon, I fear, with his gambling and carousing. I don't think you can assume that so much as a farthing will come with the place when he dies. I wouldn't be too certain that your allowance will remain at its current level, either. I must say, brother, I consider myself well out of it. Stonyfields may be a humble parsonage rather than a great house, but I do not envy you. It would be a considerable relief to know you were well married, and to an ample purse."

"I shall see what I can do to arrange matters," Mr. Crabbe said evenly. "But for now, I am looking forward to my star party. And," he added, with a stern look at his brother, "I expect payment of my quid *immediately* after. It seems I may be in need of it."

✦ ✦ ✦

"Jane, dear, do remove your bonnet. I cannot see your face at all, and you know I am anxious to be certain that you are in good looks and health."

Miss Crump's worst nightmare had materialized in front of her and was ensconced in a chair in the school's front parlor, calmly eating biscuits. Miss Crump looked around wildly, seeking escape. She clutched at her bonnet as though afraid it would be wrenched from her head by force. She and her erstwhile governess had been left alone together for this touching reunion.

"But the draft . . ." she whispered. "And the gentlemen will be here soon . . ."

"Jane!" Miss le Strange's tone altered from a gentle request to a command like the crack of a carriage whip. "Take it off. Now!"

With reluctant, trembling fingers, Miss Crump untied her bonnet and dragged it from her head. Without the huge, all-encompassing hat, Miss Crump looked oddly small and shrunken. Constant compression had flattened her already thin hair to the contours of her head.

Miss le Strange's lips curled in a slight smile. "Do you at least remove it in your bed?" she inquired.

Miss Crump nodded. "Miss Quince says I must. She fears I might smother myself in my sleep, else."

Miss le Strange gave a tiny, brittle laugh. "The woman shows *some* sense, at least. I am sorry, but I cannot compliment you on your appearance, my dear. You look quite ill. We must get you back to Baggeshotte Towers immediately where I can look after you myself."

Little Miss Crump squeaked in terror and looked up at her tormentor like a cornered mouse. "I am not ill, indeed I am not! I am growing taller and bigger, Miss Quince says so." This being one of the longest pronouncements she had ever managed to produce, it became necessary for her to take a great gulp of air before going on. "I—I like it here, and I wish to stay," she concluded.

"Well, we shall just have to see about that," said Miss le Strange, brushing biscuit crumbs off her lap onto the carpet. "I am afraid you must allow me to know best on this subject."

Seeing her hopes of freedom also dashed to the floor, Miss Crump gathered herself together for another attempt.

"And I have written to my papa, begging him to be allowed to stay," she added, not daring to lift her eyes, "and my teachers enclosed letters, too, saying what great progress I am making." She was panting with effort by now.

"Oh, nonsense!" said Miss le Strange.

Yet something about the way she said it lifted Miss Crump's heart. For once, Miss le Strange did not sound certain of her complete domination.

Miss le Strange leaned back in her chair and studied her charge. She unwound a scarf from her neck, revealing something that glittered at her bosom.

Miss Crump gasped; a tiny sound.

"What now?" demanded Miss le Strange. Following her onetime pupil's gaze, she looked down. "Oh, yes. The Bagge-shotte rubies. Don't be such a goose, child. Naturally I took them with me when I left. One cannot leave valuable items simply lying about. The servants, you know! Don't tell *me* that that butler can be trusted. Run along, dear. I wish to speak to your instructresses."

But they are not *the Baggeshotte rubies,* Miss Crump thought. *They are the Ramsbottom rubies. They were my mother's, and now they are mine! You had no right!*

However, this objection, reasonable as it might be, remained unexpressed. Miss Crump hurried from the room.

11

BOTH THE ARRIVAL of Mr. Rupert Crabbe and the proposed star party were greeted with a great deal of enthusiasm. All of the ladies suddenly discovered that they had always yearned to know more about the composition of the stars and planets. The idea of a festivity in the nighttime, out of doors, and on the rooftop of the school was so novel and, as Mr. Crabbe had suggested, so romantic that it caught the collective imagination at once. The older ladies at first fretted about the dangers of the night air and its effect upon delicate constitutions, but were persuaded that, on a fine evening in September, and in a healthy neighborhood, this would not be a serious concern. And, since the ostensible reason behind the gathering was educational, even Miss Quince had to admit that it was a worthy project.

As a creative instructor will, she adapted her teaching to capitalize upon this sudden interest in the heavenly spheres. All other scholarly pursuits were shrugged off as being petty and mundane; the celestial globe occupied pride of place in the schoolroom, and the vast expanse of space set the boundary of their discourse.

A revolution had taken place in the way Miss Franklin's fellow students thought of her. Once a despised bluestocking with no conversation and no idea of how to trim a hat or net a stylish purse, she was now the accepted authority on all matters astronomical. In contrast to the physicist Blaise Pascal, who in a weak moment had once admitted, "The eternal silence of these infinite spaces fills me with dread," their Miss Franklin contemplated the enormity of endless time and distance with a cool and considering eye. The probable temperature of the surface of the sun and the nature and number of the rings of Saturn were at her fingertips, and she could bring her fellow students abreast of the latest in modern thought on shooting stars, eclipses, and the affairs of the most far-flung planets.

Miss Franklin's view of the sum total of intelligence contained within the walls of the Winthrop Hopkins Academy did not substantially alter as a result of this change in attitude, but she *was* human, and not immune to the flattery of having her opinion sought. She treated the inquiries, from Miss Victor's "Does falling asleep in the moonlight *really* make one run mad?" to Miss Evans's rather more rational questions about the moon's gravity and its effect on the tides that washed up against the seaside cliffs of Lesser Hoo with the patient indulgence of a dignified adult dog being swarmed over by a litter of puppies. Her responses were as simple and concise as possible, and her manner warmed and softened as she pronounced them.

She alone was privileged by its owner to handle the object of her desire: the telescope. This traveled in a magnificent mahogany case to protect its expensively ground lenses and delicate focusing knob. Reverently removed from the case and assembled, it proved to be an elegant brass tube some thirty-six inches long, mounted on a three-legged stand. After considerable discussion between Miss Franklin and Mr. Rupert Crabbe as to the merits of refractors versus reflectors, the desirability of a finder-scope attachment, and the many difficulties presented by the English climate to the serious stargazer, the instrument was set up on the dinner table and aimed out an open window.

Several of the young ladies were surprised, having assumed that the scope would only work during the hours of darkness, but were pleased to line up for the opportunity to watch Mrs. Watkins, who lived in a cottage on the grounds, hang her wet laundry out to dry in the sun. The sudden magnification of Mrs. Watkins through the lens was startling; several of the girls cried out, "La! How strange!" feeling an obscure sense of trespass as they spied upon the old woman.

On the other hand, when it came to Miss Asquith's turn, she declined to observe the laundry-day routine of a cottager. Caring nothing for the feelings of either Miss Franklin or Mr. Rupert Crabbe, she grasped the instrument in both hands and swiveled it so that it aimed at the village, just visible through the trees. She bent her fair head to the eyepiece, adjusted the focus, and then, after a few moments of silence, cried out in outraged tones: "Oh, my goodness! How could he? And I always thought him such a *respectable* sort of person!"

As the rest of the party regarded her with wonder, she moved the telescope back to its former position and stepped away, her lips pressed tight together, her gaze averted and her entire posture expressive of shocking news withheld. She shook her head as the others questioned her ("What was it, what did you see? Oh, do tell us, dear Miss Asquith!") and walked away to sit in a dignified manner in a chair some distance away.

"No, I am sorry, I could not undertake to tell you—it would not be right."

Mr. Crabbe's eyes narrowed. He stepped up to his brother's instrument, moved it back toward the village, and looked. After a long silence, he raised his head and regarded her demure form, bent over some needlework in her lap.

"Ah, Miss Asquith," he said sadly, "I weep for the man who marries you, truly I do. Poor, *poor* fellow." He repositioned the telescope in the direction of some sheep that were drifting about aimlessly on the moor, and then relinquished it to the next viewer. After which, evidently forgetting about the sad lot of the man who loved and married Miss Asquith, he followed her to her corner and proposed a game of piquet.

Later, Miss Franklin took another turn at the scope and looked long and hard at the village street and shop facades visible through the gap in the trees.

"I don't believe she could have seen a thing!" she said with decision. "She made up the entire episode!"

Mr. Rupert Crabbe shook his head at this folly, and together they tenderly laid the telescope back in its mahogany casket.

❧ ❧ ❧

Mr. Hadley did not leave Lesser Hoo, in spite of his earlier assertion. He, along with Mr. Crabbe, had moved his belongings to Yellering Hall and came to call at the school as often as before. The difference was that he no longer sat with Miss Mainwaring in the drawing room, or offered her his arm on their walks to the seashore. Indeed, he avoided her and shied away from her gaze.

The only comfort for Miss Mainwaring—and it was a very small comfort—was that it was accompanied by a decided air of unhappiness. She could believe that he might be uneasy; if he wished to dampen expectations for the future by no longer distinguishing her in company, *that* could make a man feel self-conscious. But no, it was more than embarrassment; putting an end to their comfortable walks and talks had made him unhappy. He sat silent and sad, staring at the floor, or out the window, or anywhere but at her, as sharp a contrast as could be to the cheerful, talkative young man of a few days ago.

Occasionally he lifted his eyes to study—astonishingly enough—Miss Crump. That lady was aware of his scrutiny, Miss Mainwaring could tell. The unfortunate Miss Crump bent her bonneted head down to focus on her tatting, twisting in her chair so as to present only the smallest possible portion of her anatomy. After a few minutes of this, she would rise and excuse herself from the company, whereupon Mr. Hadley would sigh and return to his close observation of the floorboards.

At last, Mr. Hadley seemed to make up his mind about whatever it was that was worrying him. On the afternoon of the first viewing with the telescope, as Miss Mainwaring watched from a nearby alcove, he stood and walked decisively over to Miss Crump. He bowed and said, "I ought to beg your pardon for not saying so before, but my father wishes me to present his compliments. I have recently had a letter from him, and he tells me he is well-acquainted with *your* father." Although his voice was low, Miss Mainwaring's ears were sharp, and she could hear him quite distinctly.

"Oh! Is—is he?" Miss Crump's bonnet turned this way and that in a hunted fashion, as though one or both parental figures might leap out at her.

"In fact, it appears that my father, having heard that we are in company with each other," Mr. Hadley continued in a gloomy tone, "is anxious that we become better acquainted." He heaved a sigh. "So, unless you have any objection, I shall attempt to do just that."

If Mr. Hadley had been able to penetrate beyond the brim and interior ruffles of Miss Crump's bonnet to see the expression on her face, he would have concluded that she did indeed have an objection. Muffled sounds came from her general direction that *might* have been expressive of gratified consent, but seemed more likely to be terrified dismay. However, he did not pause to interpret them, but, like a man determined to press forward in the teeth of a howling blizzard, he lowered his head and waded in.

"As perhaps you already know," he began, "my father was an officer of the East India Company, who is now retired and come back to live on his estates in England. It is his greatest wish that, having finished my studies at Oxford, I should marry and bring a wife back to live at Rowehaven. That, of course, is our house—rather a rattletrap old place, I am afraid. It was got by purchase rather than by inheritance—ours is not *nearly* so distinguished a family as yours." Here he bobbed a brief bow in her direction and then went on, "It is situated in the county of Cumberland, near the west coast. I can*not* recommend the climate of Cumberland." He paused to look up at the ceiling. "Trapped between the mountains and the sea as we are, I should think we are quite the dampest place in all England. *We* are used to it, of course, but outsiders sometimes find it irksome. One has to keep in motion, you understand, else one soon finds mosses and lichens actually *growing* upon one's person."

As an apparent afterthought, he added, "There was an old man once, I believe, left sitting on a bench in the rain, not a stone's throw away from Rowehaven. His people forgot about him, you see, and didn't think to go back and fetch him until the next morning, by which time he and the bench were positively *fused* together, one great pile of green algae. They had to *bury* the bench with him, I am sorry to say, and it was very awkward, as it didn't fit into a coffin. Well, it's not a pretty subject. *Dreadful* place, Rowehaven. However, as I say, the pater is anxious that I find myself a bride and bring her home with me. But I mustn't talk so much about *my* affairs. Do tell me about yourself, Miss Crump."

Miss Mainwaring, who had been listening to this speech with widening eyes and parting lips, moved her fascinated stare from Mr. Hadley to Miss Crump.

Miss Crump did not accept the invitation to converse about her own life and interests. She sat motionless for a long minute, and then sagged to her right, toppling onto the floor, where she lay quite still.

Miss Mainwaring flew to her side and knelt on the floor.

"You utter cad, sir!" she whispered, casting a furious glance up at Mr. Hadley, who, to do him justice, was looking horrified. "How *could* you? Miss Crump, of all people! Oh poor, dear Miss Crump, do wake up!"

"You do not understand," cried Mr. Hadley. "I was only trying to—"

"Trying to do *what*? Give the poor girl convulsions?" Miss Mainwaring administered a series of slaps to Miss Crump's pallid hand in an attempt to rouse her. Others, alarmed by this scene, were gathering around, so Miss Mainwaring ceased her recriminations, only saying in a sharp tone, "She is regaining consciousness. Go and fetch a glass of wine for her."

Mr. Hadley obeyed, and soon Miss Crump was restored to her seat, being fanned by five or six ladies and presented with hartshorn and vinegar by two more. Seeing that the effect of the attention was to make Miss Crump even more uncomfortable, Miss Quince intervened and led her off to her chamber to lie down. As they went, Miss Crump happened to catch sight of Mr. Hadley and uttered a small, distressed cry.

"Hush, child, hush," soothed Miss Quince, but she regarded Mr. Hadley with interest.

At this point, the gentlemen decided that they had stayed long enough. They gathered up gloves and walking sticks—it had been decided to leave the telescope at the school in Miss Franklin's care to avoid further jostling about—and prepared to go. Mr. Hadley was not immediately to be found, however, and when he did appear, with disordered cravat and an anxious look, he was observed to pass close by Miss Mainwaring and bend to speak to her.

When they were gone, Miss Mainwaring went upstairs to her room. It was only once she had gained the privacy of that chamber that she smoothed out the little scrap of paper Mr. Hadley had pressed into her hand.

In hasty, ink-spattered letters it said:

Have patience, I beg. Trust me.

12

MISS PFFOLLIOTT NOW made it a regular practice to borrow Wolfie for the daily walk to the post office. Mr. Lomax, the shepherd, had two younger and smaller dogs that were far better at herding sheep. In his opinion, Wolfie was entirely too soft. He was inclined to dote on the sheep in a foolish, avuncular manner, frolicking with the lambs, nuzzling the ewes, and bumping shoulders with the rams in a companionable, man-to-man sort of way, rather than instilling the fear and respect that was the proper attitude for a flock toward its attendant sheepdogs. It was all very bad for ovine discipline.

"Leave off licking that lamb's face at once, tha' waste o' dog flesh," growled Mr. Lomax, "and go along wi' t'young lady."

Wolfie was only too pleased to comply, and whenever they encountered Mr. Rasmussen on their journeys was also pleased to greet *him*, veering off the path at an uneven, off-kilter trot, foaming a bit at the mouth and baring his overgrown yellow fangs in an affable grin. The shriek with which that gentleman responded to these overtures was almost as shrill as the shrieks with which Miss Pffolliott had been wont to greet *him* in the past.

For several days Mr. Rasmussen had remained at a respectful distance, bowing courteously as they passed; so thoroughly cowed did he appear to be that Miss Pffolliott even went so far as to grant him a small nod in return. On this occasion she collected the letters for the school and sailed past him with her head held high and a sense of growing confidence.

As she handed the post over to Miss Quince, she felt a sudden misgiving at the sight of one envelope addressed to the headmistresses of the Winthrop Hopkins Academy—it seemed familiar in some way, and it made her uneasy. She watched Miss Quince as she opened it and perused the contents. Miss Quince's eyebrows lifted and, after reading several sentences, she raised her gaze from the page.

"As you have guessed, my dear, this concerns you. It is from your father."

Her father! Miss Pffolliott did not feel equal to speech.

"He sends greetings and kind regards to us and to you, and wishes you to know that an old friend of his is visiting in our area. His name is Mr. Gideon Rasmussen, and—only fancy!— he is staying at the Blue Swan, right here in Lesser Hoo. He wishes to convey to you and to us"—here Miss Quince looked thoughtfully at Miss Pffolliott—"his strong desire that we extend every courtesy toward the gentleman. He then goes on to say, apparently apropos of nothing," she added, "that it is quite time we should be thinking of finding you a husband. And that is all, save his signature."

She folded the letter up, regarding her pupil with some concern. "You are not well acquainted with your father, I believe, Miss Pffolliott?"

"No, Miss Quince. I have never met him in my life, save for the day I was born. My mother gave up her life in giving life to me, and he sent me away to go and live with her family."

"Which family is now dead, I understand. You are alone in the world, then, except for this rather elusive parent?"

Miss Pffolliott nodded, her eyes large and anxious.

Miss Quince tapped the edge of the folded letter pensively on the top of the little table that served as her work desk. "It is your grandparents' estate that pays our fees, you know, not your father. However, he *is* your father, and as such he has both moral *and* legal rights. We would wish to cooperate in any way that is reasonable and proper. I shall send an emissary down to the Blue Swan and invite this Mr. Rasmussen to visit."

"Y-e-e-es, Miss Quince," Miss Pffolliott replied, looking at the tips of her shoes.

"However, if you should find his company or his person distasteful, we can inform your father of the fact."

Miss Pffolliott nodded silently.

"Now cease looking so glum! You have nothing to worry about."

"Yes, Miss Quince," she replied, and left the room. But in spite of Miss Quince's kindly meant reassurances, she knew that she had a great deal to worry her.

For she had at last identified the source of her unease in relation to the envelope containing her father's letter: the handwriting on it looked remarkably similar to the handwriting of one Mr. Gideon Rasmussen. And there was no way at all to explain *that* to Miss Quince.

✤ ✤ ✤

The star party was tentatively scheduled for either Friday or Saturday evening, whichever should give promise of the best weather and hence the best viewing conditions, and preparations began apace. The roof of the schoolhouse was ideal for this purpose, the building being a simple Georgian three-storied box with a parapet around. Miss Briggs's harp (for she played this as well as the pianoforte) was to be carried up to furnish an appropriately celestial musical accompaniment. This made everyone feel that a small, informal dance ought to be attempted, as well as a light supper laid out for refreshment after their exertions. Admittedly, this was straying a good deal from the educational purpose of the gathering, but the headmistresses were prepared to be indulgent, and an elegant, cultured event was anticipated by all.

Miss Franklin was so delighted to have access to a telescope that she soon prevailed upon Mr. Rupert Crabbe to allow her to use it nightly in order to test a series of mathematical calculations she was carrying out in relation to the orbit of Uranus. She had been corresponding with an Italian astronomer (signing her name as "R. Franklin" in order to disguise her sex, though she did not confess this duplicity to Mr. Rupert Crabbe) and had obtained a set of his observations taken over the course of several years. It was her belief that there was yet another undiscovered planet in the solar system, one which circled the sun in an ellipse even wider and more immense than that of Uranus, which was the farthest yet known.

"Why, Ceres was detected only a decade ago! I believe that many, many more objects exist within our own system yet to be discovered," she said.

Mr. Rupert Crabbe rather scoffed at the idea that a planet could be inferred by measuring the orbits of others. However, he allowed her the use of the instrument, examined her calculations, and checked the accuracy of her sums. He admitted that they seemed to be correct, but argued that slight variations in the trajectory of such a distant object might be due merely to errors of observation.

"Oh! I know it well, sir," she responded, raking her hands through her abundant black hair so that it stuck out at an odd angle from her head (thereby destroying the neat and artful arrangement achieved by a long-suffering ladies' maid). "I realize that only the most vigilant and persistent scrutiny can possibly validate my suspicions. That is why I am so grateful to have the use of your device whilst you remain in the neighborhood."

"You may have that, and welcome. I myself have been so discouraged by the clouds that haunt England that I do not use it so much as I had anticipated when I purchased it. *You* seem to have been able to make some observations, however." He pointed to a small notebook Miss Franklin had been using.

"Oh, I do not go to bed until I have had *some* result, even if I have to remain awake all night," she said. "However, I need an instrument of my own, rather than a borrowed one. What use are a few snatched nights here and there, when I ought to be scanning the skies nightly over a period of years? If only I could use the money spent on my attending this useless academy to purchase one!"

Several of the other pupils were nearby, and Mr. Rupert Crabbe's eyebrows lifted at the bluntness of Miss Franklin's speech. He said, "Not entirely useless, surely, since it enabled us to have the pleasure of making your acquaintance!"

"We might have met sooner if my mother allowed me to go to school in Cambridge or Oxford," she retorted. "Here I am exiled from scientific thought and opinion. There isn't a person with an ounce of intellectual curiosity inside of a hundred-mile radius. Er," she added as an afterthought, "with the exception of you, that is. But how I long to discuss my ideas with men of experience and knowledge, such as Sir William Herschel. I believe that his sister Caroline is his assistant, and has discovered a number of comets in her own right."

"Under his direction, I believe that is so. However, your mother no doubt believed your removal from distracting intellectual pursuits was in your best interests. Without an accomplished brother or male relative to sponsor you and supervise your work, it is unlikely that you would have been taken seriously, you know," he said in a gentle tone.

She stared at him in silence for a moment, and then gathered up her bundle of papers. "No doubt you are in the right. Good afternoon, Mr. Crabbe," she said.

"Wait! Miss Franklin, please do not take offense—" he began, but she had left him. He sighed, and then bent to pick up one of the notebooks that, in her hurry, had escaped her grasp. He sat for a time studying it, and then folded it and thrust it into his vest.

✦ ✦ ✦

Miss le Strange had triumphed. Through the unwilling intervention of Miss Winthrop, she had managed to get herself introduced to Mrs. Westing, mother of Lord Boring, and within a matter of a few days was moving her possessions from the despised precincts of the Blue Swan to the much more refined dower house at Gudgeon Park. Mrs. Westing, who had come to the restricted world of Lesser Hoo two years ago from the lively society of London, was frankly bored, and glad to have a new face to look at, as well as a new partner at cards. True, as the newcomer belonged to the impoverished le Strange family, she was unlikely to provide any significant income, but she soon proved herself to be a skilled and wily opponent. Mrs. Westing, who relied rather heavily on her winnings for the niceties of life, also delighted in what might be called the art and science of these sorts of games; she respected a worthy adversary.

The two ladies settled down quite happily by the fireside every evening to outmaneuver and outplay each other in an atmosphere of utmost concentration, the sound of the cards slapping down upon the table the only noise for hours at a time. Eventually, however, Miss le Strange grew restless and wished to be taken on visits about the neighborhood, so that she might commence her campaign to recapture her pupil, Miss Crump.

Annoyed by this demand at first, Mrs. Westing soon realized that her guest would form an ideal partner in four-handed games such as whist. Rather than battling each other every night, they could instead join forces and launch that brilliance, those subtle strategies and feats of memory, against their unsuspecting neighbors instead. Not only would it be most enjoyable, it might be quite profitable, as well.

She therefore agreed quite amiably, and set about introducing Miss le Strange into the society of Lesser Hoo.

13

THE NIGHT OF the star party was a lovely autumn evening. The last culinary herbs in the kitchen gardens had been newly harvested in advance of a killing frost, so the air was heavy with a delicious scent of parsley, sweet marjoram, savory, and thyme. The roof of the school had been transformed—tables, rugs, chairs, and folding screens had been carried up and arranged about the space, giving the illusion of an indoor room with the heavens above for a ceiling.

Miss Briggs, dressed in a white gown that glowed silver in the moonlight, leaned into the harp, coaxing scores of glissandi from her instrument by way of tuning up, and the servants moved decorously about, dispensing claret cup and little cakes, quite as though they were in the parlor two stories below. Enormously excited by the glamor of the whole affair, Robert was in his element. He darted here and there, replenishing plates and glasses, arranging flowers, whisking away crumbs, bowing so often and with such vigor that he made everyone feel rather seasick.

Before she was allowed to ascend to the rooftop, Miss

Hopkins and Miss Winthrop had inspected every student to make sure that she was shawled and cloaked against the treacherous night air, even though the temperature was almost tropical, and the ladies had to fan themselves in order to maintain some level of comfort. "'For all flesh is as grass,'" Miss Winthrop reminded them, tugging Miss Crump's shawl a little tighter as a shield against encroaching mortality. "'The grass withereth, and the flower thereof falleth away.'"

"How true," murmured Miss Asquith, blotting her damp forehead with a handkerchief. "I can feel myself withering and falling away even now."

Happily, as the night advanced it cooled, and the cloaks and shawls became, if not welcome, then at least tolerable. The crescent moon—merely a pallid sliver earlier in the daylight—brightened until it dominated the sky. It was now just above the horizon, a half hour before setting, which meant they could study it through the lens briefly before it sank from sight. However, Miss Franklin and Mr. Rupert Crabbe assured everybody that the other features of the night sky would be far more visible once the moon was gone, taking its crystalline light with it. The company lined up to gaze upon the desolate lunar landscape, the mountains and valleys picked out in sharp relief on the boundary between dark and light.

"The mountains of the moon! How strange and wonderful," murmured Miss Victor as she relinquished her place at the telescope. The sight of those shining highlands, so far away and so alien from daily life, imposed an awed, respectful silence upon the company until at last the orb drifted out of sight and was hidden by the western hills.

Once the moon had retired for the night, however, Miss Briggs was prevailed upon to strike up a lively tune on her harp, and three couples—Miss Victor being partnered by Miss Pffolliott—lined up for a country dance while Miss Franklin and Mr. Rupert Crabbe attempted to work out the whereabouts of the planet Saturn.

The star party had always been meant to be a small and informal gathering with the sole attendees the pupils of the school and the visiting gentlemen. However, urged on by Miss le Strange, Mrs. Westing decided that the lack of an invitation did not signify; they were entitled to attend by virtue of their combined rank (Miss le Strange) and position in the neighborhood (Mrs. Westing). They were shown up to the rooftop on the thin pretext of coming to inquire after the health of Mr. Arbuthnot, who was at present installed in a large wingback chair with his injured leg on an ottoman. Upon being applied to, Miss Evans, who rarely left his side, was pleased to oblige with an exhaustive dissertation on the course of his illness and recovery. She painted a vivid picture of their hopes and fears, their moments of alarm and despondency, yet in conclusion did justice to their gradually increasing confidence and security in the future.

"I insist upon having the dressings changed twice a day," she confided, with as much self-assurance as if she and Mr. Arbuthnot had been wed a decade at least and she were the seasoned mother of eight, "lest putrefaction begin around the wound. I am informed that the outer crust of the injury—"

"Oh, delightful! So happy to hear it. But I believe Miss Hopkins is motioning me over," lied Mrs. Westing. After that, the ladies dropped all affectation of concern and settled down to further their own interests, Mrs. Westing to try to organize a card game and Miss le Strange to tell the tale of her old and distinguished family before this new audience. It was "My sister who married the *principe*, and is *now* of course properly addressed as the *Principessa*," and ". . . the Palazzo di Funghili, in Venice, you know," on the one hand, and ". . . it is called vingt-et-un, quite a *new* game from France . . ." and "Only a *small* flutter, to pass the time," on the other.

Miss Crump, who when she first arrived on the rooftop had chosen a seat at a safe distance from Mr. Hadley, was much alarmed when he stood and changed places so he could engage her in further conversation about his decrepit family home, his irascible father ("Rather a violent temper, I am afraid, but we find that if we give way to him in all things, we can manage him very well"), and the poor condition of the farmland on his estate ("Nothing but stones, I assure you, my dear Miss Crump—quite untillable—half the time we've nothing to put on the table to eat"). The entrance of Miss le Strange under the patronage of Mrs. Westing threw her into a further agony of emotion; she could not help but feel that the sufferings of Odysseus as he sailed between Scylla and Charybdis would never have compared with her own, caught between the horrors of Miss le Strange on her right and Mr. Hadley on her left.

To add to her distress, Miss le Strange was wearing not only the necklace, but also a pair of drop earrings and a jeweled comb from the parure once owned by Miss Crump's mother. The parure was an entire suite of jewels, with, in addition to the pieces now adorning Miss le Strange's person, a tiara, a brooch, and a pair of bracelets, all magnificent examples of the jeweler's art, and all belonging to Miss Crump and not to Miss le Strange.

Miserably, Miss Crump studied this out of the corner of her eye. Any woman of spirit would have demanded that her governess hand over the jewels at once. She tried to imagine the scene, tried to frame the sentences with which she would take back her property and reduce Miss le Strange to her proper place. "Miss le Strange," she would say—No, it was impossible. She shuddered, feeling an overwhelming desire to retire to her chamber, climb onto her couch, and pull the bed-clothes over her bonneted head.

Miss Mainwaring, aware at least of the discomfort her friend experienced in Mr. Hadley's company, rescued her. She led Miss Crump away from her chair to the telescope, demanding that they be shown the rings of Saturn, as she knew Miss Crump greatly wished it. Miss Crump had barely known of the existence of the rings of Saturn before this desire was imputed to her, but she offered no contradiction. Obediently she squinted through the lens and remarked, "How . . . how interesting!"

"Did you see Cassini's Division?" Miss Franklin demanded. "I could not, myself, but Mr. Rupert Crabbe says that he can when the conditions are right."

To Miss Crump, this reference to an astronomical term conveyed nothing but the dreaded long division over which she labored in vain. She looked at Miss Mainwaring for guidance, but that lady had stepped up to the telescope and was complaining that she saw nothing but dark, empty sky.

"N-no, I don't believe I did," Miss Crump said in a faint voice. "I never knew there was mathematics in space. How tiresome for you!" She and Miss Franklin regarded each other with mutual noncomprehension for a long moment, until Miss Mainwaring, having successfully focused on the planet, called out, "Oh yes, I see! There *is* a ring! How perfectly lovely!" With a twitch of her shoulders, Miss Franklin dismissed Miss Crump as an enigma beyond her ability to crack and instead begged Miss Mainwaring to count the number of rings she could pick out.

An invitation *had* been issued to Mr. Rasmussen, and Miss Pffolliott had spent the hours before the party in a state of mild dread, rather than eager anticipation. How could she broach the subject of the handwriting on her father's letter with him? Could it simply be a coincidence? Normally every individual develops a distinct and recognizable writing style. True, it was possible to see a similarity between her grandmother's writing and her own, but yet they were different; one could not be mistaken for another.

Perhaps her father and Mr. Rasmussen had shared the same tutor and had their letters taught them in the same way? That might account for a strong resemblance. Or, being close friends, perhaps one had, either knowingly or unknowingly, imitated the other? Miss Pffolliott's father had said that Mr. Rasmussen was an old friend, and perhaps a dear one, since he so strongly urged his daughter to pay the gentleman every respect.

Yet, while this might account for the problem of the handwriting, it introduced another. Why had Mr. Rasmussen written to her anonymously and sought to meet in secrecy, if he was in fact an old and good friend of her father's? Even if her grandmother thought her father a rogue, surely she would expect her granddaughter to be obedient to a parent's wishes at least to the extent of agreeing to meet a friend of his, so there could be no reason for such secrecy.

Now she regretted the fact that she had left the sole letter she had received from her father, long ago when she was six years old, at her home in Scunthorpe. Although she had read it often at one period of her life, it was quite some time since she had looked at the brief missive, and the precise shape and slant of the letters escaped her memory. She *thought* the writing was similar to his most recent letter (and hence to Mr. Rasmussen's), but she could not be certain.

These thoughts combined to make her uneasy as she waited her turn at the telescope and watched the entrance to the rooftop, looking for new arrivals. However, the minutes and then the hours slipped past, and Mr. Rasmussen did not come.

Initially, she was relieved, but, as the evening wound to its conclusion, her relief changed to another emotion. She did not find herself much attracted to her admirer, but he *did* admire her, which was a redeeming feature. Though not a vain girl, she could not help feeling that the least he could do was to demonstrate that admiration in front of her fellow students, instead of lurking under bridges to tax her with it in solitude. This ridiculous diffidence in public did his cause no good at all, as far as Miss Pffolliott was concerned.

In short, she was at last as annoyed by his absence as she had at first been alarmed by his impending presence.

For the rest of the ladies and gentlemen in the party, it was a night to be remembered, a night of enchantment and delight: eating, drinking, and dancing under the vast vault of heaven. Miss Briggs was praised for her musical efforts, and little Miss Victor, who was allowed to stay up long past her bedtime, danced with every gentleman present other than Mr. Arbuthnot, who was unable to dance with anyone. Miss Evans did not dance, either, but spent the evening in quiet conversation with, and tending to the needs of, the man she had every reason to believe would soon become her fiancé.

Miss Asquith had danced *three* times with Mr. Crabbe. After the third occasion, Miss Winthrop drew her aside and told her to stop making a spectacle of herself; if he were to ask again, she ought to refuse. Miss Asquith smiled in response; thereafter, she and Mr. Crabbe sat out the dancing in a dark corner, talking exclusively to each other. At intervals, the sound of her laughter floated out over the air, as light as thistledown.

A wind sprang up; the night grew colder, and the older ladies stirred: ought they to allow their charges to remain out-of-doors any longer? When a malicious gust of chill air extinguished the candles, the entertainment was declared to be at an end. After many lamentations over the conclusion of a delightful evening, the telescope was taken down and stowed away. The wind was too boisterous to allow the candles to be relit, and so the servants began to dismantle the temporary drawing room on the roof in near-total darkness.

Robert was to escort the ladies of the dower house down to their carriage and see them off. Mrs. Westing had only been able to manage to coerce her hosts into playing a few hands of vingt-et-un and was in an irritable mood; Miss le Strange, who considered that her evening had been spent more profitably, followed after, offering graceful thanks for the entertainment. As Robert attempted to offer Miss le Strange assistance in descending the unlit stairway, however, she halted and clapped a hand to her throat.

"My necklace!" she cried. "It is gone!"

14

OF COURSE, AN immediate and futile attempt was made to find the necklace in the dark, which involved many stumbles and tripping over half-rolled rugs. The search soon devolved into a version of blind man's buff in which all the participants, rather than the player designated as "It," were blindfolded. The shrieks and muffled laughter that resulted convinced Miss Quince to call a halt to the proceedings, lest someone tumble over the parapet or, perhaps, use the occasion as an excuse for some undignified and improper behavior.

"Ladies! I must ask you to descend and go to the drawing room at once," she said, raising her voice to be heard over the general hubbub and the rushing wind. The consequent move toward the stairs set off another chain of collisions, but under Miss Quince's management, all were gotten downstairs without injury or impropriety. Once the company had assembled in the drawing room, the search was declared over for the night. "But my necklace!" objected Miss le Strange. Greatly daring, Miss Crump lifted her eyes to look at her governess, but that lady seemed quite unconscious of any possible offense.

"I myself shall superintend the search," promised Miss Quince. "We shall not find it tonight, unless it is brought downstairs with some of the furniture or carpets. Tomorrow during the daylight hours will be the best time to discover it."

"It was that footman," Miss le Strange said. "I know I had it up until the moment the candles blew out. He took his opportunity *then* and abstracted it."

"Oh, pray do not say so, Miss le Strange," said Miss Quince. "Robert is an excellent young man—we are all so fond of him. I cannot believe he would do such a thing."

"You doubt my word, then—the word of a le Strange—and choose to believe in the innocence of a footman?"

"Please, Miss le Strange, remember we do not know that the necklace is lost. We will most likely find it in the morning, if not tonight."

"Very well. But do not forget: I am suspicious of that footman. I felt something brush against my neck when the lights were extinguished, and he was helping me with my shawl. I have little reason to doubt that that was the instant in which he unfastened it."

"Most likely what you felt was the shawl itself, Miss le Strange," said Miss Quince coldly. "I must ask you to wait until we have had a thorough search before accusing our servants."

"And *I* must ask *you* to understand that the pendant on that necklace was a Burmese ruby the size of a quail's egg. It is part of a parure, and the necklace is the most valuable piece."

Miss Quince lifted her eyebrows. She knew something of the state of finances in the le Strange family. "An heirloom set, I suppose? Something handed down to you from your ancestors?"

"It was a gift," Miss le Strange said, in tones quite as chilly as Miss Quince's.

"Ah, I see."

"I rather doubt you do, Miss Quince," said Miss le Strange. "It was a gift from my fiancé, Viscount Baggeshotte."

For the second time that week, Miss Crump toppled over in a dead faint upon the floor.

❖   ❖   ❖

"She was unaware of your engagement?" Miss Quince asked after Miss Crump had been carried to her chamber and they were standing at her bedside, looking down at her insensate form.

"Certainly she was, and she would not be aware of it now had I not needed to defend my reputation against your insinuations, Miss Quince. I wished to allow her father to make that announcement; however, he is ill at present and unable to do so. In fact, he is so ill, he is unable to speak or move. A palsy following apoplexy."

Miss Crump's eyelids fluttered open. "My father . . . ill? Apoplexy?" She fainted for the third time; this time, at least, she was at no risk of injury from falling.

"I see you also refrained from telling your prospective step-daughter about her father's health," Miss Quince remarked, and Miss le Strange stiffened at the headmistress's tone.

"Miss Crump is a poor, feeble creature, I am afraid," she said in tones of profound contempt, "suffering from every sort of mental and emotional weakness. I feared that the knowledge of her father's illness would have a deleterious effect upon her own health. As you can see, the news has laid her out, limp as a flounder on a fishmonger's slab."

Miss Quince shifted her attack. "Your fiancé is so ill, and yet you are not at his side. I am surprised you can spare the time from him." It was not like the gentle Eudora Quince to be so combative, but really, this woman! Her heart ached for poor Miss Crump.

Miss le Strange smiled, a thin stretching of the lips. "I thought it my duty to see to the welfare of his only child. I *had* thought to convey her to her father's sickbed, but *most unfortunately* I was prevented."

"I do regret that," Miss Quince said as civilly as she could manage, "especially as you now inform me of your special relationship to Miss Crump. However, I reserve the right to take instructions only from her father, or from her legal guardian, if that becomes necessary. I know you will understand."

Miss le Strange most decidedly did *not* understand. She did not deign to answer, but left the room without a backward glance.

"That poor, poor man," murmured Miss Quince. "I cannot be surprised at his condition, under the circumstances."

✦   ✦   ✦

The necklace was not recovered, either that night or after a careful search in the morning. No one had had the heart to repeat Miss le Strange's accusations to Robert, but the whole of the servants' wing began to treat him as if he were sickening for some fatal illness. Cook presented him with three toffee apples, telling him he must keep his strength up, the housekeeper called him "m'boy" and patted him solicitously on the shoulder, and a chambermaid took one look at him and burst into noisy lamentations. Robert thanked them for these tributes, but could not fathom what had prompted them. After devouring all three toffee apples (he was a growing boy still) he returned to the search for the necklace with renewed energy, looking for it in both likely and unlikely places—inside cracks in the stonework of the roof, lying near the foundation of the school building, or caught up in the branches of nearby trees, and then, when that produced no results, rummaging through closets and kitchen cupboards to peer into hatboxes, soup tureens, and old boots.

The students, aware that an unpleasant charge was hanging over Robert's head, pleaded to be allowed to postpone their lessons and look, too. Miss Quince, who was becoming worried on his behalf, insisted on a brief French lesson, but then allowed them to disperse over the house and grounds, looking for a flash of gold or sparkle of ruby.

Even Miss Crump bestirred herself to help with the search, although she did little more than walk dully about, stirring the leaves near the perimeter of the building with a stick. She told no one that the necklace was not her father's to give—it had descended through her mother's family and had been Miss Crump's property since the day of her mother's death. To be fair to Miss le Strange, it was quite possible that she did not know this; but her father surely did.

All the pleasure of the star party seemed to have evaporated, and the scent of herbs had given way to a rather less attractive rural scent: that of the farmers fertilizing nearby fields in preparation for sowing the winter wheat. Most of the young ladies carried a handkerchief liberally drenched in eau de cologne pressed to their noses as they lifted curtains that had been lifted ten times previously and looked behind doors and under cushions that had already been turned and turned again.

With a score of people searching assiduously, it soon became obvious that the necklace was not within the building, at least not in any place where it might have gotten by accident. Reluctantly, Miss Quince spoke with her fellow headmistresses, addressing herself primarily to Miss Hopkins, whose house and whose staff it was, urging her to allow a search to be made of the servants' quarters.

"My dear Clara, it must be done," she said, speaking with great compassion, for Miss Hopkins was by now almost hysterical, alternately weeping and abusing Miss le Strange, demanding to know why she and Mrs. Westing had ever come, as they had *not* been invited.

"I don't see why it must be," said Miss Hopkins. "My servants have been with me since I was a baby, most of them, and even if poor, dear Robert *is* of unknown parentage, he has grown up in Lesser Hoo and is the gentlest and best behaved boy I've ever known."

"Don't you see? It is for *their* protection," Miss Quince said. "It is the first thing Miss le Strange will want to know, and we must be able to tell her that a search has been performed, without result. It ought to have been done sooner, so she could not say that we had given one of them time to dispose of the necklace elsewhere."

"And in addition," said Miss Winthrop, "Robert is a member of the lower classes, and say what you will, Clara Hopkins, people of that sort will get up to anything. Brought up in Lesser Hoo! Tut, what nonsense! Of course his room and his person must be searched."

Miss Hopkins regarded her friend and co-headmistress with dawning dislike, and there might have been a serious quarrel had Miss Quince not interfered.

"*All* the servants must be searched, and *all* their quarters. In truth, I would not object to being searched myself—"

An immediate outcry arose over this, however, and Miss Quince admitted that such a search might be seen as prejudicial to the dignity of the Winthrop Hopkins Female Academy. "However," she said, "some would point out that a single lady in a position such as mine might not be averse to a comfortable sum on which to retire, no matter how it was obtained."

Miss Winthrop, who had never given any thought to what Miss Quince would live on when she was too old to teach, began to eye her speculatively, but Miss Hopkins burst out with an avowal of perfect faith in her integrity.

"I won't have it!" she cried. "Perhaps you are right about the servants, Eudora, but I won't allow my trusted and valued friend and relative to be suspected. No, not for the sake of that terrible woman, even if she is second cousin to every royal house in Europe!"

Miss Quince bestowed a grateful smile upon Miss Hopkins, a somewhat frostier one on Miss Winthrop, and went to organize a search of the servants' quarters.

Feelings against Miss le Strange were running high amongst the students as well.

"I doubt that she ever wore the necklace last night at all! Quite certainly it is lying disregarded on the top of her dressing table at this very moment," said Miss Asquith. "How dare she accuse darling Robert?"

"Not '*darling* Robert,'" chided Miss Evans. "Really, Miss Asquith, he is a footman!"

"I don't care!" Miss Asquith said, and dashed away angry tears. "He is a perfectly *wonderful* footman! You know how much he loves his position. He would never do anything to jeopardize it. And taking something that does not belong to him would never enter his head."

"I'm afraid she *was* wearing it last night," said Miss Briggs. "One couldn't help but notice how that pendant ruby sparkled in the candlelight. It is a glorious necklace. I must say"—she cast a cautious glance at Miss Crump—"it was a most impressive engagement present."

Everyone went silent at this, imagining Miss le Strange as a stepmother to Miss Crump.

In a valiant effort to change the subject, Miss Victor attempted a little light teasing. "I expect you never noticed the necklace last night, Miss Asquith, because you were far too busy being wooed by Mr. Crabbe. He is a fine dancer, is he not?"

Despite herself, Miss Asquith blushed. "Hush, child, and don't presume to twit your elders and betters." Then she looked at Miss Crump in a corner, her head bowed down under the weight of her enormous bonnet. "Oh, do cheer up, Miss Crump, pray do! I cannot bear to see you so unhappy," she said. "If the worst comes to worst, we shall slip some hemlock in horrid Miss le Strange's tea, I promise we will!"

In the shadow of Miss Crump's bonnet it was difficult to tell, but a fleeting smile, like a shooting star, *might* have crossed her countenance before winking out and being replaced by all-encompassing gloom.

15

"PSSST! I SAY, Miss Pffolliott!"

Miss Pffolliott was using a walking stick to lift the ivy leaves on the outside walls of the school, hoping to see the glint of jewelry. She whirled about, the stick still raised.

"I am glad to see you have not got that fearsome dog with you," said Mr. Rasmussen, who was peering out from behind a manicured boxwood hedge. "However"—he eyed the stick nervously—"perhaps you could lower that implement? Looks a bit hostile, don't you know."

Miss Pffolliott lowered the stick a little, but kept it in readiness. "Yes, Mr. Rasmussen?" she said. Although she was not an intrepid young lady, her timidity was beginning to give way to irritation. "What is it, sir?"

"Er . . . what were you doing just now, if you don't mind my asking?"

"I am looking for a ruby necklace."

Mr. Rasmussen chuckled. It was a masculine chuckle, full of indulgence for female imbecility. "That is an original method of acquiring finery! Perhaps you think that ruby neck-laces grow on . . . er, vines?"

"No, Mr. Rasmussen, I do not believe anything so nonsen-sical. A necklace was most regrettably lost during the star party last night. If you *had attended*, as you were *invited to do*, you would be aware that it might have dropped from the roof into these vines."

"Oh! Oh, I see. How unfortunate!" Mr. Rasmussen's eye had sharpened, and he began to look about himself with a thoughtful gaze. "Valuable, was it?"

"So I am given to understand."

"I see, I see. Wouldn't mind having a look for it, myself. Grateful lady and so on—might be something in it for me," he murmured, more to himself than to her.

"If you will excuse me, I must get on," said Miss Pffolliott, turning her back to him and raising her walking stick to the task once again.

Recalled to the matter at hand, Mr. Rasmussen cleared his throat and proceeded in a playful tone, "And now you are annoyed with your poor old admirer because he didn't come to the party last night, I perceive. Well, I couldn't do it, that's all. Prior engagement. But your headmistresses did get a letter from your father? Introducing me and recommending me to your notice, and so forth?"

"They did," Miss Pffolliott conceded. She turned to look at him. "And how, pray, did you know my father had sent such a message?"

However, Mr. Rasmussen had the answer to this at his

tongue-tip. "Why, I asked him to write it, that's how. I could see you didn't care for me poppin' up out of nowhere—very proper of you, I might add, very proper indeed—so I got the old boy to send it along. Didn't want you to think there was anything havey-cavey about me. No, your father and I, we go back a long way together. Old schoolfellows."

"Then why did you not say so?" she retorted. "Why did you not ask to be introduced in the usual way, instead of sending me those extraordinary anonymous letters, sir?"

"Now, now, now, my dear young lady! No need to be so hard on a man, just because he's impetuous. Carried away by my emotions, that's all. It's dashed difficult for a fellow, all this hanging about, waiting to be introduced, having to be watched by a chaperone every moment he's in the company of a beautiful young lady such as yourself. I daresay I saw myself as a regular young Lochinvar. Ever read that poet fellow, Scott? 'So daring in love and so dauntless in war, Have ye e'er heard of gallant like young Lochinvar?'" Mr. Rasmussen stepped out from behind the boxwood bush and struck a heroic pose, one hand on heart, one hand on an invisible sword hilt.

"I am familiar with Mr. Scott's *Marmion*," Miss Pffolliott admitted. Miss Asquith had read it aloud in a dramatic rendition only a few weeks ago—the poem about young Lochinvar and his reckless wooing of the fair Ellen had become an instant favorite.

"Thought you would be. Just the sort of thing romantic young girls like—that's the way it seemed to me, anyway."

The idea that Mr. Rasmussen had been attempting to

pique her interest through letters from an unknown lover was, on the one hand, rather touching, if also rather scandalous. On the other hand, though, wasn't he a bit elderly for that sort of behavior? He seemed to be trying to paint himself as a passionate, hotheaded *young* man. Why, he himself had pointed out that he was the same age as her father. She regarded his rather puffy midsection critically.

"I must insist that you meet with my instructors before you address me again, Mr. Rasmussen," she said. "And now, I believe this conversation is at an end." She took a firm grip on her stick and turned to walk away in a decisive manner, feeling that she was at last handling these episodes with a certain degree of composure.

"Oh, of course, of course," agreed Mr. Rasmussen, trotting along behind her. "Exactly what I had planned. I'll go and pay a call right now. Er . . ." He hesitated. "You haven't any *other* callers at the moment, have you? I shouldn't want to interrupt, you know."

"If you mean anyone other than Mr. Arbuthnot, who is resident in the school until his leg heals, no, I do not believe so," she replied, still retreating in front of him.

"In that case, lead on, my fair one," he said jovially. "I shall be charmed to meet the ladies."

❧ ❧ ❧

Inside Miss Asquith there burned a flame of revolutionary indignation. It was not *right* that a woman like Miss le Strange could accuse Robert of theft, when the entire fault in the case was *her* carelessness. Or, if not that, given the extensive search that had taken place, why then, there must be *some* other explanation.

Miss Asquith found herself comparing the actions of Miss le Strange unfavorably with the sort of high-handed behavior that had precipitated the French Revolution. Twenty years earlier, France had been seized by a violent social convulsion that saw much of the ruling class imprisoned, beheaded, or unceremoniously strung up on lampposts. The highborn all over Europe had watched aghast, sensing a crack at the base of their safe and secure world.

Miss Asquith was *not* highborn; her father's father had been a small farmer, and her mother was a lawyer's daughter. At this moment she was prepared to turn her back on the gentry, raise the revolutionary banner of *"Liberté, égalité, fraternité!"* and march on Versailles like the market women of Paris.

The one factor restraining her indignation was Robert himself; his admiration for his "betters" knew no bounds. He would be the last to advocate the overthrow of the English class system, glorying as he did in his position, his duties, and his yellow silk knee breeches. To question the accepted hierarchy would cause Robert every bit as much alarm and dismay as it would any newly created knight of the realm.

Like Miss Pffolliott, Miss Asquith was engaged in walking about outside the school, searching for the necklace. In her case, she was prodding at the stones of the foundation and hunting under bedding plants. Being in a state of high indignation, her efforts involved violent thrusts at weeds and other obstructions with her parasol. Occasionally she kicked one of the smaller stones from her path with a fair degree of violence.

"Hi! I say, that hurt!" came the aggrieved voice of Mr. Crabbe. He rounded the corner of the building and stopped to rub his knee.

Miss Asquith looked at him with disfavor. Prior to the allegations of Miss le Strange, she had regarded him as by far the cleverest and most amiable gentleman of her acquaintance. Now the scales fell from her eyes and she saw him for what he was: an aristocrat. No doubt, like all aristocrats, his greatest joy lay in snatching the last crumbs of bread from the mouths of the starving poor.

"I beg your pardon, *your Lordship.*"

Mr. Crabbe's eyebrows lifted. "I feel certain you did not mean to wound me. Is anything amiss?"

"Nothing of any consequence to *you,* my Lord."

"Er, I am not a lord *yet.* So long as my father lives, I am more correctly addressed as 'Mister Crabbe.' But perhaps you could tell me what is upsetting *you?*"

"Oh, nothing at all. It concerns a servant. He will most likely be turned away to starve in the streets or else clapped in prison, but what of it? The fact that he is innocent of any wrongdoing is of no importance. He is a member of the lower classes—therefore he must be guilty of *something.*"

"And who is the servant in question?" asked Mr. Crabbe cautiously. "No, do not tell me! I suspect it is that handsome young lad in the canary-yellow livery, whose serving at table is so exquisite that it makes one feel one has inadvertently sat down to dine in the midst of a performance of the ballet."

"Pray do not make fun of Robert. He is as good-natured and honest as—as new-baked bread."

"I've no doubt of it. The look of beatific pleasure that dawns over his face every time he sees me cross the threshold gives me a most pleasant conceit of myself. I approve of Robert. What crime is the excellent Robert accused of committing?"

"Miss le Strange—"

"Ah! Miss le Strange and the affair of the missing necklace. I see. No, I do not believe your footman purloined the necklace."

Miss Asquith turned to him, her face alight. "You do not? Oh, I know he didn't! But how is it to be proved?"

Mr. Crabbe hesitated. "I can tell you why I don't think he took it, but it is not conclusive, I fear. The pockets in his breeches are barely deep enough to hold sixpence without bulging, let alone that whacking great necklace."

"Oh, you are right! Robert told me that he never carries anything in his pockets for fear of spoiling the line of his uniform. And he could not have concealed it anywhere else on his person without looking exceedingly odd, as his clothing fits him so closely. Oh, hurrah!"

"However," Mr. Crabbe cautioned, "the fact that your footman's attire is tailored to within an inch of his life will not necessarily save him. He might have secreted it somewhere, you know."

"But where? We've looked and looked! There isn't anywhere!"

He looked at her thoughtfully. "You do realize that, if what you say is true and Robert did *not* take it, and if the whole of the school has been scoured and nothing found, why, someone else must have taken it?"

Miss Asquith dropped her gaze. "Oh, I suppose you are right. But Robert wouldn't do it, I know he wouldn't!"

"May I inquire then which horse you favor in this race? For we must have another thief, if Robert is to be shown innocent."

"Oh dear! You are right—it's awkward. I think, if it has to be someone I know, that I should like it to be Mrs. Westing. I know she is a dedicated gambler, and gamblers may have dreadful debts."

He laughed. "Mrs. Westing is not a very sympathetic character, is she? However, when I have had the misfortune to sit down to play with her, I generally rise from the table a poorer man. I believe she *did* have some difficulties in that way a number of years ago, but it is my suspicion that she has of recent times made it a policy to substitute duplicity for good fortune. In short, I suspect that she cheats. Quite likely, she makes a pretty profit from her gambling habit. I will not exclude her from the starting gate—even the most skillful trickster can suffer a reversal of fortune—but I do not regard her as the favorite to win."

"But who, then?" Miss Asquith knitted her brow and concentrated. "I don't believe that any of the other servants went near Miss le Strange—Robert showed her in and served her, and then escorted her out. And the young ladies have adequate incomes—none of them would have any reason to do such a thing, or the nerve to try it. And the same is true of the headmistresses and the gentlemen present at the star party." Her certainty wavered when she thought of Miss Quince, but *really! Miss Quince!* It was quite as unlikely as that Robert was the culprit.

Mr. Crabbe pondered a moment. Then he said, not looking at her, "Allow me to offer you a truly suspicious character: myself." When she frowned at this frivolity, he continued, "I am quite serious, I assure you. You may be unaware of it—though I doubt that your papa would be—but my family is in low water financially. Lord Boring is not the only man of your acquaintance possessing a parent who cannot leave a wager alone. My father has been engaged in despoiling my inheritance for as long as I have been alive. In fact, my brother, Mr. Rupert Crabbe, came to warn me of further depredations on my holdings. As matters stand, I shall almost certainly be insolvent by Christmastime." As he came to the end of this remark, he raised his eyes and looked full at her to judge her reception of it.

"*Really?* Oh, how—That is, I am most sorry to hear it, sir," she amended, dropping her gaze. A tiny smile flickered across her face, and then was gone. She altered her tone to reflect the gravity appropriate to one who has received such a confidence. "But in spite of your misfortunes, I decline to consider you as a contestant in our horse race. You may call it a personal prejudice on my part, but I do not believe you would choose that sort of measure to solve your difficulties."

"I must confess that I believe you are in the right of it," he said. "However attractive the *idea* might have been, it would have made me most uncomfortable. I should have been terrified to look the moneylender in the face, for fear he denounce me on the spot."

Perhaps Miss Asquith *was* sorry for his financial woes, but if so, her grief was not long-lived. She smiled, turning away her head in an attempt to conceal her expression. He watched her with his head cocked to one side, considering the implications of this reaction. Then, evidently relieved of some apprehension, he returned her smile and offered her his arm. The two entered the house in perfect amity and accord.

16

AS MISS ROSALIND Franklin had barely registered the existence of Robert the footman, she was largely unconcerned about his fate. The fate of a ruby necklace—a collection of aluminum oxide crystals on a string—was even less a matter of interest to her. Her assistance in the search was therefore perfunctory and brief. She was getting little sleep these nights, as she needed the hours of darkness for observing the planet Uranus. Although her eyesight was naturally sharp, the time spent peering through a lens was beginning to take its toll in the form of headaches and eyestrain. She decided to take advantage of the inhabitants of the school being occupied elsewhere for a little rest upon her bed.

Once there, however, she could not seem to find the sleep she sought. Instead, her mind lingered upon her observations. She was a fool, she knew, to try to find an even more distant planet than Uranus using Mr. Rupert Crabbe's relatively small telescope. What was needed for the task was an instrument of much greater dimensions, located in some country with clear skies and a minimum of humidity to distort the view. No,

Mr. Rupert Crabbe was right; she was wasting her time. She needed to shift her attentions to something closer, something that might be viewed more readily with her limited tools. Perhaps the moon? Or the little planetoids that had been lately discovered between Mars and Jupiter? Yet some of her findings *had* been quite intriguing . . .

Fatigued by the effort to sleep, she rose from her bed and went to the window where the telescope awaited, poised to scan the skies. She stood looking out for some time, until a movement far off, on the high road in front of the school building, caught at her attention. Although she was by nature disinclined to pry into human affairs, some impulse moved her to pivot the telescope until it no longer aimed above, but rather at the scene below. She stooped, applied herself to the eyepiece, focused, and watched the little scene unfolding before her with a perplexed frown.

✦   ✦   ✦

Even such a naif as Robert could not remain oblivious to the atmosphere around him. He had searched diligently for the missing necklace, hoping against hope that he would be the one to find and present it to a grateful Miss le Strange. His search was not based upon any rational concept of where the necklace might innocently have gotten to; he looked in the obvious places and then everywhere else, save the bedchambers of the students and of his employers. This had led him into a number of odd corners and cupboards of the school, and he had made some surprising discoveries: a publication with rather scandalous illustrations in an old trunk, a stash of sweets under a loose floorboard in the pantry, and a collection of ancient dolls arranged around a small tea table in the attic. To his delight, he even found a necklace in the lower drawer of a sewing table, but this was revealed on second inspection as a minor object, a simple string of amber beads.

From time to time the idea that *he* might be suspected of deliberately abstracting the jewels knocked at the door of his mind, but when it did, he dismissed it. He could not imagine how anyone could think such a thing—why, a necklace was a *lady's* adornment; a man would have no use for it. The very idea was ridiculous. That one could take such an item to a moneylender or jeweler and exchange it for pounds and pence was not a notion that suggested itself to him; Lesser Hoo had no moneylenders or jewelers' shops.

"You were the only one who got close to her, m'boy," explained Mrs. Grebe, the housekeeper. "Naturally we don't think it for a moment, not for a moment!"

"The clasp must've broken, it must have," sobbed the chambermaid.

No one said anything. Because if it had fallen underfoot, why had it not been found? Responding to this unspoken comment, the chambermaid, whose name was Annie, said defiantly, "And then anybody could have taken it! *Anybody!*"

"Now, now, then," said Robert, patting her hand, "nobody thinks anybody *took* it! Why, that would be *stealing!*"

The other members of the staff looked at him pityingly and shook their heads.

❖ ❖ ❖

The news of the loss of the necklace spread through the neighborhood. Sir Quentin and Lady Throstletwist were distraught when they realized that Robert had been accused. He had been raised in their household, indulged and cosseted like a favorite dog, and only reluctantly allowed to leave in order to work at Miss Hopkins's establishment. Mrs. Fredericks of Crooked Castle shook her head and said to her husband, "I *told* you it was a mistake hiring a handsome young man like that to work in a girls' academy," although how his personal beauty had any impact on the current situation was unclear. Lady Boring said that she had always considered the management of the servants both at Yellering Hall and at the school to be almost criminally lax, and her mother-in-law, Mrs. Westing, agreed. It did not surprise either of them in the least that the footman had taken to stealing valuable necklaces.

"If I were Clara Hopkins I'd have that brooch of hers looked at as well," said Lady Boring to Mrs. Westing. "I've no doubt he's pawned every scrap of gold he could get his hands on and replaced it with pinchbeck. And I have also heard that there is an excellent market in used buttons, whether of metal or bone, and so I should recommend a careful examination of every garment in the house."

Mr. Bold, the vicar, had had it in mind to preach a sermon

that Sunday on how the worth of a virtuous woman was above rubies and how spiritual riches were far greater than precious stones. However, after an unnerving encounter with Miss le Strange, he decided that instead, a resounding denunciation of dishonesty, bearing false witness, and ingratitude amongst the lower classes would be the wiser path.

Mr. Godalming, who was magistrate for the district, began to feel a nervous conviction that he had better do *something* definite, and soon. But what ought that to be? If he sent a constable to arrest young Robert, half the gentry hereabouts would be livid; if he did not, the other half would be. Upon further reflection, however, he concluded that the pro-Robert forces outnumbered the anti-Robert faction, and, as he was busy selecting trees to fell in the woodlot on the eastern side of his property, decided not to make any rash decisions but to sleep on it and hope that the blasted necklace would show up on its own.

Miss le Strange, as the chief member of the anti-Robert faction, was not backward in making her wants known. She said in loud and ringing tones that she wanted her necklace returned, and inquired how, precisely, the ladies of the Winthrop Hopkins Academy proposed to accomplish this.

Swallowing hard, Miss Hopkins asked after the precise value of the piece.

"As to that, I could not say," Miss le Strange said coldly. "It was not a subject Lord Baggeshotte would discuss with me."

"It is difficult then to know how you expect to be compensated," began Miss Hopkins, but Miss Quince interrupted with, "In truth, I believe we shall have to contact Lord Bagge-shotte. Although I realize he is ill, he deserves to know that his gift has been lost."

"Have I not explained that he is unable to speak?" asked Miss le Strange, who sounded as if she did not care for the term *lost*, implying as it did possible carelessness on the part of the one who had lost it. "It will do you no good to contact him."

"In that case, it is his lawyer we must inform. Unless he has made special arrangements to allow you to act for him, his lawyer will be responsible for any decisions during his in-capacity. Even if the worst should happen and he dies without being able to communicate, Lord Baggeshotte's lawyer, acting for Miss Crump, will no doubt be the executor of his estate. Since you are not, in fact, his legal wife, your rights and duties are limited."

Miss le Strange frowned and made an impatient gesture, as though waving away a cloud of irritating gnats. "I tell you, he *gave* me the necklace. It is my property, and I am his affianced bride."

"Pardon me," asked Miss Quince, "but have you any proof of that? Perhaps he had begun the process of working out the marriage settlements and his legal counsel would be able to confirm it?"

Miss le Strange's countenance settled into lines of yet greater hauteur. "No. I told you. It was as yet unspoken beyond our two selves."

"Then did he not give you a ring or some token by which to solemnize the engagement?"

"He gave me the necklace!"

"Nevertheless, I believe we will contact Lord Baggeshotte and his lawyer before we take any further action."

Miss Quince and Miss le Strange stared at each other across a few yards of air that appeared to harden into ice crystals. The onlookers waited in silent awe for whatever the outcome might be.

"Little did I think that I would come to an establishment that purports to provide young Englishwomen with an intellectual and *moral* education and be robbed blind with no recompense or satisfaction offered," said Miss le Strange. "You have not heard the last of this, I assure you," she said magnificently, if somewhat unoriginally, and swept from the room.

The three ladies sat in silence for a moment, looking at one another. Then Miss Winthrop put into words the sentiment that her co-headmistresses were feeling, but reluctant to express aloud: "For all that she's so well-bred, she's nothing better than a governess! I cannot *think* how we have allowed ourselves to be so bamboozled!"

✦ ✦ ✦

At dinnertime, perhaps in an attempt to break the tension and lead everyone's thoughts and feelings in a new direction, Mr. Arbuthnot and Miss Evans formally announced their engagement. The news surprised no one; they had been waiting for confirmation of Miss Evans's father's approval. However, a letter had arrived that afternoon giving his consent, and, having crossed that not-very-daunting hurdle, the young people were free to announce their happiness to their friends.

Miss Evans's father had, in fact, been delighted; Mr. Arbuthnot's family and estates were rather better than what he might have expected to get for his daughter through marriage. He rarely thought about her from one month to another, but by this feat she had managed to elevate her position in his esteem tenfold, and, had his natural indolence not been so great, he might have exerted himself to the trouble and expense of traveling twenty miles to tell her so.

Everyone was pleased for the young couple; they were acknowledged to be uniquely suited to each other. With upright characters, good moral sense, and an almost total lack of imagination, they were certain to make a united and devoted pair.

At nineteen, Miss Evans had been the oldest of the students; it was fitting that she should be the first to wed. The younger girls smiled and whispered in one another's ears and wondered when it would be their turn. Miss Franklin alone could not comprehend how Miss Evans could let anything interrupt her schooling—she did not mean to leave them until she had mastered Italian, did she?

"Indeed she does," said Mr. Crabbe, laughing. "They will travel to Italy itself, and that will be a much better method of perfecting Miss Evans's Italian than any tutor."

Oh, how delightful! Italy! All that could be wished for! As her fellow students expressed their envy and delight, Miss Asquith leaned in to speak privately to Miss Franklin.

"I understand that your studies are all-important to you, but will you not admit that marriage and family have their own value in the lives of *both* men and women? After all, if there were no family life, quite soon there would be no human life at all. Children must be born to replace those who die!"

Miss Franklin smiled. "Oh, Miss Asquith, of course you are in the right, yet I cannot help but feel that the minds of these young women are being wasted, trained for nothing but household management and child-rearing."

"When *you* marry, of course, you must choose someone who shares your interests and intellect. He must be a scientist like you, one who can appreciate your mental endowments as well as your more personal charms." Here Miss Asquith looked at Mr. Rupert Crabbe, who was sitting alone in a corner, regarding the celebrations with an air of benign detachment.

Miss Franklin blushed and looked down at her lap. The heightened color was not flattering to her rather severe beauty; too, it appeared to be a source of discomfort, and she pressed her palms to her flaming cheeks.

"I have always believed it best that I not marry at all," she said, not meeting Miss Asquith's eyes.

"Ah, but that is easy to say when one has not met a gentleman who would make a good husband, is it not?"

"Perhaps. I do not know. I do not feel certain of Mr.—of the gentleman's motives and feelings."

"In that case, allow me to explain them to you: he likes and admires you very much. Why, he barely even speaks to anyone save yourself and, rarely, his brother. When I attempt to make a little polite conversation with him, he looks at me as if I were speaking in ancient Egyptian. But with you, he is at ease—the two of you are generally so deep in discourse that I am amazed to have this opportunity to converse with you whilst he is present."

"I—I do not know." Miss Franklin shook her head.

"And I tell you, I *do*! I advise you to prepare your mind for a proposal, my friend!"

17

THE LAST DAYS of October were waning, but the weather was still warm, with one fine, dry day succeeding another. A few days after the announcement of his engagement, Mr. Arbuthnot demanded to be allowed out of his invalid chair. Leaning on two sticks and aided by his betrothed, he staggered some five paces across the parlor floor before staggering back to his seat. Flushed with triumph and the unaccustomed exertion, he asked to be wheeled out-of-doors, and he and Miss Evans settled down in a spot in the sun-dappled shade of the orchard by the high road.

When the gentlemen from Yellering Hall came to call, as they did most afternoons, they and the rest of the school went in a body to join the couple for a nuncheon alfresco. Thanks to the efforts of Miss Quince and the distraction of the Arbuthnot and Evans engagement, the affair of the missing necklace had dropped into the background of everyone's mind.

Several of the ladies, both the younger and the older, sat in the sun and sewed. Miss Franklin bent over a small hand-stitched notebook, writing line after line of densely spaced prose interspersed with numbers, Greek letters, and arithmetical symbols, flicking the pages over as they were filled. The gentlemen lolled about doing not much of anything, a little stupefied by the autumnal sunshine with its false promise of endless warm days to come. Miss Victor was engaged in sketching a ragged clump of Michaelmas daisies as Miss Briggs sang an old country ballad about doomed lovers. Her fresh young voice lofted up over the little gathering and blended with the sound of the wind stirring the fallen leaves and the calls of doves.

Into this idyllic scene two figures appeared on the high road that ran in front of the school. From small, indistinct dots they grew larger and clearer as they approached, resolving into Miss le Strange and her maidservant. They marched past the school grounds, turning their heads to stare at the group under the apple trees. Miss le Strange gave one curt nod to acknowledge the acquaintance, and then walked on.

A cloud blotted out the sun; the doves stilled their cries. Miss Briggs's song faltered and broke off. In the silence, it was possible to hear the rustle of the skirts of the interlopers and the muffled thud of their heels hitting the dusty road. Their backs, as they moved onward toward the village of Lesser Hoo, were rigid with disapproval and hostility.

Miss Victor dropped her sketchbook and crayon and began to sniffle, her eyes welling up ominously. Miss Crump took the fine white shawl from her shoulders and wrapped it around her bonneted head so that she looked like an oddly shaped ghost cowering in the shadows. The ladies lowered their mending and watched the small parade as it dwindled again in size and disappeared around a bend. Even Miss Franklin paused in her furious scribblings and looked up to see them go.

"Who was that lady, pray?" she inquired.

"Oh, for goodness' sakes!" cried Miss Asquith, exasperated with her friend. "That was Miss le Strange, author of all our woe. *Do* pay attention, Miss Franklin!"

"So that is Miss le Strange," Miss Franklin said thoughtfully.

Soon thereafter, everyone present found a compelling reason to leave the sunlit orchard and return to the house. Apparently preoccupied by the discovery of Miss le Strange's identity, Miss Franklin got up without remembering her notebook of formulae, leaving it abandoned under a tree. However, this was of no import, as Mr. Rupert Crabbe slipped it into his waistcoat pocket and followed after her.

✦ ✦ ✦

At the house, they discovered that Robert had been on the point of coming to fetch them, or at least to fetch Mr. Crabbe and his brother, Rupert. After the passage of Miss le Strange and her servant, the party had spied someone else approaching, this time on horseback, but it had been assumed that this person was riding on toward Lesser Hoo and would not pause. It was, however, a messenger, sent by express with a letter for Mr. Crabbe. The urgency of such a missive must be assumed; everyone save Mr. Crabbe, Mr. Rupert Crabbe, and Miss Asquith soon quitted the room to allow the brothers to discover in privacy whatever calamity it might reveal.

Miss Quince paused at the doorway, calling in a low tone, "Miss Asquith, please come with us. We will commence our lessons upstairs in the music room."

Miss Asquith responded, "Pray do not press me, Miss Quince. I *must* know what the matter is, or die of my ignorance." There was no sign of levity on her usually merry countenance, and her tone gave assurance of the gravity of her feelings.

Sighing with vexation at her pupil's willfulness, yet unable to avoid some stirrings of sympathy, Miss Quince remained in the doorway to ensure the propriety of such a conference, and thus was unable to avoid hearing all that passed.

"I see it comes from our father's solicitor," said Mr. Rupert Crabbe. "Do open it, Henry, and end this suspense. Our father's not writing it himself is such a frightful omen—tell me quickly! Is he dead?"

A long silence followed this plea, as Mr. Crabbe perused the message. At last he handed the letter to his brother and said, "T'would be better if he were, I daresay, but he is not. Not yet, tho' perhaps he soon will be, once the court of assizes has heard his case."

"His case! What *can* you mean, court of assizes? That is only for the most serious of criminal cases—you cannot be suggesting—!"

"Stop arguing with me, Rupert, and read the letter. As I come to think of it, it is worse than that. It will have to be the Lord High Steward and the House of Lords," growled Mr. Crabbe. His gaze lit upon Miss Asquith's serious face, looking up at him with compassion and concern. "I do not grudge you hearing this, Miss Asquith. No doubt most of England knows it already. Our father has—"

"He has *killed* Sir Grimm! After losing to him at cards! Sir Grimm, our old neighbor! Oh, the disgrace of it, and me a clergyman!" cried Rupert. "And he did the deed in front of witnesses, too!"

Mr. Crabbe gestured toward his brother, who was clutching at his hair with one hand and crumpling the letter with the other. "As my brother informs you, we are now the sons of a murderer, and a murderer so addlepated as to commit his crime in front of two maidservants, the local doctor, and a justice of the peace."

"We are ruined! Ruined! We shall never be able to hold up our heads in public!"

"Again, my brother expresses the matter concisely," said Mr. Crabbe. "I hope you will understand that we must leave you, Miss Asquith, and—is that you, Miss Quince? Pray give our apologies to the other ladies, but we must be off at once."

Miss Asquith placed her hand on his arm and said, her eyes meeting his, "I am more sorry than I can say for your pain. I wish there were a way I could offer you some aid."

Mr. Crabbe looked down at her small white hand on his sleeve. "I—I thank you for that, Miss Asquith. However"—here he raised his gaze to hers again, his voice became more formal, and he moved away a space so that her hand fell—"I doubt anybody can do anything for us at present. We shall have to take the kicking fate has in store for us, I fear. Good-bye, Miss Quince, Miss Asquith. Rupert, come along."

Rupert looked distractedly about himself. "Wait!" he said. "I beg your pardon, brother; there is one thing I—" He darted into an adjoining room, but returned shortly.

Miss Asquith, regarding him with pity, said, "I believe I know whom you seek. I will tell her that necessity prevented you from doing so. She is not someone who demands that the proprieties be observed—she will readily forgive you. Neither she *nor* I am conventional, you know. Now go, and do not worry any further about us. Good-bye, good-bye! Please travel safely, and . . . I pray your journey's end will show you a better circumstance than you at present expect."

And with no more than a scant few words more, they were gone, and within an hour, gone altogether from the village of Lesser Hoo.

*   *   *

Quite naturally, a great deal of curiosity about the nature of the events that had so abruptly deprived them of the company of the two brothers had been aroused, and after some deliberation, Miss Quince decided to reveal the shocking story, albeit in as dull and drab a way as possible.

"I gather that the Baron is a man of very little self-command," she said, "prone to any number of petty vices and a great source of worry to his friends. There was a quarrel, I believe, with the result that a gentleman has most unfortunately died, and the law is likely to make a great deal of tiresome fuss. Mr. Crabbe and Mr. Rupert Crabbe have quite properly gone home to try to lend some assistance in the matter. As soon as the House of

Lords can be convened to hear the case it will all be settled, and none of us need give it any further thought."

Everyone exclaimed over the matter, but as Miss Quince had rather made it sound as if the Baron were a naughty child who had broken a piece of china in a fit of temper, the horror of the event was lessened. Mr. Hadley took himself off, feeling that he might be able to help his friends in arranging their departure, or at least in smoothing over matters with the Throstletwists.

Miss Asquith had retired to her room after the two brothers' departure, only pausing to squeeze her friend Miss Franklin's hand and murmur, "They had to go, and immediately—Miss Quince will explain why. There was no time for farewells. He sought you, before they left, without success. But we will see them again, I assure you, my dear Miss Franklin."

Miss Franklin nodded and returned the pressure on her hand. "Perhaps we shall. You must go to your room and have a little weep. I do not find release in tears, myself, but I am informed that many women do. I will come to you later and see to it that you have something to eat and drink."

Miss Asquith thanked her friend and indeed did retire to her room for a short spell of tears, and remained there until the next day.

✦ ✦ ✦

Mr. Rasmussen soon called, eager to be introduced to the young ladies and to discuss the scandal, which formed the sole subject of conversation in the neighborhood. While he had already made the acquaintance of the three headmistresses, he was unknown to several of the students. They cast curious glances in his direction, which then slid over to Miss Pffolliott, who sat in a corner, paying great attention to a pelisse she was engaged in altering.

Under the influence of these interested female eyes, Mr. Rasmussen expanded. He spoke of his estates, his travels, his friends in high places. He even, winking, hinted at conducting amours amongst the "ton," the most fashionable set of people in England. Miss Winthrop and Miss Hopkins seemed willing to hear more, but Miss Quince soon quashed this subject of conversation, and so he reverted to the safer topic of well-known and well-born friends.

"Knew that fellow Baron Hardcastle, father of your young friend, Mr. Crabbe. Knew him well, in fact; I went to school with him. What a rascal!" And Mr. Rasmussen laughed uproariously and slapped his knee.

"Oh?" said Miss Quince in a chilly tone. "Then you are no doubt distressed at his current predicament."

"Ah, well! It won't surprise anybody who ever met him that Hardcastle ended up in a deuced bad way. He always was a bit of a loose fish—no wonder then that he finds himself in hot water now! Pretty good, hey? Loose fish, hot water? What? What?" He laughed again. "And I expect the sons are no better than they should be either, hey? Personally, I shouldn't believe a word either of them said." Here he paused to look around and judge the effect of his words. Never a man sensitive to nuance in human expressions, he continued, "Pair of rapscallions,

I should think, and they've been found out now with a vengeance. No one will pay either of *them* any mind in the future."

Miss Quince said, "No one, Mr. Rasmussen, save people of sense and observation, I suppose. *We* have been well impressed with *both* young gentlemen."

Miss Franklin cleared her throat. "As to the character of Mr. Crabbe the elder, I have no complaint to make, other than to a certain levity and lack of serious thought. However, I do rather object to the behavior of Mr. *Rupert* Crabbe."

The entire company regarded her with astonishment. Those who had thought about Miss Franklin and Mr. Rupert Crabbe at all had assumed that she, like Miss Asquith, must be in a state of deepest mourning at their absence.

Miss Hopkins, suspecting that revelations of an indelicate nature were about to be divulged, made an attempt to head Miss Franklin off. "You shall tell us about that presently, my dear," she said. "But I wish we could change the subject for now . . . What say you to, er . . . telling us about the calculations you have been working on . . . Oh! I suppose we shall have to send Mr. Rupert Crabbe's telescope after him, shan't we, and then you will lose the use of it. How unfortunate for you!" Miss Hopkins, who considered Miss Franklin's calculations and her work with the telescope to be a monumental waste of time, was being less than honest here, but would much rather talk of the gentleman's telescope than of any failings of the gentleman himself.

"I am unable to refer to my calculations, or even to duplicate them using Mr. Rupert Crabbe's telescope," Miss Franklin said. "Apparently, in the moments after reading the letter from his father's lawyer, he made arrangements with one of the maids to have his telescope conveyed to him at Yellering Hall. And then he pocketed the notebooks filled with my work and took them away with him as well."

"But . . . but why should he do that?" demanded a stupefied Miss Winthrop.

"I expect he wanted to take credit for my discoveries," said Miss Franklin. "And now, if you don't mind, I believe that I, too, will retire to my room."

18

MISS ASQUITH, UPON rising from her bed on the morrow, was all indignation and outraged friendship when she heard the tale of the perfidious Rupert Crabbe. The sheer effrontery of his actions was such that she almost agreed with Mr. Rasmussen that the entire Crabbe family was a band of knaves and rapscallions—but no, she could not think poorly of the elder brother, however wicked his relatives might be.

Miss Hopkins and Miss Winthrop refused to believe that Mr. Rupert Crabbe's carrying off seven or eight little booklets of Miss Franklin's notations could be anything other than an error—perhaps he had mistaken them for his own work. Miss Asquith, however, required no proof from Miss Franklin that it was a deliberate act. Everyone knew those little books of hers; she had been chaffed about them often enough, and in Mr. Rupert Crabbe's presence. He must know, as everyone did, that they were her astronomical observations and deductions.

"Really, Miss Franklin, Miss Asquith, I am afraid that you both think rather too highly of the value of these little experiments," scolded Miss Winthrop. "Why should a clever young man such as Mr. Rupert Crabbe wish to trouble himself with a few notations by Miss Franklin?"

"Because clever young Mr. Rupert Crabbe was quite intelligent enough to recognize genius when he saw it," retorted Miss Asquith. Remembering that she was a well-behaved and dutiful young gentlewoman, she added, "That is, if you please, Miss Winthrop." She bobbed a quick, mollifying curtsy, then remarked, "No doubt he hopes to write a monograph and present it to the Royal Society using Miss Franklin's discoveries, claiming they are his own."

"Oh, tosh!" said Miss Winthrop angrily. "What nonsense!" Miss Quince looked grave, but offered no opinion.

Miss Franklin said calmly, "I ought to have kept a better watch on them. He had picked up one or two earlier and did not return them, so I should have known. I did not anticipate his abrupt departure, or that he would act so decisively." Then she sat down and began to make up a new little notebook, laying out the papers, folding them, and sewing the spine with neat, precise stitches, as though losing weeks of work did not matter to her.

"At least we have taught her to sew a straight seam," murmured Miss Winthrop to Miss Hopkins. "If you recall what a hodgepodge her needlework was when she came here!"

Miss Asquith waited until the conversation had drifted to other topics and she and Miss Franklin were alone and unobserved in their corner. Then she said, "I do not wish to tempt you into the 'slough of despond,' dear Miss Franklin, but surely you must feel *something* in this matter! I know that you were uncertain about Mr. Rupert Crabbe's true intentions, and it appears you were in the right *there*, as I was wrong. But, even if your vanity and your heart are untouched, you must feel dreadful about losing the documentation of so much patient thought and observation. If you desire not to speak of it, I will respect your wishes, but if it would ease your mind or heart to unburden yourself to me, I am entirely at your command."

Miss Franklin was silent a moment. "You are very kind," she began, and then, turning to study her companion with her large dark eyes, went on to say, "Yes, you *are* very kind, aren't you? It is rather unfair of you to be kind to me, you know, Miss Asquith. The behavior of Mr. Rupert Crabbe had convinced me that I was right to turn my back upon any hope of love or trust in humanity. I have been sitting here congratulating myself upon becoming insentient—on growing a carapace as hard and impervious as that of a tortoise. And here you are, insisting upon acting as my friend, caring about my sorrows and disappointments." She shook her head. "You are undoing all the good that Mr. Rupert Crabbe's betrayal has done me. Perhaps I shall not be able to *quite* wall myself off from human affections. I shall have to leave one small chink in my armor open, for your friendship."

Uncertain whether to laugh or weep at this unexpected reproach, Miss Asquith begged her to at least give the assurance that her heart was not blighted. "For I feel most dreadfully guilty at having encouraged you to expect a declaration from him. I was wrong, and I regret it bitterly."

"I do not think you were wrong, Miss Asquith—your name

is Emily, is it not? May I call you by it? Mine is Rosalind, and I hope you will so address me."

"Oh, pray do! But what do you mean, Rosalind?"

"I believe he *had* in fact decided to make me an offer. My fortune is ample, and I suppose he assumed I would make a useful assistant in his scientific studies, in between bearing his children, managing his congregation, and sewing his shirts. If I should manage to make any discoveries worthy of publishing, he could always write them up and claim the credit, as it would have been his legal right to do.

"It was the news of his father's crime that caused him to abandon that plan. He knew my mother would never consent to a marriage with the son of a notorious gambler who had killed a man in a brawl. No, not even tho' he *was* the son of a peer of the realm. Perhaps," she said with a slight smile, "Mama might allow me to marry the *elder* of the Crabbe brothers, he who will be the baron one day, but never a younger son, a clergyman who is apt to lose his position after all this scandal."

Miss Asquith's hands twisted in her lap. "But you of course—"

Miss Franklin laughed. "Fear not! Even if I had had it in mind to be so faithless a friend, Mr. Crabbe the elder has never once looked at another woman so long as you were in the room. No, Mr. Crabbe and I should be unsuited to each other. It was only Rupert Crabbe I ever thought of."

She sighed. "I will own, Emily, that my vanity, if not my heart, was touched. I wondered if I could subjugate my will to a man's, in return for the comfort of being a natural, a *normal* woman, and living the life of a wife and mother. Yet, while I could tell that he was considering making me an offer, I could not decide if there was any real affection in the impulse, or merely calculation. He valued me, yes: I am young, attractive, with considerable mental attainments and a substantial dowry. But I could not tell whether or not he loved me. Being genuinely loved would have compensated for some sacrifice of independence on my part.

"And then one day I lost one of my little booklets of calculations. I returned to the room where I had left it to find no trace of it. I recollected seeing Mr. Rupert Crabbe pick something up off the floor as I left the room, but when I taxed him with it, he denied finding a notebook.

"After that, I wondered. Some days later, I left another completed booklet where he might find it, and observed him from a place of concealment. He took it up, looked long at the work inside, and then secreted it upon his person. Again, he denied knowledge of its whereabouts. Mr. Rupert Crabbe's behavior in absconding with my other material does not surprise me at all. I assumed that, when once he had proposed and I had rejected him, he would do precisely that."

"Then—then you were determined to refuse him? Of course you were, since he could act in such a low and duplicitous manner! But how strange that he should purloin your work like that when he had hopes for your future together! I do not understand it at all."

"I believe I do. He could not be certain of me, you see. I did not behave with the deference he thought due to his sex and position. And so he sought to—I believe the term is 'hedge his bets.' If I agreed to marry him, all well and good: he would have access to my work, both present and future, as well as to my fortune and my person. If I did not agree, he would at least have my formulae upon which he could base a learned paper, and thereby win himself a name."

Miss Asquith could not help but smile a little at Miss Franklin's serene assumption that any paper based upon her formulae would of course result in renown and respect for its author. However, the fact that Mr. Rupert Crabbe had put himself to the trouble of stealing it rather lent weight to the assumption.

"But since you knew he was stealing your notebooks . . . ! Pray forgive me, Rosalind, but why did you not better guard them? How often have I observed you leaving them in a small heap on a table in the parlor! Will this not be a dreadful loss to you?"

Miss Franklin picked up a fan from the table next to her, discarded by one of the other young ladies, and began to thresh it back and forth in front of her face, which had the effect of shielding her expression from Miss Asquith's gaze.

"I did indeed invest a great deal of time, thought, and effort in those notebooks," she admitted. "However, I have decided that, since I do not have access to a telescope of my own, it will be best if I shift my explorations from astronomy to a science that does not require such expensive equipment—at least until I get some control of my own money, that is. I had thought of botany, which merely requires a garden. I am much interested in the variability of species, and I might be able to do something with fast-growing plants that could be selected for some specific trait, you know, which would—"

Miss Asquith reached out and seized hold of her hand. "Pray stop waving that fan about, Rosalind. I cannot see you properly, and it is not *that* hot in this room. What was in those notebooks that Mr. Rupert Crabbe stole?"

"Observations on the orbit of Uranus," Miss Franklin responded, "and a theory that certain perturbations in that orbit might indicate the existence of another planet beyond it in our system. The equations and the observations used to expound the theory, all of which are reported in the notebooks, would appear to bear it out." She gazed wide-eyed at Miss Asquith.

Miss Asquith studied her face. "You say 'a theory.' And the equations 'would *appear* to bear it out.'" She frowned in concentration and then went on, watching Miss Franklin carefully. "No, I do not believe it can be a tarradiddle, a nonsense you made up to impose upon him. He is far too intelligent and knowledgeable in the discipline to be gulled by some rubbish you invented. So I see that you are quite truthful in saying that you spent a great deal of time and effort on those booklets, ensuring that they were convincing to an informed and powerful intellect. Then, in fact you do *not* believe that there are any planets out past Uranus?"

"Certainly I do," responded Miss Franklin. "And if only I had regular access to a good lens, somewhat *larger* than Mr. Rupert Crabbe's, I should prove it."

"Ah, I see! You would prove it, *if only you were given the opportunity*. But, as you have not had the opportunity, your notebooks do not in reality prove any such thing?"

Miss Franklin looked down at the fan, resting inert in her lap, a small smile flickering across her face.

"Perhaps there might be some errors in the pages of those notebooks," she conceded. "One who is anxious for fame in scientific circles, who is unwilling to do the lengthy work of checking my observations and deductions, *might* be misled into believing that I had proof. However, I am sure that Mr. Rupert Crabbe would never be so foolish as to take the unsupported word of a mere woman and simply attempt to publish my findings as his own without extensive review."

Miss Asquith regarded her in silence for a moment.

"Do you know, I am often thought to be rather daring in my attitudes and my manner. But I must say, my dear Rosalind, you quite outdo me. You *are* rather a devil, aren't you?"

Miss Franklin smiled, but said nothing.

"Very well. I shall not wrack my feelings on your account. You have lost nothing of worth and are heart-whole. Now, if only we could resolve the matter of Miss le Strange's necklace as satisfactorily as that, I should be much relieved, and fully *two-thirds* along the road toward perfect happiness."

"Do you know—I had quite forgot—there is something about Miss le Strange I meant to tell you. I probably ought not to speak of it, however."

As Miss Asquith considered the best way in which to pry loose this interesting secret from Miss Franklin's rather undeveloped sense of propriety, an interruption occurred.

"Mrs. Fredericks of Crooked Castle," announced Robert, beaming all over his handsome face, and ushering the new mother, making her first morning call after her confinement, into the parlor with an extravagant bow. "*And* Master Rodney Fredericks, I believe!"

"Yes, here we are, and I have *so* much to tell you all!" said Mrs. Fredericks, flinging her bonnet, gloves, and parasol hither and yon with great abandon. "I have brought Rodney along with his nursemaid, as I find I cannot bear to be parted from him for long, so we shall keep our visit short, lest he should grow testy. He's rather a poppet, but when he feels he is not being appreciated, *look out!* is all I can say."

The young ladies gathered around to admire the young man and the blooming health of his mother.

"Oh, I am excessively well—both my son and I are positively bursting with vigor and well-being. You need not concern yourselves with *us*. But listen! Now that I am allowed to get up and exert myself, I have determined to make a stir in the neighborhood.

"My dears, I intend to give a ball! This week fortnight!"

19

AND YET, DESPITE the raptures lavished upon Mrs. Fredericks for her kind intentions, several of the young ladies appeared to be less delighted than they ought to be.

Quite naturally, some, like Miss Victor, were euphoric. At her age, any entertainment more sophisticated than watching Cook pluck a chicken for supper was an extravagant and urbane delight. And although professional musicians would be in attendance, Miss Briggs had already been asked to perform as well; she was therefore pleased and gratified. Then, of course, even though Mr. Arbuthnot was not yet quite well enough to dance, it would be the engaged couple's first official appearance together in public; he and Miss Evans were calmly looking forward to the event.

On the descending scale of happiness, Miss Pffolliott was divided in her feelings. On the one hand, Mr. Rasmussen was her admitted suitor, so she would have a partner, and not have to suffer the indignity of sitting by and watching others dance. On the other, she could not bring herself to *like* her parentally endorsed admirer; by turns, she both smiled and sighed.

Miss Asquith was grieving for the loss of Mr. Crabbe, yet such was her nature that she could not help but look forward to any form of merriment. Miss Franklin was indifferent; she planned to smuggle a treatise on the cell division of plants into the ballroom to entertain herself whilst her fellow students frivoled the night away. And, at the nadir of this list of pleasurable anticipation, Miss Crump was made miserable by the thought that she might be expected to perform, either on the dance floor or in conversation.

Although the Fredericks had agreed that its stated reason was to celebrate Miss Evans's and Mr. Arbuthnot's engagement, it was Miss Mainwaring whose happiness the ball had truly been meant to promote. Thus, Mrs. Fredericks's eye was on her niece as she made her announcement, and she was concerned to note that Miss Mainwaring did not appear elated by the news.

"Oh yes. How delightful," she said. "What could be more exciting?"

"As you are so enthralled by the idea, Cecily, perhaps your teachers will excuse you from lessons this afternoon so that you can be my assistant and run errands and so forth?" Mrs. Fredericks looked at her stepsister and her stepsister's friend with lifted eyebrows.

"Oh, certainly!" said Miss Hopkins. "I know Miss Mainwaring would enjoy helping you with the preparations."

If this was true, Miss Mainwaring did not display any signs of it. She avoided her aunt's eyes. "Miss Quince said I ought to spend more time practicing my French," she objected.

"We shall speak nothing but French the whole of the afternoon," Mrs. Fredericks replied with decision. "Come, Cecily! Go and get your bonnet on. I wish to speak with you. *Dépêche-toi!*"

Reluctantly, Miss Mainwaring fetched her bonnet. Little Master Rodney stirred in the nursemaid's arms as she stood, preparing to leave. Robert, who had been making ridiculous faces at the baby behind the nursemaid's back, said, "Diddle-ums! Kootchy-coo!" and wiggled his fingers in front of the child's face. The nursemaid stepped away from Robert with an air of snatching the baby out of range of some malign influence. Rather startled by this evasive action, Robert drew back to allow them to precede him, his smile slipping from fatuous glee to anxious uncertainty.

Mrs. Fredericks, who had placed a hand at the base of Miss Mainwaring's back in order to propel her out of the house, spared a moment to note this small interchange. When they had gained the front walk, leaving Robert drooping like a wilted begonia in the doorway, she decided to tackle this mystery first, before interrogating her niece.

"Agnes, why did you behave just now as if that good-looking young footman was breathing the plague over my son?" she demanded, looking hard at the girl. Agnes was new to the household, having been brought up from London to care for Master Rodney.

"Oooh, Ma'am!" replied the girl, attempting to curtsy while walking with her arms encumbered by the baby. "I know they say in the servants' hall that he's honest as the day is long, but what *I* say is, there's no smoke without fire!"

"Ah. The matter of the necklace, I suppose. Even I, in the midst of my maternal preoccupations, have heard about that," Mrs. Fredericks said thoughtfully. "What say you, Cecily? Do you believe that Robert took those jewels? You were present, after all."

Diverted from her own worries, Cecily shook her head so decisively that her curls bounced about her face. "Certainly not! The servants' hall is quite right. Poor Robert would not dream of doing it. No one likes that Miss le Strange in the least, for all she is so well-born."

"It is unlikely she would steal her own necklace, however," said Mrs. Fredericks. She turned back to Agnes. "You heard what Miss Mainwaring said. Kindly do not spread any rumors. We must hope that the necklace turns up on its own."

Agnes did not quite dare to sniff, but she looked as though she was considering it. As a citizen of the great city of London freshly arrived at this little tin-pot village in Yorkshire, she felt herself to be a woman of the world in comparison with these naïve country folk. In Agnes's opinion, even Mrs. Fredericks, pleasant lady that she was, had no more sense than a day-old chick when it came to the wicked ways of footmen. Once, Agnes had loved a handsome footman, only to be spurned and to see her tenderest feelings trampled upon. Agnes considered that she knew everything there was to know about footmen, and judged accordingly.

Once at the Castle, Mrs. Fredericks sent Agnes off to the nursery to put young Rodney down for a nap, and prepared to pry open the oyster that was her niece.

"Well, Cecily—" she began.

"En français, non?" inquired Cecily.

"What? Oh, good heavens no, you foolish creature! I merely said that to get you away. I am afraid I am not up to a discussion of your happiness in a foreign language, even if it *is* the language of love. And now, tell me in plain English why it is that you are facing the expectation of a ball with all the enthusiasm of a patient waiting to have a tooth extracted."

"Oh, Aunt Althea . . . !"

"You are in love with that young Mr. Hadley, are you not?"

"Aunt Althea!"

"Don't be such a goose. I am not more than three years your senior, but I feel a hundred. I expect it comes of my being such an old married woman now—it has a terribly aging effect on one, having to put up with the whims and foibles of men and babes. Come now! It is obvious that you love him. You go red and white by turns every time he enters a room. It is true that I have had my attention rather on other subjects of late, but I should have to be blind not to notice *that!*"

"Well . . . yes, but—"

"And what is wrong with that? In spite of what I said just now, I approve of matrimony. And motherhood as well, altho' at times I do wish that babies would not cry *quite* so loudly, but that is neither here nor there. From all that I can tell, Mr. Hadley is a very decent young gentleman, and, assuming his prospects are as good as I have every reason to believe, I intend that you shall marry him. You want to, do you not?"

Miss Mainwaring's eyes misted up and threatened to overflow.

"Oh yes, most dreadfully!" she cried, but at this point she was interrupted by the entrance of her uncle Fredericks, carrying a messy stack of papers that looked as though they had been disinterred from a badger's den.

"Oh, *do* go away, Mr. Fredericks!" cried his affectionate wife. "I have got your niece to admit that she wants dreadfully to marry Mr. Hadley, and now you must come barging in and ruin everything!"

"Hadley? Hadley, do you say? Not Caruthers Hadley, surely?" demanded Mr. Fredericks.

"I do not believe so. The given name of your beloved isn't Caruthers, is it, Cecily?" Mrs. Fredericks inquired of the now openly sobbing Miss Mainwaring.

"No, certainly not," she replied, mopping at her tears with a tiny handkerchief more composed of lace than linen. "His name is Arthur!"

"Oh, good, good!" exclaimed her uncle. "Shouldn't think you'd want to marry old Caruthers. Must be fifty if he's a day, and the most awful scoundrel I ever met. Tried to cross me in that indigo deal—you remember, Althea—swore I'd never have dealings with the man again. Ha! Caruthers Hadley! The old crook!"

"As the gentleman you mention is *not* the gentleman in question, perhaps we could delay discussion of his various crimes until a later time?" inquired Mrs. Fredericks.

"Oh, indeed. Don't you even think of marrying Caruthers Hadley, though, Cecily! Greatest villain un-hung in England. That being understood, I believe I will allow you two ladies to sort out your various problems on your own," and Mr. Fredericks hastened out of the room again, shedding several dog-eared and dirty pages as he went.

"Now we have got rid of him, I believe we may find we have need of him after all," reflected Mrs. Fredericks as she pressed her own, rather more practical, handkerchief into service for her niece-by-marriage's tear-spattered face. "I want him to inquire into Mr. Hadley's parentage and financial situation, and nobody is better equipped to find out about finances than your uncle. However, do not fret, Cecily dearest, we will know all about him soon, I assure you. Pray tell me your grief and we will see what can be done to assuage it."

And so Cecily Mainwaring told her of her growing fondness turning to love for the man who had seemed so interested in a childhood spent on an Indian indigo plantation, and whose father was heavily invested in the East India Company. This connection had seemed to draw them together, until quite suddenly he had begun making the most extraordinary overtures to Miss Crump.

"And she hates it, Aunt, she *hates* it! Poor, dear Miss Crump cannot bear these—these peculiar stories he tells her about his home and his family. He draws the most *bizarre* picture of his circumstances, apparently in an attempt to woo her. Only, it seems to me that he actually wishes to repel her. Oh! It is so confusing!"

"I see," said Mrs. Fredericks thoughtfully. "Or I think I do. At least, I have an idea. We shall have your uncle initiate a bit of research into Mr. Hadley's background. That is the first step."

Her niece blotted her eyes with the handkerchief and sighed.

✦ ✦ ✦

The date for the ball was set, and preparations began in earnest. Not Miss Mainwaring alone, but all of the students were pressed into service to run errands, choose music, help to plan the menu for the dinner, and sew silk flowers as decoration. When not actually engaged in helping to ready the Castle for the celebration, they mended and refurbished their best gowns, experimented with new hairstyles, and tried on one another's gloves and petticoats.

A letter came from Lord Baggeshotte's attorney, stating that the Viscount was still living, but too ill to speak. If valuable property had been stolen, the attorney recommended that the guilty party be handed over to the local magistrate. If an engagement had occurred between Miss le Strange and Lord Baggeshotte, the attorney knew nothing about it, and neither, upon being questioned, did any of the Viscount's servants or family connections. Miss le Strange's position as fiancée was therefore unsupported by any evidence, and her possession of the necklace conceivably unauthorized. Here the letter became vague; his lawyerly caution dreaded possibly offending his employer's rightful bride, yet the idea that an imposter had managed to gain possession of, and then lost, a precious family heirloom was not to be contemplated, either.

In a frenzied attempt to avoid taking a stand one way or the other without first consulting his noble client, the attorney's communication degenerated into near gibberish. At last, he inquired: Why they did not ask Miss Crump, who *must* know about the matter?

This missive was shown, without comment, to Miss le Strange, who read it, also without comment, although her face tightened as she read the lines containing the words *imposter* and *unauthorized possession*. Miss Quince continued to be surprised that she did not leave Lesser Hoo for the bedside of her fiancé where she could better protect her interests, or so it seemed to Miss Quince, at least. However, she did not say so, and indeed the entire meeting between the two women was silent, even though the air between them crackled with suppressed emotion.

"We must wait for the Viscount either to regain the power of speech or else to be forever silenced by death," said Miss Quince in tones that brooked no contradiction. Miss le Strange said nothing, but left the school immediately, without even attempting to see her charge, Miss Crump.

✦ ✦ ✦

"The swine! The utter swine! How dare he—or his blasted son—come sniffing around my niece? My own sister's daughter! Well, I'll see him in Hades!"

It was a week and a half since Mrs. Fredericks had made Miss Mainwaring admit to the true state of her affections. Mr. Fredericks was gripping a letter in his hand and pacing in an agitated manner about the great hall of Crooked Castle.

"Hush, my dear. Please calm down. You'll do yourself an injury. Sit down, and press this damp cloth against your head. That's right. Are you better now?"

"I am *not* better, nor do I intend to be so until Cecily gives up any idea of marrying the son of this—this cad, Caruthers Hadley!"

"Then he *is* the father of Arthur Hadley?"

"He is, devil take him."

"But there is nothing against the lad himself, and Cecily loves him. I find that my stepsister and Clara Hopkins and, far more importantly, Miss Quince like him very much. He should have a future with the East India Company, as his father holds such a high position there."

Mr. Fredericks ceased pacing long enough to fix his wife with a stern eye. "If Cecily marries Arthur Hadley," he said, in the tone of voice he might have used to attempt to explain quadratic equations to one of his dogs, "that will make *me* his uncle, which is tantamount to making me brother to Caruthers Hadley. Quite out of the question."

Mrs. Fredericks regarded him thoughtfully. "The fact that you are behaving like such a great gawby, my dear, leads me to believe that he must have bested you in the indigo deal you mention. Nothing else could explain such vituperation."

"He did nothing of the kind!"

"Are you aware that, from all appearances, Mr. Hadley Senior is every bit as much opposed to the match as you are? It is my personal belief that he has forbidden his son to make an offer to Cecily, and has instead ordered him to pursue Miss Crump, Viscount Baggeshotte's daughter."

Mr. Fredericks rounded on her. "Why, the dirty dog! How dare he think my niece not good enough for his boy?"

"I rather suspect it is because he thinks that *you* bested *him* in the indigo deal, and he cannot bear the humiliation of meeting you again." Having delivered herself of this opinion, Mrs. Fredericks folded up her mending and left the room, feeling that it was best to allow her husband to think on this aspect of the situation in solitude.

"Humph!" said Mr. Fredericks. Then after a pause for reflection, he began to chuckle. "Ha! Poor old Caruthers Hadley!"

20

MISS PFFOLLIOTT WAS missing the dog, Wolfie. Since Mr. Rasmussen had assumed a more respectable position in her life, she had not needed canine companionship on her daily walks and, to her surprise, she found herself quite desolate without his undemanding presence. His size was such that she need not bend to pat him; the palm of her hand rested on his huge shaggy head as they walked along together down the lanes, and his company made her feel she was fit for anything.

Now, though Mr. Rasmussen had ceased to waylay her, she felt lonely and exposed out on the fells without her friend. At the field where she had been wont to see Wolfie she paused, hoping perhaps to offer him a kiss and a caress.

"If tha' wants him, tha' can have him," said Mr. Lomax from his habitual recumbent position on the shady side of the stone wall. Miss Pffolliott uttered a shrill squeak at this unexpected remark. However, Wolfie lunged into view, expressing his joy at this reunion by gamboling noisily about, looking and sounding like a bear undergoing a seizure of some description.

As usual, the sight of the dog cheered and heartened her,

and she calmed. She greeted the shepherd, adding, "What do you mean, Mr. Lomax?"

Mr. Lomax spat in disgust. "Pardon me, Miss, but that dog is useless. T'other dogs can run rings about him, and he eats like a prize hog. *You* take him, Miss. Tell Miss Hopkins he'll be right handy for scarin' off vagrants and suchlike—least, so long as they don't get too close and he starts fawnin' all over 'em."

"Oh, but . . ." As the words formed on her lips, it occurred to her how much she would love to have Wolfie by her side every day. She had not made any close friends at the school—her relations with the other girls were cordial, but distant—and the thought of having Wolfie's affectionate presence on a regular basis was very sweet. Indeed, she realized, she valued his company far more than the company of her beau, Mr. Rasmussen. She stooped and wrapped her arms around the big dog's neck.

"There's a fox been after t'hens of late," said Mr. Lomax, watching her shrewdly. "Daresay Miss Hopkins has been troubled, like most folks. You might mention that to her when you bring him back. Fox won't want to come around where Wolfie's been, and you needn't worry about him with the fowl. He's right gormless when it comes to chickens—thinks they're puppies or summat. You'd undertake to feed and water the beast, wouldn't you?"

"I would, Mr. Lomax," Miss Pffolliott said, nodding her head.

"Well, then, that's settled. Get along w'you, Wolfie. You're t'young lady's dog now."

Wolfie greeted this news with a series of howls and a delighted, lumbering dance around his new mistress, and the two set off in the direction of the post office in a state of considerable contentment.

✦ ✦ ✦

"I say, what a very fierce-looking dog! Is that not Lomax's sheepdog?" The gentleman who thus addressed Miss Pffolliott as they left the village shop had stopped to admire Wolfie, offering the dog his hand to sniff and drool over.

"Oh, how do you do, Mr. Godalming? Yes—er, that is, no, not anymore," said Miss Pffolliott. She explained the transfer of ownership and, as Mr. Godalming seemed quite interested, shyly admitted to being nervous about Wolfie's reception at the school. "He is so terribly *large*, you see. And, as you say, he does not appear nearly as sweet-natured as he is. But he *is*, truly he is very, *very* affectionate and friendly." She spoke pleadingly, as though if she could convince Mr. Godalming she would therefore be able to convince Miss Hopkins to let her keep him.

Mr. Godalming laughed and scratched behind Wolfie's ears. The grain had been got in weeks ago, the fields manured, the vegetables and fruits harvested and preserved, and he was now, if not quite a gentleman of leisure, then a much more relaxed and genial soul than he had been in September. "He's got a savage look to him, fair enough, but I believe you are right, and it is all a sham! You're nothing but a great baby, aren't you, Wolfie? I've heard Lomax complaining about him as a sheepdog—said he was eating him out of house and home and wasn't worth the price of his feed—so it does not surprise me that he has pushed him off onto you. Still, he ought to be worthwhile having about in a houseful of women—you've just the one male house servant, haven't you?"

Miss Pffolliott agreed that Robert was their only indoor man.

"Why then, Miss Pffolliott, if you will allow me to escort you and your new dog home, I think I may be able to be of assistance to you. I had planned to walk over to the Castle to speak with Mrs. Fredericks about the ball, and I might as well see you back on my way."

Miss Pffolliott expressed herself as happy to accept his arm on the way to the school, but wondered aloud what he could mean by the phrase, "may be able to be of assistance to you."

"It is this, Miss Pffolliott. You are aware that I am magistrate for this district?" When she nodded, he continued, "As magistrate I get to know the crimes and misdemeanors going on in the area. And"—here he leaned in closer and spoke in a lower tone—"I do not mean to alarm you, or any other of the ladies, but there have been several house-breakings at Allingham, which as you know is a mere six miles away. I shall make sure to draw your Miss Hopkins aside and tell her that I strongly recommend she get herself a good, fearsome-looking watchdog. In fact"—and here he looked down at the anxious face gazing up at him—"I shall tell her it was my idea to begin with, if you like!"

"Oh, would you, Mr. Godalming? Would you?"

"Of course, m'dear. Happy to!" He patted her hand and steered her around a small puddle in the road. This Miss Pffolliott was a nice little creature, he thought, and it was pleasant to do her this small favor. She seemed fond of her dog, which he found rather touching. He himself was devoted, in his way, to his own dogs. He rummaged around in his mind for a topic of conversation.

"Don't suppose you care for sheep at all," he suggested diffidently. "I find them fascinating, myself, but ladies may not think much about them."

Miss Pffolliott replied that her knowledge of sheep was not extensive, but expressed a willingness to learn. This attitude in a young lady was so novel that Mr. Godalming began to think her quite exceptional. Using the flocks by the side of the road as a sort of visual aid, he waxed eloquent about all matters ovine as Miss Pffolliott listened, her head tipped to one side.

She was reflecting that, for all Mr. Godalming was a rather ugly man and, yes, definitely inclined to run on a bit about sheep, he was kind. In these ways he could be said to resemble her dear Wolfie, and after all, sheep *might* have points of interest hitherto unsuspected.

✢ ✢ ✢

The reason that Miss le Strange—having been prevented from taking repossession of her pupil—had not left Lesser Hoo and traveled to Lord Baggeshotte's bedside was simple: she had not the funds to do so. Much to the governess's fury, Mrs. Westing had managed to best her at cards time and time again, gradually shifting the contents of Miss le Strange's purse into her own. In fact, Miss le Strange had suspicions of her hostess's honesty. However, even if she could prove actual cheating, the result of exposing the lady would be to make an enemy of her only ally in the neighborhood, and to deprive herself of a roof over her head. She held her tongue and watched her last few resources dwindling away.

Her regular stipend as a governess would not be payable for several months, and as long as Lord Baggeshotte remained unable to speak, it was unlikely that his lawyer would be willing to advance her any money based upon her unrecognized position as the Viscount's fiancée. She had hoped that the Misses Winthrop, Hopkins, and Quince would be willing to pay some portion of the necklace's value to avoid any scandal, but they had remained obdurate, so *that* source of ready money had dried up. And the other arrangements she had made to ensure her future, in the event that Lord Baggeshotte should die without making provision for her, were not proceeding as smoothly as she could wish.

Her lip curled. How *could* she have been so careless as to allow his Lordship to have a seizure before announcing their engagement? She ought to have insisted he make it public immediately, before he had a chance to reconsider. Once it was proclaimed abroad, there would have been no going back, but his sudden illness—immediately after the proposal she had managed to bring about with much toil—had allowed him an out.

She must regain guardianship of Miss Crump. It was for this reason that she had journeyed to Lesser Hoo in the first place. So long as she had control of the girl, she would also have some control over the father and, additionally, control of the girl's purse strings. No one could argue that, as the governess charged with bringing the poor child to her father's sickbed, she should purchase the coach fares and inn accommodations. She would pay for them from the child's allowance, which she happened to know was both generous and rarely touched.

Miss le Strange's eyes brightened at the thought of the pleasant little pile of silver and gold Miss Crump was sure to have amassed here in quiet Lesser Hoo, where it was difficult to find any shops in which to spend one's money. Thank goodness the child was far too stupid to learn how to play card games, or no doubt Mrs. Westing would have nosed out the existence of that allowance and managed to strip her of it—and her dowry as well, for that matter.

She considered the best way to manage. There was no point in appealing to Miss Quince; their enmity was both fixed and mutual. And the other two headmistresses would not want to lose the pupil whose presence lent such prestige to their establishment. No, she would have to swallow her pride and convince Miss Crump to place herself under Miss le Strange's guardianship again.

Miss le Strange was not a fool. She knew quite well that her prospective stepdaughter both feared and disliked her. In the past this had not seemed of much importance, as the girl could be relied upon to do whatever she was told. Now, however, all that was required was for her to continue to express a preference to remain in Lesser Hoo, and the ladies of the

Winthrop Hopkins Academy would refuse to relinquish her.

She paid a call on the school and requested a private interview with Miss Crump. However, when Miss Crump appeared after a long interval (during which Miss le Strange minutely examined the room for evidence of slovenly housekeeping, without success), she was accompanied by Miss Mainwaring.

Miss le Strange peered at this interloper through the silver lorgnette she kept on a chain around her neck. She in fact possessed excellent eyesight, but found that being scrutinized in this manner was apt to make social inferiors uneasy. Miss Mainwaring, who had had some experience of tigresses in her former life, remained unperturbed. Instead of offering any excuse for her presence, she sat down beside her friend, took a piece of embroidery out of her workbag, and began to thread her needle.

"I know you will understand, Miss . . . Miss . . . er, hmm," said Miss le Strange through gritted teeth, "when I ask you to leave me alone with my ward. We have a number of things to discuss that are not for strangers' ears."

Miss Mainwaring looked up from her work. "Oh, I am so sorry, Miss le Strange!" she said in apologetic and deferential tones. "But, you see, Miss Crump asked me particularly to come with her to this interview, and as we are *most intimate friends*, I could not think of disappointing her. You do not wish me to leave, do you, dear Jane?"

Miss Crump shook her bonneted head violently. "No," she whispered. "No, no, I do not wish you to leave. Not at all!"

And she clutched Miss Mainwaring's arm as though Miss le Strange might attempt to separate them by brute force. Miss Mainwaring smiled, and bent once more to her embroidery as though the question were settled.

Miss le Strange's eyes narrowed. It did indeed seem as though physical means would be required to remove Miss Mainwaring from the room, and that, of course, was out of the question. The best she could do was to pretend the little chit did not exist. She turned toward her former pupil, fixing her with the flat stare that had so often reduced the child to tears.

"Your father is ill," she said in a level voice. "He may die at any moment. You will want to go to him, I know, but of course you must have a companion on the journey. I am ready to accompany you to Bath—you need only speak the word, and we shall be off."

"Oh, but—"

"Do you not love your father, Jane?"

Miss Crump cast an agonized look at her friend. Miss Mainwaring folded her embroidery and crossed her hands over it on her lap.

"Miss Crump has written to her papa," said she. "We understand that his health is improving. Although he still cannot speak, he was able to make his desires about his daughter known. He wishes her to remain in Lesser Hoo until he sends for her."

"*What?*" demanded Miss le Strange. "And how was he able to make these '*wishes*' known, if he was unable to speak?"

"We understand—" began Miss Mainwaring, but she was interrupted by a loud scream, followed by a number of other excited vocalizations immediately without.

The door to the room flew open and an enormous creature galloped in, all eyes and teeth and long, pointed claws. The two girls drew back into their chairs, terrified. Even the indomitable Miss le Strange gasped. She stood up and braced herself, ready to do battle against this nightmarish monster, like Saint George facing the dragon.

And indeed, it seemed to be Miss le Strange the beast sought. Gathering itself together, it leaped toward her, mouth agape and drooling, every tooth it owned on display, its massive paws aimed at her shoulders as though to bring her to the floor.

Uttering a strangled cry, she turned and fled, with the fearful apparition close behind. Out the front door she ran, down the drive to the main road. She did not stop to rest until she was convinced it no longer followed her, and she leaned, gasping, against a stone wall a quarter-mile from the school. The tigress had been routed by the wolf.

"Wolfie! Bad, bad dog! Oh Wolfie, how could you behave so?" wailed Miss Pffolliott. "Just when I wanted you to make a good impression!" She dragged the dog back into the house by the simple expedient of grasping at the loose skin around his neck and tugging. "I am so dreadfully, dreadfully sorry, Miss Hopkins, Miss Winthrop! Oh, Miss Quince, I do apologize! It is only that he is so friendly, you see!" And she burst into tears.

Here Mr. Godalming interceded, explaining the situation to the astounded inhabitants of the school. "And I thought

Wolfie here might be quite useful in the event that a house-breaker came prowling around," he concluded.

"Or a fox after the chi-ickens," sobbed Miss Pffolliott.

Miss Quince was the first to recover. She gazed at the open front door whence Miss le Strange had made her hurried departure.

At last she spoke. "I should say that Wolfie has already proved his value."

21

THE HEADMISTRESSES OF the Winthrop Hopkins Academy dispatched Robert to the dower house at Gudgeon Park the next day with a note of apology. The dog, they explained, was new to their establishment and not yet trained. As he was intended to be a guard dog, they must ask their neighbors' indulgence while they struggled to curb the animal's rather *savage* propensities. No doubt, in time it would be safe to accept visits from people the dog did not know, but for the moment they must ask for a period of forbearance until the animal settled in.

Miss le Strange, who received this apology in the morning room, regarded Robert with hatred. *Of course* it was a coincidence that this new guard dog—to frighten off house-breakers, they claimed—had first arrived as she was attempting to detach her pupil from the school. Oh, certainly.

"*You* ought to be in prison," was her reply, and she left the room. Robert, who had managed to forget about the necklace and the unpleasant emotions associated with it, regarded her retreating back with concern. Was the poor lady perhaps going a bit daft?

"Yes, Ma'am," he said.

✢   ✢   ✢

Miss Franklin was now engaged in a contest of wills with Cuthbert the gardener, who managed the hothouse at the school. It was Cuthbert's unenlightened opinion that this building, so costly to build and to heat, was only to be used for the purpose of providing out-of-season fruits and vegetables, and not for experiments, no matter how scientific. As the growing season was drawing to a close, Miss Franklin's eye had fallen upon the hothouse as the proper place to begin her inherited variability studies.

It took quite an hour's argument, during which she trailed him relentlessly as he went about his autumn tasks, to convince him that her experiments could be combined with his goal of supplying bunches of grapes, tender lettuces, and French beans for the table during the winter months. Perched on a limb harvesting late apples, he found himself quite literally treed, with Miss Franklin haranguing him about pea plants on the ladder below. Unable to descend the tree without pacifying her, in the end he capitulated.

Perhaps, *perhaps*, if Miss Hopkins agreed, then a small section of the space might be allotted to Miss Franklin's foolishness. However, the plants chosen must be something that Cuthbert himself approved, must be something he would have grown in any event.

Oh, certainly, *certainly*! Miss Franklin had little doubt of carrying her point after this concession, and graciously moved aside to allow her victim to climb back down to earth.

On her way out of the orchard, she paused and pulled a small notebook and pencil from the pocket of her apron skirt. How could she utilize the space given to her to the utmost and still allow her plants the necessary air and light? She bent over her notebook, sketching out plans. At last, satisfied for the moment at any rate, she straightened.

Her eye fell upon an old, gnarled apple tree that, like an elderly woman needing the support of a cane, had gradually transferred much of its weight onto the wall that enclosed the orchard and separated it from the main road. Something about the tree stirred a memory in Miss Franklin's mind. Something . . . something odd . . .

Ah! She had it now. She left the orchard and turned down the drive to walk out onto the road. Soon she came abreast of the tree, which was leaning out over the thoroughfare, its scanty but sweet apples a temptation for a hungry passerby. Looking toward the school from this vantage point, she could see sunlight winking off the ranks of bedroom windows on the third floor. Her own room, third from the left, commanded an excellent view of the place where she stood right now, particularly when seen through a telescope.

And, yes, as she had suspected, there was a hole in the trunk of the tree. A person in her present position could have easily reached up and placed a parcel inside without ever entering the school property. Putting this thought into action, she climbed atop a boulder next to the wall and thrust her hand into the hole, indifferent to the possibility that some small creature might have made it a home. Immediately her fingertips met the surface of an object wrapped in cloth, invisible to anyone passing by, even those on horseback.

She pulled it out and, remembering how she herself had observed the person who had placed it there, thrust the bundle casually into her apron pocket for later inspection. A brief consideration of the propriety of her behavior did not worry her much. If one party secretes an object inside a tree belonging to another party and then abandons it, surely it must now belong to the second party, must it not? If the item appeared to be of any interest she would present it to Miss Hopkins, on whose property the tree stood.

She was about to retire to her chamber to examine it when she noticed Miss Quince sitting in the parlor correcting some Italian conjugations. Deeming it wise to get Miss Quince on her side before the matter of the hothouse was broached to the other two headmistresses, she postponed the unwrapping of the parcel until a later time. And once she had done with explaining to Miss Quince and gone back to her chamber, a great improvement in plant racks occurred to her and, fetching paper and charcoal, she began to sketch it out. At last, on being called to dinner, she cast off her apron, with its lumpy pocket, and hung it on a hook in the back of her wardrobe.

By the time she laid herself down on her bed that night,

her mind filled with visions of hundreds and hundreds of tiny seedlings, each meticulously labeled and documented, she had forgotten the existence of the parcel found in the old apple tree.

✦ ✦ ✦

Miss Asquith was unhappy. Even the approach of the upcoming ball could not rescue her from periods of despondency and gloom. She laughed less, smiled less, made fewer extravagant remarks, and ceased playing pranks altogether. She disliked the person she was becoming, and attempted, by dint of much silent scolding, to shame herself into happiness again, but to no avail. She *would* find herself staring into space, hands and thoughts idle, sunk in melancholy.

Some fifty miles from here, *he* was also presumably sitting and thinking wretched thoughts about his father, whose case was even now being decided by the House of Lords. Notwithstanding the fact that Lord Hardcastle was a peer of the realm, his crime had been committed in view of several respected members of the community, and there was no help for it: he must be punished. If the death had occurred as a result of a duel, or if, like the great-uncle of the poet Lord Byron, he had merely shot his coachman or some other person of lowly position, the matter might have been hushed up, but Sir Grimm was a man of some consequence, and his family was clamoring for justice.

So wretched was Miss Asquith that Miss Franklin discovered her in tears only a short time before the ball. Even Miss Franklin was unable to ignore this obvious sign of suffering, and sought an explanation for it in her own feelings.

"Oh, pray do not distress yourself so, my dear Emily," she urged her friend. "The ball will be over soon enough, and then we can return to a more rational way of life. You must claim to be indisposed, and I daresay no one will insist that you dance."

This was enough to make Miss Asquith laugh through her tears. She embraced Miss Franklin, causing that young lady to blush and grow confused. "You silly!" Miss Asquith cried. "Do you still not understand what a frivolous creature I am? I love to dance above all things! Given the opportunity, I should dance from morning until night without ceasing to take breath."

Miss Franklin attempted to sort out this contradictory information. "But why, then, do you weep? Have you got a pain somewhere?"

Miss Asquith met this simplicity with some of her own. "Yes, my dear, I do have a pain, in my heart and my head. I weep because I am missing Mr. Crabbe, and because I fear that he is undergoing a dreadful ordeal, listening to his father be roundly abused by the Lord High Steward and the entire House of Peers. Oh! If only I could know what the verdict is! For he *must* know by now."

"Oh, I do beg your pardon, Emily! I had quite forgot about the two Mr. Crabbes and their troubles. Why do you not write to him and ask? I've no doubt we could learn his address from his friends Mr. Arbuthnot and Mr. Hadley."

Miss Asquith looked at her in wonderment. "I believe you tell the truth! I believe you *have* forgotten about Mr. Rupert Crabbe and his abominable behavior toward you, Rosalind. Happy woman, to be able to dismiss such an unpleasant memory, and replace it with plans for a study of the characteristics of French beans!

"But no," she continued with a rueful smile, "I could not write to Mr. Crabbe. Even *I* have not the courage to fly so determinedly in the face of convention. I shall learn soon enough, I suppose—it will be the latest scandal, and sure to be much talked of. Still, I fear I am not a patient woman."

Miss Franklin considered this. "I am sorry you should be so unhappy, Emily. In a matter where your peace of mind is so much at stake, I cannot understand why we should not ignore society's strictures. However, I will believe that you would not find such a letter easy or comfortable to write. If there is anything I can do to help you, believe me, I will do it."

Miss Asquith embraced her friend again and, to show her appreciation, began to make the minutest inquiries as to Miss Franklin's plans for the corner of the glasshouse that was to be dedicated to her pursuits.

✦ ✦ ✦

Mrs. Fredericks was little more than a blur of movement and sound in the great hall of Crooked Castle as she directed her minions hither and yon. "Raise that bunting a bit higher, Gladys! On the right side. No, no, not my right, *your* right! Don't you know your right from your left, child? Oh, don't cry about it, but ask Greengages to teach you, there's a good girl. Or Cook. Cook is an educated woman. Agnes look at how creased that tablecloth is! Take it away and press it again. And Tom"—here she looked down upon the kitchen boy, who was carrying a platter of comestibles through to the kitchen—"if you so much as *think* about nibbling on those cheeses I shall know it, I promise you, and my wrath will be awe-inspiring, all-encompassing, and quite possibly fatal."

Tom the kitchen boy let out a high-pitched giggle and escaped to the nether regions of the Castle with his cargo of cheddar and blue cheeses.

"Cecily! My dear girl, where have you been? I have been waiting for you this past hour at least." Mrs. Fredericks swooped down on her niece as she slipped through the front door and began threading her way through the bustling crowd, all engaged in polishing, dusting, sweeping, or decorating. "Come with me at once. I wish to have a word with you. Quickly, quickly! Here comes Lady Boring, and I do so want to dodge her if I can."

Obediently, Miss Mainwaring followed her aunt into the small drawing room that, in comparison with the public rooms, was an oasis of calm and silence.

"I must say this as speedily as I may, Cecily, before Charity hunts us down in our lair. I want you to arrange matters so that Mr. Hadley is left alone with Miss Crump for oh! at least half an hour's time. Do you understand? I don't want anyone to interrupt them."

Miss Mainwaring's mouth fell open. "You—you want me to arrange a tête-à-tête between Mr. Hadley and Miss Crump?"

"Yes. Can you do it?"

"You want me to make it easier for . . . for Mr. Hadley to propose to Miss Crump?"

"Precisely!" Mrs. Fredericks beamed approval at this ready comprehension on her niece's part.

"But—but I don't *want* him to propose to her! Oh, Aunt, how can you be so unkind?" And Miss Mainwaring began to look a bit tempestuous.

"I want to get it over with, silly girl! We need to move past the proposal before we can do anything of value. Once he has proposed—"

"So here you are, Althea!" Lady Boring pushed her way into the little room, seeming to take up far more than her fair share of space. "Hiding away and allowing the servants to mismanage everything! I might have known. If *I* were giving this ball—"

"But as you are not, Charity," responded her stepsister, "perhaps you could lend me your valuable assistance. There are several stacks of linen napkins that require mending—your sewing skills were always far better than mine."

"You want me to mend your old linens? I think *not*! Althea, our relationship requires that I allow you a great deal of latitude, but no one could possibly blame me for taking offense. Your behavior is such that—"

And berating Mrs. Fredericks, Lady Boring followed her back to the great hall, leaving behind a sorely puzzled Miss Mainwaring.

22

"MR. HADLEY, DO sit by us," called Miss Mainwaring, making room on the small bench by the rose garden and beckoning the gentleman closer. It seemed to her that she was beginning to understand why her aunt wanted Mr. Hadley and Miss Crump left alone together, and she had decided to obey her instructions. "Oh, Miss Crump, pray do not go, I wanted to speak to you about the trim on my bonnet—you are *so* clever with bonnets."

Miss Crump, whose ever-present bonnet had kept the same trimmings since it was purchased, cast a desperate glance toward the entrance to the schoolhouse. Miss Mainwaring took her hand and gently tugged her back onto her seat. Mr. Hadley looked somewhat surprised at being summoned from afar, but approached and sat down on the bench without argument. There was little to see in the rose garden at this time of year, and so none of the other students or teachers was nearby; most were playing at *paille maille*, or lawn billiards, visible in the distance but barely audible. It was a pleasant autumn day with blue skies and a bright sun, which made it possible to sit out-side in comfort.

"I have heard you speak of your lovely home to Miss Crump, Mr. Hadley," Miss Mainwaring continued, "and I know I should love to see that part of England. The Lake District is thought to be very beautiful, is it not? Although I believe it does receive a great deal of rain."

Mr. Hadley approached this conversational gambit with caution. "Er . . . that is so, Miss Mainwaring. I think perhaps *you* would enjoy the Lake District. But it is not for everyone. Someone like Miss Crump here might find it entirely too damp for her health." This thought appeared to be a happy one, for he went on, inspired, "*You*, Miss Mainwaring, who have spent time in foreign climes rigorous enough to try the constitution of an ox, you who have told me about the rainy season in the country of your birth, *you* might find the Lake District conge-nial. But Miss Crump, I do not know how you would like to find a slick of moisture on every surface in every season, and your dresses falling apart from rot. Are you at all inclined to respiratory conditions, Miss Crump? I fear a move to my part of the country might even be fatal to one like yourself who is clearly in delicate health."

Miss Crump declined to have a positive malady of the lungs, but agreed with the proposition that she was not par-ticularly robust.

Miss Mainwaring looked full at Mr. Hadley and said in friendly tones, "I would enjoy visiting your home someday. I hope I will get the opportunity. And now," she added untruth-

fully, "I believe I hear Miss Quince calling my name. However"—here she fixed Miss Crump with a stern look—"*you* must
stay here with Mr. Hadley until I return."

In vain did Miss Crump struggle; it all was for naught.
Miss Mainwaring stroked her trembling hands and Mr. Hadley
was quick to beg her to remain. He gave Miss Mainwaring a
grave and questioning look; she replied with a reassuring smile
and a nod. It was their first collaboration as a couple; they understood each other without words.

"Be gentle," she murmured to him as she stood, "she is a
dear creature." To Miss Crump she said, "I shall be but a few
moments, I promise."

She walked away, feeling like a beast for putting her poor
friend in this position. However, a proposal would at least bring
about a resolution to a situation that she knew Miss Crump
found upsetting. If she would remain, hear him out, and then
give her response—the only response she *could* give—it would
be over. Mr. Hadley could report to his father quite truthfully
that he had proposed and been refused; even Mr. Hadley Senior could not argue with a lady's direct rejection.

She walked about the lawn for some moments, scarcely
conscious of her whereabouts, getting in the way of the *paille
maille* players and annoying the onlookers. Poor Miss Crump!
Perhaps, when Miss Mainwaring and Mr. Hadley had at last
found their way to wedded bliss, they could invite her to visit—
assuming that Mr. Hadley's contrary wooing had not put her
off the district altogether.

Soon, much sooner than she could have expected, a glance

in their direction revealed Mr. Hadley standing and beckoning her to approach.

Anxiously she studied her friend as she walked toward them. Even if she was not prone to respiratory weakness, she *did* seem to faint quite easily. However, she was sitting upright and, so far as it was possible to determine with a figure so heavily shawled and bonneted, she appeared to be in full possession of her faculties.

She shifted her gaze to Mr. Hadley. Never of a ruddy or bronzed complexion, Mr. Hadley's face appeared to be . . . not precisely white, but rather ashen. Misgivings stirred within her.

"How . . . ? Are you well, Mr. Hadley? Miss Crump? Jane?"

"Miss Crump has done me the honor," said Mr. Hadley in a strained voice, "of accepting my proposal of marriage. We shall be wedded, subject to her father's approval, as soon as possible, so that Miss Crump can accompany me to our new home before the winter weather sets in."

Miss Mainwaring, who had faced down tigresses, both literal and figurative, who had suffered great loss and journeyed from far lands to the place where she now stood, did not faint. She turned and walked away, leaving the happy couple alone, without a word of congratulation.

✦ ✦ ✦

"I say, Miss Pffolliott, I wonder if I may be so bold as to ask you if you would be so kind as to save a few dances for me at the ball? I should like it awfully if you would."

Miss Pffolliott blushed, not because of any refined sensibility, but because, although she seemed to possess not one, but *two* suitors, neither would be likely to arouse feelings of envy in the hearts of the other girls at the school. One of the men claimed to be desperately in love with her, but she could not believe in his assurances. Having lately had a chance to spend time with him in company, she had seen the way he looked at a blackberry trifle with rum sauce, and suspected that she knew where his passions really lay. And the other suitor, the one who importuned her now in front of *everyone*, was the widely despised Mr. Godalming.

The lawn billiards players seemed all to have heard the inquiry. They were too well-bred to stand and stare waiting for the answer; the sense she received was of heads tilting, ears tuned to hear her reply. Miss Pffolliott blushed again.

No, Mr. Godalming was not handsome or dashing or— or *desirable* in the usual ways that schoolgirls swooned over, but . . .

The truth was, she realized, that he liked and admired her, in much the same way as he liked and admired her dog, Wolfie. He thought her congenial and pleasant to talk to. He looked at her, Miss Pffolliott, and saw an ordinary, good-natured young woman well-suited to country life and country concerns. And that was a true assessment of who she was. Oh, she was pretty enough in the usual way, but she was not the heroine of a novel, fit for drama and a life of extraordinary joys and griefs. No, she was one who would find contentment as the wife of a gentleman landowner and farmer, a magistrate and person of importance in a small country village. She was cut from a simple, strong cloth that would wash and wear well, with modest trimmings for a holiday; she was not a fragile velvet or satin that must be kept for best.

She lifted her chin and said, in the face of all the interested onlookers, "Yes, Mr. Godalming, I should be delighted."

He was anxious to tell her about one of his bitches that had whelped, and in fact, she found the discussion engrossing and pleaded with Miss Hopkins to escort her on a visit to see the pups as soon as possible. Wolfie, she thought, would make a doting uncle to the little ones and would greatly enjoy the outing.

She smiled on Mr. Godalming as he offered to run to the house for a cold drink to refresh her. No, his ugliness was of no consequence at all; it only made him more dear, in the same way that Wolfie's hideous leer made her smile.

❧ ❧ ❧

How all of creation conspires against me! thought Miss le Strange. She glared at the *paille maille* players on the lawn. With much hilarity, they were endeavoring to propel a ball through a hoop with wooden mallets, and were thus unaware of her baleful gaze, at least for the moment. She had hoped that the inhabitants of the school would be inside, perhaps doing something of a scholarly nature, instead of assembling en masse here, almost on the very spot where she had intended to carry out a covert act.

However, she would not allow her plans to be thwarted. Or, at any rate, thwarted any more than they already had been, she amended, grinding her teeth with a harsh sound that made her servant, Maggie, standing next to her, shudder. She had received a letter an hour ago that had made it clear that all her strategies and designs were as nothing, as thin and insubstantial as dust, and about to be blown away on the wind.

The letter was from Viscount Baggeshotte. In staggering letters that were barely legible, he repudiated the engagement she had worked so hard to achieve. Her lip curled in contempt as she read the words: . . . *must have misinterpreted something I said . . . hold you in the highest esteem, but . . . a deathbed promise to my dear wife . . .* A deathbed promise, indeed! The old reprobate! The man was a cad, pure and simple.

And now he was removing Miss Crump from her care and control as well. *As you have seen her placed in a school of good repute . . . the child informs me that she is happy and does not desire to leave . . . letter of recommendation to help settle you . . . employment with an excellent family in Wales.*

Wales! *Wales!* As if Yorkshire was not enough of a comedown! Wales! A place where they were so poor, they ate cheese instead of butcher's meat and called it "rabbit." So poor that they could apparently not afford any vowels but instead spelled everything with an incomprehensible string of consonants! Miss le Strange spit upon Viscount Baggeshotte's "excellent family in Wales."

At least she had her insurance plan, tucked away in the

event that the tide of fortune should turn against her, which it most assuredly had. She meant to secure it without further delay and leave this place at once.

By an ingenious arrangement involving a mirror hidden in a shawl, she had managed to cheat her hostess out of a neat little sum of money last night. Imagine! A le Strange reduced to cheating at cards in order to scrape up enough money for coach fare! Still, cheating a cheater did not count as a moral failing, not in Miss le Strange's opinion. The money she had won from Mrs. Westing was her own, taken from her by depraved and wicked means.

However, it was essential that she get away from Lesser Hoo as swiftly as possible, before Mrs. Westing had the opportunity to win it back. To that end, she and Maggie were loitering in the road next to the school, and she was wishing that the ground under the *paille maille* alley would open up and swallow every one of the players and onlookers. The alley consisted of nothing more than a long green stretch of mowed lawn, with a large hoop set into the ground at each end. It was situated right across the drive from the orchard, which was where Miss le Strange needed to make a discreet retrieval.

"Go and distract them," she ordered Maggie. "Faint, or something of that nature."

Maggie's opinion of the gentry's concern for their inferiors was not high. She doubted a fainting servant girl would disrupt an agreeable afternoon's entertainment, and therefore chose another tactic. Like her mistress, she disliked dogs; she looked around for Wolfie, without result. Then she advanced to stand in front of the lawn billiards alley and, pointing away from the orchard, screamed as loudly as she could.

Startled, the young ladies and gentlemen looked up.

"The dog! The one that looks like a wolf! It's killing the chickens! Oh, shoot it before it destroys them all!"

Although Maggie was pointing in a different direction from the chicken coop, which was tactfully hidden behind the house with the other unaesthetic aspects of a functioning country estate, it was impossible to entirely dismiss her accusations as a bag of moonshine; the group began to drift in the direction she was pointing.

Miss Pffolliott was sitting apart with Mr. Godalming, thanking her stars that Mr. Rasmussen had been prevented by business from paying a visit today and wondering how she could maneuver Mr. Godalming into proposing as soon as possible so that she would be able to send Mr. Rasmussen away. She was therefore slow to realize that her dog was being most unfairly slandered. When she did realize, she leaped up from her bench and spoke Wolfie's name. He rose up from his place of concealment behind the seat, looking like some demonic apparition erupting from the infernal regions into modern-day England. Even though by now they had good reason to believe in the dog's essential kindliness, several of the more delicately strung young ladies shrieked at his sudden emergence.

"He is not doing anything of the kind," Miss Pffolliott said indignantly.

"No, indeed, he is not," Mr. Godalming agreed. "That dog wouldn't kill a chicken if his life depended on it."

"My mistake," said Maggie, having ascertained that her mistress had concluded her business at the apple tree. "Beg pardon, I'm sure." She bobbed a curtsy and departed the scene, following in Miss le Strange's footsteps back toward the dower house.

Well before she had caught her up, she realized that her mistress was in a temper. Maggie had seen the signs—the clenched fists, the stiff shoulders, the fast, angry step—far too often to be mistaken. Prudently she held her tongue and waited for Miss le Strange to speak.

Which Miss le Strange did soon enough: "The scheming little s-s-snake!" she hissed, too angry to speak without sputtering. "She *knew*! She bided her time and then she crept out here and *t-took* it! The little viper!"

Maggie, who had a fairly good idea of what had been hidden in the apple tree, was not about to admit to it. Innocently she inquired, "Who, Miss? Who took it? Was it anything of value?"

Miss le Strange was too furious to be cautious.

"Anything of value?" Miss le Strange snarled. "It was the necklace, you fool! And of course it was the Crump creature. She had the temerity to look affronted when she saw me wear it! I had every intention of letting her have the rest of the parure—they were lesser pieces anyway. But that necklace was magnificent."

Maggie considered saying *I see, Miss* in a neutral tone of voice, but thought better of it and remained silent.

"I want that necklace, and I mean to get it back," Miss le Strange said, striding along and breathing heavily, like a prize hunting horse that has been run neck-or-nothing across hill and dale. "I *deserve* that necklace, after the way I have been treated."

This time Maggie deemed it safe enough to say, "Yes, Miss."

23

THE NIGHT OF the ball was upon them. Mrs. Fredericks had spoken lightly of limiting the guests to the members of the Winthrop Hopkins Academy and their visitors, but of course it could not be done; the whole of the landed gentry for twenty miles around had to be invited, dignitaries were summoned from London and York, and in the end invitations, beautifully inscribed on thick, cream-colored paper, were sent to everybody from the village and environs who had any pretensions at all to gentility. As the Fredericks were by far the wealthiest family in the district, an entertainment like this was anticipated to be grand indeed. Unlike the star party, which had achieved elegance by the simple expedient of decoration with the heavenly lights, the Crooked Castle ball was to glitter with more earthly, and more costly, adornments.

In the past year, the Castle had undergone substantial renovation, amounting in fact to demolition and reconstruction on another location. The Fredericks had chosen to honor, and even to exaggerate, the whimsical nature of the building, which was not truly ancient, but rather a romantic's dream of a medieval fortress. They had added a great number of spurious towers, crenellations, flying buttresses and carved archways, increasing the architectural confusion of the original. It was a structure of considerable charm, which, now she had married and no longer lived in it, Lady Boring called *vulgar*.

Tonight Crooked Castle wore its festive attire; everything that tapestry, bannerettes, flowers, and candlelight could do to make it ready for a gala had been provided. The great hall was decked in feudal splendor, a feast fit for a twelfth-century royal court had been prepared for the guests, and a full orchestra was quartered in the little drawing room, playing a Haydn concerto. A trotto or a passamezzo might have been more appropriate for the medieval theme, but, as Mrs. Fredericks explained, they made her feel as if she ought to be wearing a jester's motley and a belled cap instead of a ballgown.

Mr. and Mrs. Fredericks stood in the hall greeting their guests as they arrived, making each welcome regardless of rank or station. Owing to the short notice, Mrs. Fredericks's mother and stepfather—the Marquis and Marchioness of Bumber-shook, who lived at the extreme opposite end of the country— had been unable to attend. There would therefore be nobody ranking higher than a baron present, which meant that the complex rules of precedence could be a *little* less in evidence and the gathering a *little* less formal.

Mr. Fredericks had insisted upon including some of his business cronies; these persons, never having been in the company of so many blue bloods and landed proprietors in their lives, huddled together and talked shop in sepulchral tones.

The ladies from the school were embraced by Mrs. Fredericks, divested of their wraps, and had glasses of claret cup, enlivened with French champagne, pressed into their hands. Soon the hall had filled up; the older ladies and gentlemen began to think about repairing to the card room for a hand or two of whist, while the younger set arranged itself in readiness for a country dance.

The Boring party arrived late, evidently in an attempt to indicate Lady Boring's independence. Lord Boring was pleasant and friendly, as always. His mother, Mrs. Westing, went to the card room, explaining that Miss le Strange was indisposed and had begged to be excused.

"Poor creature, she does feel ill," said Mrs. Westing as she sat down to a table and began shuffling a deck of cards with the unnerving expertise of a professional sharper. "Lately she has not even been well enough to join me in a pleasant game of chance, however hard I importuned her. *Quite* unfair, as she has recently won a large sum from me and now refuses to give me the opportunity to win it back."

"Tasteless ostentation! Oh, these *nouveau riche*, so gaudy, so common!" Thus amiably, and none-too-quietly, spoke Lady Boring, the stepsister of the hostess. "And look at that perfectly dreadful man! I do believe he's a bookmaker at a racecourse, or a moneylender. What *could* have possessed dear Althea to allow him in the door? The woman must be mad!"

The man in question, who had indeed at one stage in his career been known to lend money at a rather high rate of interest, hunched over a little more in an attempt to disappear, and wondered if these excursions into high society were worth the discomfort. His wife, who had had great ambitions for the evening, eyed him accusingly. However, the merchants and their wives soon found a safe harbor in a small chamber off the great hall, which had been fitted up as a sitting room.

While they were actually experiencing the Crooked Castle ball, it provided these worthy merchants with only moderate pleasure, but in years to come they recounted its glories, speaking as though they had, for this one night, been on equal terms with the gentry and nobility of Northern England. By the time they had grown old, it had become elevated in their memories to one of the great events of their lives.

Mrs. Fredericks was observing her party with a hostess's eye. By and large, she was content with what she saw. She had known quite well that it was too much to expect the local elite to mix with her husband's business friends, and was glad to see they had found a refuge whence they could watch the rest of the company unseen. She sent a footman to attend to their needs and then forgot them. Soon enough her husband would join them, and she would have much ado to make him remember his duties as host.

It was Miss Mainwaring who concerned her, and Mr. Hadley. She had been unable to snatch a moment's private conversation with her niece before the ball, and was reduced to making deductions based upon observation. Miss Mainwaring was pale and unhappy. She was lovely in white, her hair and toilette simple, unassuming, and exquisite, but there were blue shadows below her eyes, and her lips were downturned.

And Mr. Hadley was not behaving like an ardent swain at all. He did not make any obvious attempt to woo either Miss Mainwaring or Miss Crump, but stumped gloomily along behind the latter, scarcely speaking or raising his gaze from the floor. He never once looked at Miss Mainwaring that her aunt could see. Miss Crump, of course, was an enigma. Who could judge what emotions flitted across the face of one so heavily shrouded? Even here, in the ballroom, where a bonnet was unacceptable, she had managed to make herself invisible in a veil of diaphanous muslin of the most delicate weave, draped over her head and shoulders.

In Mrs. Fredericks's opinion, her niece's romance was not prospering.

Miss Crump was, in fact, very uneasy. Before the ball, she had begged for Miss Mainwaring's assistance. Not only did she want her help with the recalcitrant head covering, but she hoped to unburden herself to her friend, who had so suddenly and unaccountably turned uncommunicative.

"Oh, yes," said Miss Mainwaring dully, "I should be happy to do what I can," and indeed, she did an excellent job swathing Miss Crump in the material and pinning it so that it would not come undone.

"I know you are likely quite surprised that I have accepted Mr. Hadley's offer of marriage," Miss Crump murmured, feeling as though the effort to confide was like the effort of rolling an immense boulder up a hill, "but I hope that you, my friend, will not condemn it. You see . . ." She paused, seeking a glimpse of Miss Mainwaring, whose face was turned away and who seemed out of sorts. "I confess I do not . . . I do not love him, whatever that may mean. Indeed, he startles and confuses me with his endless talk of rain. But . . ." This was one of the longest, and certainly most difficult, speeches she had ever made in her life, and Miss Mainwaring was not helping at all. Miss Crump began to feel aggrieved. She had come to expect more of Miss Mainwaring. "In fact, I am marrying him to remove myself from Miss le Strange's control. She . . . she terrifies me, far, far more than Mr. Hadley. If I am married, she can have no dominion over me. If my father wishes to make her his wife, it is not my place to object, but as a married woman myself, I can limit my visits to my father's household. I can plead . . . oh! All sorts of reasons why I do not wish to go and see them."

She drew a deep breath and soldiered on, pushing her boulder uphill, with Miss Mainwaring silent at her side.

"I am at peace with my decision, save for one thing. Miss Mainwaring—that is, Cecily," said Miss Crump, attempting to get her friend to look at her, "do you believe it is wrong for me to abandon my father to that woman's mercies?"

Miss Mainwaring uttered a small sound, like a despondent bird. She turned and looked full at Miss Crump. "Thank you for explaining your actions to me, Jane. I will allow that I *had* wondered. I had thought you immovably opposed to his suit. I understand you now, and I cannot find fault with what you have done. Your father must look out for himself. In general, I believe that fathers are loath to take advice from their daughters on these matters, so I doubt in any case that he would listen to your protests. Mr. Hadley is—is a kindly gentleman who will treat you well." Here she broke off and, stifling a sob, was forced to leave the room.

Miss Crump drew what comfort she could from this conversation, as meager as it was.

✦　✦　✦

Miss Pffolliott would have been enjoying the ball, if only Mr. Rasmussen were not present. His manners, never polished, had deteriorated drastically when he discovered he had a rival. Miss Pffolliott had hoped that the matter could be handled without drama, but Mr. Godalming was by now deeply in love, and quite as outraged by the presence of Mr. Rasmussen as the latter gentleman was infuriated by his.

Contrary to the usual expectation, Miss Pffolliott was not made happy by having two men quarreling over her. She stood as if between two enraged bulls, her own small person the sole impediment preventing them from locking horns in a battle to the death. Both men loomed over her, one on her left and one on her right, each demanding in a loud voice to be allowed to bring her refreshments, each adamant that she dance with *him* first.

"But, Mr. Rasmussen, you know I have already told you that Mr. Godalming engaged me several days ago for the first two dances. *You* did not ask me until just now."

"Well, I didn't know I needed to, did I?" he demanded belligerently. "How was I to guess this bracket-faced bumpkin was going to turn up? I don't know how a pretty girl like you can even contemplate dancing with an ape like that. I should think the very idea would make a young woman of sensibility come over faint and have to lie down."

"Mr. Rasmussen, pray keep your voice down. He hears you."

"So I should hope. Old chawbacon! Who is he, anyway? Some yeoman or small freeholder, I expect—Fredericks doesn't seem to care *who* he invites to his house."

This was too much for Mr. Godalming. He had been able to control his temper when his appearance was insulted; he was wholly unable to do so when his large and prosperous estate, all three thousand acres of it managed by the latest and most advanced methods, was referred to as a "small freehold."

"What I am, Mr. What-Have-You, is the magistrate for this district, and I shall have you up on charges if you continue to annoy this young lady. And, as I *am* the magistrate, and as the law and order of this neighborhood is in my care, I would like to ask a question. Nearly every soul in this ballroom knows *my* name and *my* reputation. So tell me, who are *you*?"

Mr. Rasmussen flushed at this challenge, and retorted, "One who is well known to the girl's father, that's who. One who is being encouraged to court her, *by her own father*. Show him the letter, Miss Pffolliott! Show it to him, by gad!" He snorted and pawed the ground, further enhancing his resemblance to a bovine male.

"I—I did not think to bring the letter to a ballroom, Mr. Rasmussen. In any case, it was not addressed to me, so—"

"Never mind that," cut in Mr. Rasmussen. "Miss Pffolliott can show you the letter on another occasion. The point is that there *is* a letter. You agree that there is a letter, do you not, Miss P?"

Miss Pffolliott, who decidedly disliked being addressed so informally, agreed that there was a letter.

"Ha! Told you so. Take *that*!"

Both men were still flanking Miss Pffolliott. Behind her back Mr. Rasmussen's leg shot out viciously.

"Ow! I say, he kicked me! He kicked me in the shin! That's assault, Rasmussen!" roared Mr. Godalming.

Their host, who had been greeting a tardy guest, was alerted to this skirmish by his lady wife and began to move in their direction across the crowded room.

"*Please*, Mr. Rasmussen! This is most unseemly! I must ask you to go away immediately. And yes, there was a letter, but I might add that it appeared to be in *your* handwriting," said Miss Pffolliott, who was so distressed that she gave no thought to the possible repercussions of divulging this.

Mr. Rasmussen reared back and stared down at her, his face blotched and empurpled. She could not imagine how any-one could think him to be even passably good-looking. "Oh, so that's how it's to be, is it? Trying to make out I wrote that letter, are you? Listen here, Godalming, ask yourself how she would know what my handwriting looks like. I'll tell you how! She's been receiving letters from me for the past two months on the sly, that's how! Little Miss Butter-Won't-Melt-in-Her-Mouth here has been turning up to secret rendezvous with *me* out on the moor. And now that she's tired of me, she thinks she'll have *you* instead, you great simpleton!"

Miss Pffolliott gasped. She began to feel a black tide rising before her eyes. She staggered and felt someone take her arm and support her. She was guided to a chair and all but fell into it, her head sinking to her knees.

"Why, the blackguard! You are a villain, sir! I'll see you horsewhipped for this!"

To Miss Pffolliott's immeasurable relief, the voice berating Mr. Rasmussen and the hand under her elbow both proved to belong to Mr. Godalming. This discovery was so heartening that she sat up and viewed the scene.

Astonishingly, few people had noticed her collapse or were casting inquiring glances in her direction. Mr. Godalming was keeping his voice low, perhaps to avoid attracting further attention, and Mr. Rasmussen's response was in a low tone as well.

"What do you say, Miss P? Will you have me, or will you not? It won't be long before your knight errant here begins to wonder about what I said about you, and you'll regret not marrying me."

Miss Pffolliott could not speak. She shook her head. At last, finding her voice, she whispered, "No! Not under any circumstances. *Go away!*"

"Rasmussen, Godalming, are the two of you making a bear garden out of my great hall?" It was Mr. Fredericks, his voice mild.

Both men looked up to face this new element in the conversation.

Behind Mr. Fredericks, yet another voice spoke.

"Hullo, Spotford. What are *you* doing here? I should have

thought you'd have been hanged by now." The newcomer was Mr. Crabbe. *He* was the late-arrived guest, Miss Pffolliott realized, whom Mr. Fredericks had just welcomed.

If it were possible to do so, Mr. Rasmussen's face would have darkened still further. His mouth twisted, and for a moment it looked as though he might expectorate onto the floor. "Oh, so it's Crabbe, is it? I thought we'd got shot of you," he said. "No, they haven't hanged me yet. How about your father? Or will they let *him* off with a fine, since he's a baron?"

"The latter," replied Mr. Crabbe coolly. "Miss Pffolliott, Mr. Godalming—I do not know who you think this man is, but I can assure you he is not who he says he is. I can also assure you that anything, *anything* he says is false."

"It is false, it *is*!" Miss Pffolliott turned to Mr. Godalming. "Yes, he sent me letters, that is true, and I know I ought to have told Miss Quince about them. But I told him he must not attempt to meet me until he was properly introduced, and we were chaperoned, indeed I did!"

"Of course you did," agreed Mr. Godalming, whose soul was on fire with newfound chivalry. "The man's an absolute rotter."

"Oh, if you're going to believe *her* . . ." Evidently at this point Mr. Rasmussen realized that they *did* believe her, and that, added to the recollection of what Mr. Crabbe could tell them about his past crimes and misdeeds, convinced him to give it up. "Very well, I'll go. I wish you good luck of that bit of muslin, Godalming."

They watched as he pushed his way through the crowd, no longer bothering with the slightest affectation of good manners, not hesitating to step on toes or prod with his elbows in order to speed his progress.

"Well! What was *that* about? How do you do, Mr. Crabbe? How *very* delightful it is to see you again." Miss Asquith had approached unnoticed, and stood with her head tilted quizzically to one side. "And ought not Mr. Rasmussen be apprehended and arrested, Mr. Godalming? He has rather the look of a criminal fleeing the scene of his crime."

24

"MISS ASQUITH, YOU look enchanting," said Mr. Crabbe. "And as usual, you are in the right. Mr. Rasmussen, known to me as Spotford, and probably also known under a great many other aliases, *is* a criminal. I hope we have unmasked him before he had the opportunity to commit any more crimes. I beg you will tell me that none of you has given him any money. He had a good deal from my father before I saw him off the estate and told him to return at the risk of a thrashing. He was the readier to leave in that he had discovered by that time that my father had nothing left to steal."

"He has been pestering Miss Pffolliott in the most dastardly manner to marry him," said Mr. Godalming. "She has refused him."

Mr. Crabbe nodded in approval. "An excellent decision, Miss Pffolliott. I doubt you would be happy, yoked for life to a thief and a cheat. He often impersonates a lawyer, although he has had no training. I trust he has not got anything to do with the management of your affairs."

"I do not think so, and yet . . ." Miss Pffolliott's voice trailed off. In a moment she said, "It is only that I have realized why his handwriting looked so familiar to me when I first saw it. It is the same as that of my father's attorney, who wrote to me after my grandmother died."

"Oh, lord! That's unfortunate. I fear you'll find your father's financial health will have suffered a great blow, with Spotford in charge of it. I strongly urge you to write to your father and bid him look into the disposition of his funds."

"I will do it, if you will allow me," said Mr. Godalming.

"Do you know, I wish you would," said Miss Pffolliott after some thought. "I am so little acquainted with my father that I cannot guess how I could convince him of the seriousness of my concern. I suppose," she said slowly, "Mr. Rasmussen, or whatever his name may be, was in a position to know that my father was unable to touch my fortune, that it could only be gained by marriage."

"That seems likely enough. When is the last time you heard from your father?" Mr. Crabbe asked.

"Not for many, many years. I was but a small child when I received the only communication I have ever had from him."

Mr. Crabbe looked grave. "I should waste no time in inquiring about Mr. Pffolliott, Godalming." Then, looking at Miss Pffolliott as she leaned on Mr. Godalming's arm, he smiled. "In any case, I suspect you will have a need to talk to that gentleman soon on another subject."

"Quite right, quite right," said Mr. Godalming, growing

pink in the cheeks. "And now I think I will get this young lady something to eat, so we shan't have her fainting in a public place, *if* you will excuse me."

Miss Asquith and Mr. Crabbe expressed a willingness to do so, and, when he had returned with some refreshments, they soon found a pretext to leave the couple alone to settle their future.

"Never, *never* would I have thought that I could witness a nice young girl like Miss Pffolliott in imminent danger of becoming engaged to Mr. Godalming and simply walk away, leaving her to her fate!" marveled Miss Asquith as they found a pair of unoccupied chairs in a relatively quiet corner of the room.

"I will admit that he's hardly a Beau Brummell for looks, but he seems harmless enough. What's wrong with him?" inquired Mr. Crabbe.

"As you are not a romantically inclined young schoolgirl, I suppose I will not be able to explain it," she replied. "However, I must admit that he seems much improved of late. No doubt true love has made a gallant of him. Hooray for Miss Pffolliott!"

They were silent a moment, smiling at each other.

"How good it is to see you again!" burst forth the irrepressible Miss Asquith at last. "I know I ought not to venture upon delicate ground, but I fear I cannot help my nature. Do I . . . do I understand you to say that your father has escaped imprisonment? That he is merely to pay a fine?"

"You do. Is it fair? Is it justice? I doubt it. That a man should be able to kill another in a fit of temper and be obliged to give up nothing but a few hundred pounds, simply because he is a peer of the realm, is hardly an example of the finest in English jurisprudence. However, I will own that, for the sake of my brother and me, I am glad of it."

Miss Asquith's democratic principles suffered a bit of a dent; she, too, could not help but be glad of it, if not for dreadful Mr. Rupert Crabbe, then for his older brother.

"You will be surprised—"

"It surprised me—"

Both broke off and laughed uneasily. After a somewhat awkward pause, Mr. Crabbe pressed on. "You may have received the impression when last we met that I was determined to remove myself from your life and never trouble you with my presence again."

"I did," murmured Miss Asquith. "And I was sorry for it." ·

"That impression was correct. The shame and infamy that was bound to descend upon my name was such that I did not feel I could offer it to any decent young woman, let alone one for whom I—I desired only the best and happiest of futures. I have since . . . I have since been persuaded to change my mind and to put my happiness to the test. Miss Asquith, will you, could you possibly consider becoming my wife, even though it will mean allying yourself to so disgraceful a family?"

Miss Asquith closed her eyes in relief and sighed. "Why, *of course* I could, Mr. Crabbe, and of course I will! I did everything but tell you so the last we spoke. But since my pleadings did not move you, I will own that I would like to know what or who it was that persuaded you."

Mr. Crabbe drew in a sharp breath. "You *would?* Truly, you would marry me? Then she was right!"

Miss Asquith stared at him. "*She? Who* was right?"

"Why, your friend, Miss Franklin. She wrote to me, fairly demanding that I return and propose marriage to you. Her way of phrasing the matter was refreshingly open and logical. She explained that, under the current foolish social system prevalent in England today, you, being the daughter of a gin merchant—however wealthy he might be—would normally be unlikely to marry the heir to a barony. However, as I was both impoverished *and* disgraced, the marriage would be considered perfectly equitable and suitable on both sides. She added that, since your father is a successful businessman, no doubt he would see it in the same light, and she hardly thought I needed to ask permission of *my* father, under the circumstances."

Miss Asquith pressed her hands over her mouth to stifle her laughter. "Oh, darling, darling Rosalind! How I love her! And what do I not owe her? My whole life's happiness! If only *she* could be as happy as I am now." And, becoming more serious, she told her fiancé the unpleasant truth about the relations between Miss Franklin and Mr. Rupert Crabbe.

Mr. Crabbe was much grieved, and for a time despondent. "Yet *another* reason why you might not wish to be welcomed into my family. I do not deserve you, indeed I do not. I am sorry to say so, but I find that I readily believe it of my brother. I recall that he *did* speak of writing a monograph on the subject of a possible planet beyond Uranus, using calculations he says *he* made whilst here this fall. It is a sign of Miss Franklin's breadth of mind and spirit that she would work to promote *my* cause with her friend. Do you suppose we can ever persuade her to visit us when we are married?"

"We shall arrange never to have your brother and my friend visit at the same time, that is all. However, I think that, even if by some mischance their paths were to cross, *she* would carry it off with far more aplomb than *he*." It seemed to her inadvisable to reveal the trick Miss Franklin had played on her erstwhile suitor; if he took the trouble to verify her calculations, he would not suffer, and if he did not—why then, he deserved to.

"No doubt," Mr. Crabbe agreed.

"And, do you know, I do not think that marriage would suit Miss Franklin. There are certain almost inevitable consequences of marriage—you know to what I refer—that would seriously hamper her scientific endeavors. Until the day comes when a woman can choose how large a family she will have, it is best, I think, for someone like Miss Franklin to keep her intelligence and energy free for her work, rather than squandering it on a new baby every year."

"Perhaps so," he responded.

"Now, I, being the amiable nitwit that I am, can squander *my* intellectual capital on an infinite number of infants, without depriving the world of one scintilla of brilliance."

Mr. Crabbe shook his head at her. "'O, she doth teach the torches to burn bright,'" quoth he. "That is you. Your brilliance may not serve to expound the stars, but it lights up my heart and my life."

"Ah, I know a man is truly in love when he quotes Shakespeare," she replied with a smile. "Pray do write to my papa when you get home, however late it may be, and beg for his approval—I will give you his direction. I believe that Rosalind is right, and the title will soothe any concerns he might have about the scandal. You must put it all in as good a light as you can, of course. I have little fear he will refuse. Shall you write to *your* papa for permission to wed, or, as Rosalind suggests, simply announce it as a given fact?"

"Oh, I expect I shall follow the usual forms and ask his blessing. Then I'll remind him that he has likely not *got* a few hundred pounds with which to pay his fine and thus avoid imprisonment. However, if he is very, very polite to his future daughter-in-law, she *might* be induced to pay it so that he can attend our wedding."

"An excellent idea, my dear. I foresee that we shall make a formidable pair."

✤ ✤ ✤

Miss le Strange was *not* ill. While most of the inhabitants of Lesser Hoo and its environs danced and ate and played at cards in the newly renovated Crooked Castle, Miss le Strange hurried alone through the darkened countryside toward the Winthrop Hopkins Female Academy. She had chosen not to trust even Maggie on this particular errand, telling her that she would be in her room nursing a headache. When she judged that the school would be empty, she slipped away. Donning a large black cloak that helped to disguise her sex and made her less visible in the dark, moonless night, she hurried down the road, hoping to go unnoticed.

On the same road, coming from the other direction, was Mr. Rasmussen, known to Mr. Crabbe and his family as Spotford. Like Miss le Strange, he kept to the shadows, avoiding curious eyes.

Each had, on a prior visit, noted and remembered various entrances at the school that were likely to be unwatched and unbarred. So careful were they to remain silent and undetected that neither noticed the other, although they entered at the same time.

They were correct in believing the school to be nearly deserted. Most of the staff were at the castle, where they were lending a hand with the cooking and serving, and incidentally eating and drinking and making merry in the servants' hall. The only person left was an elderly maid-of-all-work who had been given leave to slumber by the kitchen fire, being too old for late hours and strenuous work.

Miss le Strange let herself into the building by a door that opened up onto a terrace on the western side; Mr. Rasmussen crept in through a humbler entrance to the scullery. He was then forced to tiptoe through the kitchen behind the sleeping servant's back, skulking up the rear stairs, which creaked alarmingly. Miss le Strange, taking a more direct route, reached her destination several minutes before Mr. Rasmussen.

That necklace, both reasoned, had to be *somewhere*. Mr. Rasmussen assumed that the footman, Robert, had taken it, since that was what he himself would have done given the opportunity, and began searching the servants' rooms. Miss le

Strange, who *knew* Robert had not stolen it, went straight to the chambers in the front, looking for the one that belonged to Miss Crump.

Neither had ever been in the private rooms of the house, and so had no certainty which one belonged to their quarry. Mr. Rasmussen had an easier job, as the servants' bedrooms were smaller and less filled with possessions than those belonging to the students and the teachers.

Both being methodical by nature, at least when it came to the pursuit of their own best interests, they took each room in turn, working slowly, one from the front of the house and one from the rear, gradually coming closer and closer to each other.

Down in the kitchen, sleeping beside the maid-of-all-work and oblivious to the invasion of his home, Wolfie was dreaming about sheep. The sheep were running, and Wolfie was running, too, running joyously in the sunshine, barking. Eventually his dream-self barked so loudly that he woke up.

Wolfie lay still for a moment, meditating. First he considered the question of whether or not he was hungry, and decided that, yes, of course he was hungry. Then he began to speculate on where Miss Pffolliott had got to, and why it was so silent in the usually busy household. Listening intently, his sharp ears began to note stealthy little rustles coming from above. He stood up, pleased. There was someone upstairs for him to go and greet.

25

MISS LE STRANGE had her hand in the pocket of an apron she had found in the back of a wardrobe in one of the students' rooms when she heard the sound of toenails clicking on the stairs, approaching the third floor. Instinctively her hand closed upon the wrapped bundle she had discovered and she drew it forth, clutching it tightly as she stayed her breath, listening.

Miss le Strange had not forgotten the existence of her enemy, the dog. On the contrary, she had been surprised not to encounter him before this, and she had come prepared. She moved silently toward the hallway, still holding the bundle. With one part of her mind she had registered the fact that the cloth-wrapped parcel was identical in appearance to the one she had secreted in the old apple tree some weeks ago.

When she reached the darkened hallway she saw two things. The first was the enormous, hairy mass of Wolfie cresting over the top of the stair, filling the entire stairwell so that she could not pass. The second, which she had little leisure to consider, was another dark mass, this one human in shape, coming up the hall from the back of the house. This, of course, was Mr. Rasmussen, who had just experienced a sensation like the kick of a horse to his chest upon stepping out into the front hall and confronting Wolfie and the shrouded figure of Miss le Strange.

Mr. Rasmussen, a man of far lesser intellect than Miss le Strange, had forgotten about Wolfie, and had not considered how he should react if challenged by that singularly ferocious-looking animal. He stared, fascinated, as the cloaked figure held something up and tossed it in the direction of the dog.

The object thrown at Wolfie's head was in fact a bread roll that had been soaked in enough laudanum, or liquid opium, to fell an elephant. As Miss le Strange was not knowledgeable about dogs, she did not realize that most will swallow bread as willingly as a lump of beefsteak. She had taken the precaution of smearing it with a coating of mutton fat, which she believed would prove irresistible to any canine of normal appetites.

In this calculation, she was correct. However, to her consternation, instead of lying down to chew on the odoriferous, sticky sphere, he merely opened his jaws wide and swallowed it entire. And instead of his being halted by the consumption of such a large wodge of fat, bread, and soporific drugs, it did not even slow his advance. Having gained the upper hallway, he leapt ecstatically at Miss le Strange, anxious to extend to her the courtesies of the house.

Miss le Strange uttered a shrill cry—unheard by the maid-of-all-work in the kitchen, who, besides being asleep, was deaf as well—and lunged to the left. This had the effect of disconcerting Wolfie for a vital few seconds, and Miss le Strange was off like a shot, running down the stairs without the least precaution taken against noise. Her goal was to escape with the lumpy package she held in her hand back to the dower house, where she hoped to lie low until she and her maid and the neat sum of money she had won from Mrs. Westing could make a discreet departure.

Wolfie paused, irresolute. On the one hand, the kind lady who had given him such a tasty treat was hurrying away, and he wished to catch her up. On the other hand, someone else lingered in the hall, who *also* ought to be given a greeting.

Mr. Rasmussen, whose wits had been sharpened by the crisis, used this hesitation to hurl himself down the stairway after Miss le Strange. Not only did he wish to avoid the attentions of Wolfie, but the cloth wrapped around the bundle in her grasp had been briefly illuminated by faint starlight coming in through a window, and he had jumped to a conclusion. Here was someone else in pursuit of the necklace, and furthermore, that someone else had found it and was preparing to make off with it.

Had that person seemed to be a large and muscular male, Mr. Rasmussen might, like the bard, have decided that the better part of valor was discretion, and retired from the fray. However, even though the figure was obscured by a long cape, there were several indications that this was instead a female, or at least a youth of slight build. He meant to follow and see if he could wrest it away from him or her.

Wolfie was delighted. If there was one aspect of his former

life that he missed, it was the opportunity to run full-out, galloping over hill and dale. Now these two visitors were obviously inviting him to an exhilarating game of tag in the nighttime. As well as the pleasure of a romp through the countryside, Miss le Strange, since she had been carrying a ball of mutton fat in her pocket this past hour, smelled intoxicatingly both of sheep *and* dinner. He began to descend the stairs.

Now, large dogs do not descend staircases as readily as they ascend them. Their own weight renders them awkward and, fearing a fall, they tend to go slowly. This allowed both Miss le Strange and Mr. Rasmussen a good start, and they were well away from the school by the time Wolfie erupted through the side door, which they had left swinging wide in their hasty exits. However, Wolfie's nose was up to the task of tracking Miss le Strange's lovely scent, and he soon picked up speed on the flat ground.

On the horizon, a crescent moon was rising, and this, added to the starlight, made the landscape and the contestants in this race much more visible. Miss le Strange twitched at the hood of her cloak, the better to hide her features. The temperature was dropping, and a frost by dawn seemed certain.

To the east, the road that ran past the school went toward Crooked Castle and Gudgeon Park, and, to the west, toward Lesser Hoo. Miss le Strange was headed east, planning to turn off onto the drive to Gudgeon Park and its dower house before she reached the Castle. Taking a hurried glance over her shoulder, she saw no Wolfie behind her, and entertained the unkind hope that, with luck, she had fed him enough laudanum not only to disable but to kill him. What she *did* see instead was the masculine figure she had encountered inside the house, following her. Cursing under her breath, she redoubled her efforts.

In fact, the amount of opium Miss le Strange had provided was far greater than necessary for her purpose, either of insensibility or of assassination. Wolfie's organs of digestion responded to the receipt of such an overwhelmingly toxic morsel by rejecting it in an emphatic manner. He halted, made some terrifying noises, and then relieved himself of the contents of his stomach. Being of an iron constitution and, like most dogs, largely unmoved by the experience of vomiting, he resumed his former activity. With great leaps and bounds he closed the gap between himself and the two humans. Soon he was loping along at their sides, turning to regard them with eyes that glowed orange in the moonlight and a fiendish grin that exposed all his teeth and allowed gobbets of saliva to trail out in the wind behind him: in short, a creature born of nightmare.

Wolfie had caught up with them before the turnoff to Gudgeon Park, and, as he was keeping pace on their right side, he blocked the way to Miss le Strange's destination. Realizing this, and also that, should she make the turn, her human pursuer would inevitably guess at her identity, she resolved to continue on toward the Castle. There, she hoped to mingle with the crowd and thus escape detection until the time came to return home. How she came to have arrived alone and unaccompanied in the dark might be difficult to explain, but she was past being concerned about that now. The great thing, so far as Miss le Strange was concerned, was to escape from the horrible, apparently immortal, dog and to stop running, to ease the dreadful stitch forming in her left side.

Unfortunately for this plan, Mr. Rasmussen was gaining on her. Although not particularly fit, he was attired in far more practical footwear for running, and was not encumbered as she was by her skirts and the voluminous cloak that hampered her at every step.

Thus it was that first Miss le Strange, then Mr. Rasmussen, and finally Wolfie burst into the Crooked Castle ball, racing over the open drawbridge, through the portcullis, and under the heavily carved archway into the great hall. Their impetus carried them past the small groupings of guests who stood near the door and into the center of the enormous room, colliding with an elderly local dignitary in the act of performing a graceful allemande in the dance known as Lord Nelson's Hornpipe and depositing him in an undignified heap on the floor.

Miss le Strange and Mr. Rasmussen managed to skid to a stop, but Wolfie kept on, gamboling about the room, alternately baying and barking, half out of his mind with excitement. It was possible to follow his path through the crowd by tracking the screams and shouts of panic as he lumbered into new clusters of revelers. Eventually, having made a full circuit of the room, he returned to his former companions in the middle of the dance floor.

Miss le Strange, seeing him approach, flung up her hands in an instinctive effort to ward him off. This caused her to lose her death grip on the white parcel she had removed from the schoolhouse. It flew out to land on the floor; the force of the impact was such as to tear asunder the loose stitching securing the cloth around its contents.

Onto the polished oaken floorboards slid the Ramsbottom necklace in all its glory. The pendant stone, large as a quail's egg and cut so as to make the most of every ray of light, glittered like a miniature bonfire. The guests shifted their gazes from Wolfie to the barbaric splendor of some six hundred carats of rubies winking up at the great central chandelier.

Miss Franklin and Miss Asquith, who had been conferring about the latter's newly engaged status, drew near, gaping like everyone else. Miss Quince also advanced and looked at her old antagonist, who was panting hard and pressing one hand to her side, her eyes slewing this way and that, seeking an avenue of escape.

"So you found the necklace after all, Miss le Strange," said Miss Quince in a flattened voice.

"Yes," gasped Miss le Strange, "I did." Her eye fell upon Robert, who was peering out from behind the baize door to the kitchen. She lifted her arm and pointed an accusing finger in his direction. "I found it in *his* room. I knew you would not search it properly. I *knew* you were swayed by a foolish fondness for that—that common serving boy. So I made it my business to look in his room, and I found it!"

Miss Quince shook her head. "You are wrong, Miss le Strange. All the servants' rooms in the school were closely searched at the time the necklace went missing. We were anxious to clear them, and especially Robert, of any suspicion."

"And, in fact, you did not find it there," agreed Miss Franklin. "You could not have. I now realize it was in *my* room these past few days. I saw you hide a cloth-wrapped parcel in the old apple tree at the school some weeks ago—*this* cloth-wrapped parcel. Quite recently, I recalled seeing you do so and had the curiosity to remove it. I had intended to examine it, but put it away and forgot about it."

Miss Mainwaring spoke up, remembering a conversation with her aunt. "But . . . if the necklace belongs to Miss le Strange, why would she steal it from herself?"

At this, Miss Crump found herself to be wretched. She knew she should speak; she knew that it was the right thing to do, and possibly the only way to protect poor Robert, who was most certainly innocent. Yet to make a loud assertion about her ownership of the necklace in front of this crowd of people . . . How could she do it? Her former governess stood there, defiant and scornful, a figure of terror.

Yet . . . She was to be married soon, and to have her own damp, algae-encrusted home, where Miss le Strange would not be allowed entry unless Miss Crump—Mrs. Hadley!—willed it. Yes, she could be brave. She could do it.

She tugged on Miss Mainwaring's sleeve. Miss Mainwaring bent close to listen, and Miss Crump whispered in her ear. Miss Mainwaring's lips parted and her eyes rounded in surprise. She patted her friend's arm and lifted her voice so that it could be heard through the chattering, buzzing sound of the crowd.

"This necklace does *not* belong to Miss le Strange, whatever she may say," she said. "It belongs to the Honorable Miss Jane Crump, daughter of Lady Baggeshotte. These rubies are handed down through the female line, *not* the male line. They came to Lady Baggeshotte from her mother, and on her death they became the property of her daughter, Miss Crump. Miss le Strange claims they were given to her by Viscount Baggeshotte, but," she finished triumphantly, "he was legally unable to dispose of them in any such manner."

Then Miss Mainwaring stooped and picked up the necklace. Miss le Strange took a step forward, as though to snatch it back.

"He *didn't* give them to you, did he?" said Miss Mainwaring in a low voice, without looking at her. "He became ill and you simply took them, believing that, as his fiancée, you deserved to have them."

"Of course I did," Miss le Strange replied through gritted teeth. "How was I to know they belonged to that little milksop?" White with fury, she turned to face her former pupil. "How glad I am that I shall never know the humiliation of being your stepmother. Your cad of a father has chosen to go back on his word of honor. I will bid you farewell—you'll not see me again. I leave for Wales in the morning." Her back as rigid as that of an offended cat, she stalked from the room, only saying to Mrs. Fredericks as she passed, "I require an escort back to the dower house. *Not* that dreadful Robert—I want another servant to see me safely there."

Mr. Rasmussen, observing this drama openmouthed, hastened after her. "Do allow *me*, Miss le Strange! I say, you are a remarkable woman, a very remarkable woman indeed! What style, what *panache*! Oh, my heart!"

Miss le Strange lifted haughty eyebrows, but assented, and the two departed the Castle in a much more sedate and seemly manner than they had entered it.

Miss Mainwaring took her friend's arm and pulled her away from the tight knots of people discussing recent events.

"Here, my dear," she said. "Let me help you put on your lovely necklace." She gently removed the gauzy wraps around Miss Crump's head so that she could slip the blazing string of crimson stones around her neck. "Come and see how it looks." She led Miss Crump to one of the mirrors that reflected and amplified the candlelight in the room. "You are magnificent!" she said. "Now, you must leave off the scarf—it quite spoils the effect of the necklace. You've never worn it before, have you?"

Miss Crump shook her head.

"Why, this is the perfect night to wear it for the first time. To toast the departure of Miss le Strange, and, of course"— here Miss Mainwaring could not stop her voice wobbling with emotion—"to celebrate your engagement."

A large tear brimmed in Miss Crump's eye, reflecting the scarlet of the rubies. Slowly, it traced a course down her cheek and landed on the necklace.

"Now, now, you silly thing, you mustn't cry! Everything has turned out for the best," Miss Mainwaring scolded.

"But—but I only said yes to Mr. Hadley in order to get away from Miss le Strange," wailed Miss Crump. "Now that she is going to go away and I shall never see her again, *must* I marry him and go to live in his horrid house?"

Miss Mainwaring laughed and wrapped her arms around her little friend. Tears started up in her eyes as well.

"No, my dearest, you shall not, not if you do not want to. It is the lady's privilege to change her mind. Mr. Hadley could not, not without opening himself up to censure, but *you* may do so at any moment up until the ceremony. Come, I will help you. Do not fret; I feel certain I can explain it to him so that he will harbor no resentment toward you at all. You need say nothing—I will tell him you have reconsidered."

And tugging an embarrassed and distressed Miss Crump behind her, she sought out Mr. Hadley. Judging by the expression on that gentleman's face as she talked, it would be possible to conclude that the news did not quite break his heart.

26

EVIDENTLY, MRS. FREDERICKS was right: a young girl in love needs a ball like a flower needs the sun and the rain. By the conclusion of the Crooked Castle ball, four out of the eight students at the Winthrop Hopkins Female Academy were engaged, either formally or informally.

Miss Evans, of course, being a sensible, level-headed young woman, had required no outside assistance to obtain her happiness. However, three proposals of marriage were issued and accepted during the festivities, and while none of these three couples could formally announce their plans until relatives could be contacted and made to take an interest in the lives of their daughters, there was much whispering and merriment in the students' bedrooms that night, and for many nights afterward.

A happy marriage confers a great advantage upon all members of the union: the wife, the husband, and any children in their care. It is not essential for fulfillment in life; both sexes may live singly and be well satisfied with their lot. And not every marriage is happy; many married people must seek their contentment elsewhere. Yet where a sturdy bond *does* grow up between a wedded pair it becomes a source of strength and joy their whole lives through. These four young women likely stood as good a chance at that happiness as any; they married not only for love or expediency, but also for liking and respect.

Miss Pffolliott still had cause to fret for the immediate future. At the end of Wolfie's mad dash across the country and into the ballroom, he lay down by her side and promptly fell into such a deep sleep that he could not be roused to go home. Miss Pffolliott spent an unsettled night alternating between rejoicing at the state of affairs between Mr. Godalming and herself and fearing for the life and well-being of her dog. Mrs. Fredericks, whose dog, Fido, was very dear to her and who therefore understood Miss Pffolliott's feelings, gave orders that the giant beast—who had, after all, rid the community of two pestilential characters—was to be left to slumber undisturbed in the midst of her great hall. The servants were thus forced to tiptoe around his massive body to clear away the chairs and tables and dirty crockery, whispering in order to avoid awakening him. Mr. Godalming called early the next morning at the Castle (far earlier, in fact, than the residents of the castle might have preferred after such a night), and was able to bring a revived Wolfie back to his mistress. He appeared to be none the worse for having had a good night's sleep, and no one ever guessed that Miss le Strange had meant to kill him.

The news Miss Pffolliott eventually received about her father was less favorable. Friends of Mr. Pffolliott expressed shock that his daughter was unaware that he had died several years before. His lawyer was assumed to have informed her, and to have settled her deceased parent's estate upon her. Upon investigation, it became clear that by now there was no estate to settle; it had been spent by the lawyer, who was discovered to be no lawyer at all.

However, as the fortune passed down to Miss Pffolliott by her grandparents was quite adequate and Mr. Godalming's income considerably more than adequate, and as Mr. Pffolliott had hardly been a doting father, she could not summon up much grief on his account. The excitement of inspecting her future home and the planning of her wedding pushed unpleasant thoughts from her mind.

Miss Mainwaring's happiness took a little longer to achieve. Mr. Hadley's father, while forced to accept that his son's proposal to the wealthy and well-born Miss Crump had met with no success, was still opposed to his marriage to a niece of Mr. Fredericks. After a good deal of prodding by Mrs. Fredericks, her husband managed to arrange a business deal that greatly benefited the senior Mr. Hadley. This produced a softening, and by the next spring, when Miss Mainwaring had achieved her seventeenth year, the young couple was able to join hands in matrimony, leaving after the ceremony to travel to the groom's home in the Lake District, that scenic, but decidedly damp, region in the west of England.

Miss Crump *was* coaxed into visiting them at Rowehaven. Her friend, now Mrs. Hadley, also managed to convince her that she could go bareheaded from time to time without any dire consequences. As Mrs. Fredericks had had the foresight to send a servant after Miss le Strange and Mr. Rasmussen the night of the ball to take possession of the rest of the Rams-bottom rubies, Miss Crump was sometimes also persuaded to wear the entire parure in their ballroom, to the amazement of her friends and connections. She gained in poise through her friendship with the couple and, while she would always be reserved, eventually reached a level of assurance enabling her to express a clear preference for either baked fish or fowl when interrogated by an unfamiliar footman at the dinner table.

The publication of a paper on the subject of *Perturbations of the Orbit of Uranus* by one Rupert Crabbe occasioned a little arid amusement on the part of Miss Franklin when a funda-mental error in the calculations was pointed out. The paper was scathingly reviewed, and the Reverend Mr. Rupert Crabbe thereafter abandoned the writing of scientific papers in favor of composing sermons for his congregation promoting honesty and fair dealing.

Miss Franklin soon took over the entire care and direc-tion of the school greenhouse, having proved to the satisfaction of Cuthbert the gardener that she could produce both scien-tific data *and* exceptionally large and succulent fruits and veg-etables for the consumption of the Winthrop Hopkins Female Academy. She began working on a theory of inherited traits as demonstrated in scarlet runner beans, and became so im-mersed in this study that she almost never looked up at the stars again, save occasionally on a frosty, clear night in winter.

Her prediction about the parental response to the Asquith-Crabbe engagement was accurate. Miss Asquith's father calcu-lated that the personal habits of the current Baron Hardcastle made it unlikely he would live much longer, and after his death he and his crime would be forgotten. On the other hand, the idea that he, Angus Asquith, gin distiller, might someday be grandfather to a peer of the realm filled him with glee. He gave his consent without a murmur and congratulated his daughter on a remarkably clever coup.

Baron Hardcastle had flattered himself that he would have free play with his daughter-in-law's fortune soon after the wedding, but somehow or other he never seemed to receive more than just enough to enable him to live like a gentleman. How this could be he never knew, but it did not turn him against that young lady; she knew exactly how to amuse and cajole him so that he quite forgot his grievance. He always went contentedly home after a visit to his son's establishment.

Miss Asquith had proposed that Mr. Crabbe hire Robert, as she feared she would miss him dreadfully when she went away. However, Mr. Crabbe protested that the last thing he required in his household was an exceptionally handsome and saintly footman to whom his future wife was devoted. Robert therefore remained on at the school. He took on the role of a butler in time, and married Annie the chambermaid, who was an excellent cook and a fine woman.

The headmistresses of the Winthrop Hopkins Female Academy now had a much diminished list of pupils. They applied to friends and relatives for referrals and, by spring, found themselves with six new pupils, for a total of *ten* young ladies, all of whom were to be equipped with some knowledge of geography, French, Italian, mathematics, and some decorative and artistic skills that would enable them to procure a husband.

Their relatives did not seem to have noticed they had sent them to a corner of England with almost *no* eligible bachelors. Even Mr. Godalming was no longer single, but married and looking forward to the birth of a son or daughter by midsummer.

"Mark my words," said one Miss Susanna Billings to her fellow pupils one day, when the fact that most of the inhabitants of Lesser Hoo were married couples, maiden ladies, or farmers eking out a bare existence had finally sunk in. "If something drastic is not done, *none* of us shall ever marry!"

FIN

AUTHOR'S NOTE

THE BOOK FROM which the opening quotation is taken (*The Watsons*, by Jane Austen) was never completed. It has five chapters, was begun in 1803, and was abandoned sometime in 1805.

The character of Miss Rosalind Franklin is named in tribute to the real Rosalind Franklin, who lived in the mid-twentieth century and was a British biophysicist and X-ray crystallographer. Overcoming parental prejudices to become a scientist, she made major contributions in several areas of this almost exclusively masculine field before dying of cancer at the age of thirty-seven. Her X-ray photographs of DNA brought her very close to solving the mystery of its structure. While she was producing these images, Maurice Wilkins, a scientist working in the same lab on a different project, showed the photographs without her knowledge or permission to a rival team of scientists. They quickly used the information so gained to publish their own conclusions. The three men, James Watson, Francis Crick, and Maurice Wilkins, later received the Nobel Prize for the discovery. Perhaps they might have eventually come to the same conclusion without her work, but on the other hand, she might have scooped them all—we'll never know. In any case, this is all too typical of the treatment women of intellect and accomplishment have received throughout history.

There *were* women working in the sciences in the nineteenth century, and they were not often granted the respect that they deserved. Mary Anning would have been close to the age of Miss Rosalind Franklin in *A School for Brides*. An uneducated child of the lower classes, she assisted her father in the collection of fossils to be sold to tourists in their seaside town of Lyme Regis. She was soon classifying her finds and offering many insights into the lives of these extinct animals. She discovered the first ichthyosaur and plesiosaur skeletons, and the first English pterosaur. As a woman, she could not join the Geological Society and rarely received formal credit for her discoveries, although she was known worldwide in geological circles for the breadth and depth of her knowledge. The extreme danger of fossil collecting (the best time was in winter, when the unstable cliffs were subject to landslides) would have made it a nearly impossible career for an upper-class woman like my character Miss Franklin.

Miss Franklin was, of course, correct. There *is* another planet beyond Uranus. Neptune was discovered in 1846.

ACKNOWLEDGMENTS

A LARGE BOUQUET of thanks to my editor, Sharyn November, and to Janet Pascal, the production editor who helps me to get it right.

TURN THE PAGE TO READ A SAMPLE OF
THE EQUALLY HILARIOUS AND CHARMING
COMPANION NOVEL

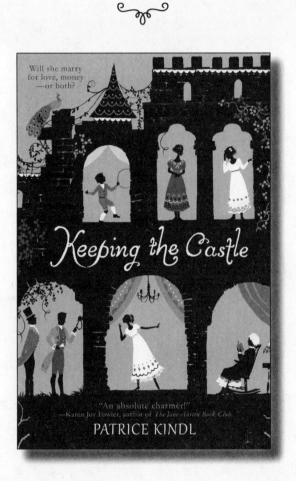

1

WE WERE WALKING IN the castle garden. The silvery light of early spring streaked across the grass, transforming the overgrown shrubbery into a place of magic and romance. He had begged me for a few moments of privacy, to "discuss a matter of great importance." By this I assumed that he meant to make an offer of marriage.

"I love you, Althea—you are *so* beautiful," murmured the young man into my ear.

Well, I was willing enough. I looked up at him from under my eyelashes. "I love you too," I confessed. I averted my gaze and added privately, "You are *so* rich."

Unfortunately, I apparently said this aloud, if just barely, and his hearing was sharper than one would expect, given his other attributes.

"I beg your pardon? You love me *because* I'm rich?"

"Not *only* because of that," I hastened to assure him. He also was reasonably amiable and came of a good family. He admired me and was apparently willing to over-look my lack of fortune, all points in his favor. And, yes, he was rich. Quite enough to turn the head, and capture the heart, of an impressionable and impecunious young girl such as myself.

"So . . ." He thought this over. "If I lost my money, you wouldn't love me anymore?"

"If I became ill," I countered, "so that my hair fell out in clumps and my skin was covered with scabs and I limped, would you still love me?"

"Egad!" He stared at me, evidently attempting to pic-ture this. He turned a little green.

"But," I said, "most likely those things will not hap-pen. You are rich and I am beautiful. We should make an excellent couple. Our children will have my looks and your money." At least, so I hoped. Only imagine a child with his lack of neck and my lack of funds! The poor man's head looked exactly like a melon, or perhaps one of those large orange gourds from the Americas, bursting out of his cravat. And he had such big red lips, which he licked incessantly.

We each were lost in our own separate thoughts for a moment, I mourning the fate of these hypothetical offspring, he, as his subsequent commentary proved, considering the finer distinctions of desire and avarice.

"It's not the same thing," he said at last, looking sulky. "Admiration of a woman's beauty in a man is . . ." he waved a hand, searching for the mot juste . . . "it's spiritual. It shows that he has a soul." His gaze swept up and down my form, lingering regretfully on my bosom, which was exposed enough for interest and covered enough for decorum. He licked his lips. "But," he went on, withdrawing his gaze, "any consideration of the contents of a man's purse by a lady he is courting is—I regret to say this to one I held in such high esteem only a few short moments ago, but I must—it is mercenary and shows a cold heart. I must withdraw my protestations of ardor. Good evening to you."

He bowed, turned, and stalked out of the garden. I sighed. When would I learn to speak with a tactful tongue? There went another one. I kept forgetting how ridiculously sensitive and illogical men were. He assumed that his fortune would buy a beauty; I assumed that my beauty would procure me a rich husband. It seemed much the same thing to me, but evidently what was permissible in a man was not in a woman.

Ah well. There was yet time; I was but seventeen.

❦ ❦ ❦

"My dear, Mr. Godalming just hurried away. He was almost *rude*. You didn't say anything to upset him, did you?"

It was my mama, appearing at the entrance to the shrubbery accompanied by my small brother, Alexander.

"Yes, I am so sorry, Mama, but I am afraid Mr. Godalming has discovered that he has a soul above marriage to such a one as I. We have parted forever, I fear."

"Oh dear, and he seemed so devoted!"

"Yes, Mama, but you would not have enjoyed being patronized by *his* mama; you know you would not."

"My love, I could bear anything for your sake."

"Well then, *I* could not bear to be patronized by his mama. It is for the best. We shall do much better by and by," I said, linking my arm with hers and drawing her back inside the castle walls.

"I certainly hope so. To be honest, I do not think Mr. Godalming is a man who could make you happy," she said, putting my brother down on the frayed carpet. "So I am glad you are not to wed him. However," she admitted, "the whole east wing *does* need a new roof, or so I fear." My mama cast her eyes upwards to a tracery of green mold on the stone walls.

"Oh," she added, "and that balcony out over the guardhouse is sagging; the wooden framework is rotten."

"It would be easier to tear it down than to replace it," I suggested, and Mama agreed.

Our home was not a real castle in the sense of being ancient and fortified. My great-grandfather had been a romantic, fond of reading about the gallant knights of the Round Table, and it had been his childhood dream to build a castle by the sea. While influenced by the ruins of Castle Scarborough some miles away, he had not been a stickler for historical accuracy. Indeed, much of the structure was nonfunctional in any but a decorative sense, with winding stone stairs leading to nowhere, murder holes so improperly placed that they could pose no danger even to the most oblivious of intruders, and a hodgepodge of towers and battlements sticking out at random. He called it Crawley Castle, but such was his love for the picturesque that the building produced was immediately and invariably known as "Crooked Castle."

My great-grandfather had sold most of his holdings in order to build this fantasy on a hundred-foot cliff over-looking the North Sea, and then spent most of the rest of his fortune furnishing it. Since he had exchanged rich farmland for barren chalk cliffs, our family's financial situation has yet to recover from this architectural extravagance. Now our home, as inconvenient and eccentric as it was, made up nearly the sum total of our wealth, save for a pittance in rents, and for a time following my father's death our retaining even *that* was in doubt. His decease took place shortly before the birth of my brother, and for several months we lived in suspense. Had the child been a girl we would have had to leave our home and go, who knows where, in order to make way for the male heir, Charles Crawley, a second cousin none of us even knew, living somewhere in Sussex.

The birth of dear little Alexander saved us from that fate, and ever since his birth it has been the object of all our care to save the property for him (and incidentally for ourselves) when he shall be of an age to hold it.

Two years ago my mother remarried, to a man of fortune but no property named Winthrop. Mr. Winthrop was a widower with two daughters, both several years older than myself, and he had had great plans, enthusiastically seconded by my mother, to repair and refurbish the castle.

Neither Mr. Winthrop nor his plans survived the first month of marriage. He began to cough as he walked my mother down the aisle and did not leave off until a renowned physician, summoned from York at vast expense, closed his eyes in death two weeks later. His money descended to his daughters with only a pittance to us, and we therefore found ourselves in much the same situation as before the marriage with the exception of having two more mouths to feed. My stepsisters did feel *some* obligation to contribute towards their upkeep, but the sum was ever in dispute, and tardy in payment.

We could not afford to live in and maintain the castle; neither could we quit it. In order to lease it out to a tenant it would be necessary to make some rather expensive repairs, and even had we wished to sell it we could not: it belonged to little Alexander. Other than abandoning it to tumble into the sea, we had no other alternative but to live in it as cheaply as could be contrived and put our hopes in the future, which, sad to say, looked little brighter than did the present. We had no aged, wealthy relative teetering on the brink of eternity, and it would be many years before Alexander could make any attempt to repair our fortunes. Besides, we doted on him and did not like to think of his risking his life and health in the gold fields, or at the helm of a privateer sailing the high seas.

No, our only hope was in marriage. Mine.

I smiled upon my mama. "We shall have a new roof, the furniture new-covered, and three elegant gowns, all for you, upon the occasion of my wedding, you'll see," I assured her. "Perhaps I should consider an elderly suitor," I mused. "They are more easily managed, I believe. And *they* often have defective hearing, which might be quite an advantage."

My mother was shaking her head, but I went on, unregarding.

"Then too, you know, if I chose a man of great age and infirmity I might become a wealthy widow quite soon after the wedding. And then we could have the drawbridge over the moat replaced immediately rather than having to wait for him to recover from the wedding expenses; it has become a bit infirm of late."

"Oh, I believe it would be better not," interrupted my mama, "not until we have no other options. Best to aim for a younger man. You see, dearest, there are certain aspects of marriage—" She bent her head as she helped Alexander to climb up upon her lap—"it is not proper for you to know about them yet, but you must trust me to know what I am speaking about—that make a young man much more pleasing."

"Mama." I took her hand and pressed it, speaking earnestly. "I well understand that the pursuit and acquisition of a wealthy husband is my lot in life, and that achieving that goal is our only chance of assuring ourselves a comfortable future. I shall not disappoint you, I promise."

"Occasionally," my mama said, with a hint of defiance in her voice, "I wonder if it would not be possible for a lady to make her way in the world without a husband or inherited fortune. I feel that you and I are *nearly* as clever as most of the men we know."

"Oh, my dear madam! How you do go on!" I laughed and squeezed her hand. There were times when I felt as if I were her elder, wiser sister. Indeed, my life would have been a good deal easier in many respects if she had been a more worldly, realistic woman, but in spite of this failing, I loved her dearly. "You know quite well that it has been scientifically proven that a woman's small brain is not capable of understanding much beyond matters of the household. Tho' when I think of Mr. Godalming's brain . . . But no, intelligence is not all that counts in life, but power as well, and a woman without money has none." I gave her hand another squeeze. "I will find some-one, do not fear."

She smiled then, and laughed a little. "You are right, of course, as always. I am a lucky woman to have such a daughter. Both lovely *and* practical."

"Only lucky to have a daughter like Althea? What about us, Stepmother dearest?" My stepsisters, Prudence and Charity, entered the corner of the great hall that stood duty with us for a drawing room. I sighed. I believe my mama did as well, but hers was a tiny, noiseless sigh in comparison with my gusty exhalation, which was powerful enough to flutter the lace on my bodice.

"You know I consider myself lucky to have *all* my daughters, Prudence," she said.

"Yes, I should think you might, Madam," said Charity, smiling unpleasantly. Prudence smirked.

These sneers at my mother referred to the fact that *their* incomes were essential to keeping the walls about us standing. If one or both married, the castle most likely would fall down around our ears. As things were, they were unwilling to open their purses or to authorize any purchases not for their own comfort or pleasure.

Quite providentially, my stepsisters were both disagreeable and incapable of disguising the fact. Whenever they went to call upon ladies with marriageable sons or brothers, the young men would turn pale and bolt out of doors even into a driving rain, claiming to be going out with the dogs. They knew, you see, how determined the Misses Winthrop were to marry and establish independent households. Of course, given the size of their dowries, they would no doubt succeed some day.

"I saw Godalming leaving," observed Prudence. She was the elder, with a broad, flat face and figure, and few pretensions to beauty. Her favorite pastime was collecting quotations on the subject of death and mortality. She wrote them out in an elegant hand, decorated them with sketches of weeping willows and mourning urns, bound them up in an album labeled "Memento Mori," and then gloated over them. "He seemed in a bit of a hurry. I trust you did not chase him away with that indiscreet tongue of yours, Althea."

"Indeed, I am afraid I did, Prudence. We shall see him no more."

Charity seemed much put out. "I call that selfish of you, Althea! If you didn't want him, it might have occurred to you that Pru and I . . . well, *we* enjoyed his company. He is a most eligible young man." Charity was several years younger than her sister, with a graceful figure, a great many spit curls plastered over her forehead, and a mean little face like a gooseberry.

"My apologies," I said, bending my head to hide a smile. I was quite certain that Mr. Godalming's proposal had been as slow in coming as it was only because he found it a struggle to make up his mind to marry into a family containing such as Prudence and Charity. "Perhaps you will see him at Lord Boring's ball. I promise to fade into the background so that he will not be frightened away."

Charity said, "See that you do, then. I know that Prudence is partial to him," and she cast a sly smile at her sister. Prudence preened herself.

My mama and I exchanged glances. Of the two sisters, Charity was by far the more attractive—if it were possible to ignore the sharp expression in her eyes and the pinching of her lips, one might call her pretty. She compensated for this, however, by possessing a character as acerbic as undiluted lemon juice.

My mother was all kindness, as always. "I hope you both will have a delightful ball. Indeed, I may say I hope everyone does; we need a little gaiety after the long winter."

"I am looking forward to it," I said, which was an understatement. Lord Boring's upcoming ball was likely to bring whole flocks of eligible men from London, most of whom had yet to lay eyes on any of us. In light of this fact, it was almost a blessing that I had not thrown myself away on the likes of Mr. Godalming.

On the other hand, up here in the North of England, in a small, rural neighborhood, there were few single men with either a name or an income sufficiently good to make an offer of marriage to us. Mr. Godalming had been one of those few, and I had frittered him away. I could not blame my stepsisters for being annoyed with me.

Still, Lord Boring's upcoming ball was to put all to rights; we smiled upon each other and thought of eligible men.

PATRICE KINDL is the author of *Keeping the Castle*, which is also set in Lesser Hoo, as well as *Owl in Love*, *Goose Chase*, and other award-winning novels. She has shared her 1830s home in a small village in rural upstate New York with a wide variety of creatures: monkeys (she trained them to be aides to quadriplegics), birds, cats, dogs, hamsters, and a son. Her current household contains a singing, dancing, talking parrot, two Cavalier King Charles spaniels, and a very tolerant husband.

www.patricekindl.com